THE KNIGHTS CONTINUE

The Knights Continue

Dria Andersen

Adrienne Andersen

Dedication

To my husband, who was my sounding board, my cheerleader, my critique partner, and all the things I needed to finish this project. I appreciate every hour, every word of input, and most of all, your unwavering support.

To my family, who had to deal with mommy being on in another world for hours at a time. Thank you for your patience.

To my sister Tina, who reads everything I write and gives me honest feedback and encouragement, thank you mucho mucho. I appreciate your continued support and cheerleading! To my aunt Cathy who gave me my first love of romance stories, I thank you for allowing me to raid your bookshelf.

Thank you to every fan who continues to stick with me while telling the stories playing in my head. I appreciate each and every one of you. Also, I would like to give a special thanks to Pikko House for the feedback and help I get from your alpha readers.

Author's Note

Firstly, let me say that content warnings abound for this story. There is mention of child abuse, domestic abuse, and drunken abuse. Though it doesn't happen on page, some of it is spelled out, though not graphically. Rocco has gone through some stuff and it has shaped him. That trauma may be a little rough for some to read, but I try not to be too explicit. As usual, there is a lot of cussing in this book, y'all know how I do. There are sex scenes, with explicit language, and there is violence. If I miss any, please feel free to let me know. I try to be very careful about it warning readers.

The story is novella length, so short and sweet. These two were fairly easy to write and I love when that happens. As usual, it's an easy and fun love and I hope you guys enjoy. Thank y'all for taking this ride to back to Eastfield with me!

Contents

2
For Her Peace ... **121**

1

For Her Protection

one

The crush of the crowd was instantly familiar. Strangely, it was one of the things Julissa missed about Motsi gatherings. Animal shifters of all types gathered in the ballroom, dressed in the various hues of red, celebrating…what in the world were they celebrating now? She shook her head and took another sip of champagne. She honestly didn't know, and frankly, most of those in attendance probably didn't care. Any reason to gather, gossip and show-off. It was one of the perks of being a part of high shifter society.

Her father was on the Tri-council, and her family was one of the founding members of the Motsi society. Micah's position afforded Julissa many privileges that she'd enjoyed over the years. The lavish parties, the safety and protection the insular community granted had all been at her fingertips.

The tri-council, or ruling three as they were called, was responsible for controlling and governing the shifters of Eastfield. The city was divided into three parts, the cats on the Southside, bears on the North, and wolf shifters on the Eastside. The West side was neutral and home to humans and some shifters who kept themselves separate from the Motsi, though they still answered to the council. Her father had been in his job since she was born, holding on to that position with a firm hand that meant strength for some, and fear for others.

Julissa was happy to be home. For a year after law school, it had been touch and go. She'd traveled for that year, appeasing her mother under the guise of figuring out what she wanted to do with her life. But she already knew. It took her months of begging her father and

Silas Knight's assistant to get her an interview with him. Finally, after a year, she'd gotten the job she most wanted. Silas Knight was liaison to all the shifters in the country, and he worked with the government in their favor, creating laws and amendments that benefited their people. She wanted to be a part of that, and finally, she would be. She couldn't wait to start her new job next week.

Tonight was the first time she'd been to a huge Motsi event in years. She'd gone to small parties here and there when she came home to visit, but she had been serious about her school work. Now that she had her dream job, she had planned to change her lifestyle, and these big events weren't on the list. Except, in exchange for her father helping her land her new job, he required her presence at her parent's side during the more significant events. Julissa knew what that meant.

Micah Crespo was ready to marry off his only daughter.

She sighed and drank some more champagne. Her father hadn't said that in so many words, but the parade of eligible men started from the moment she'd stepped through the door. She assumed knowing her plans would be enough to deter her father, but alas. She looked around the crowded room, skimming the golden décor. The ballroom was teeming with power and crackling energy, the sound of the many conversations bouncing off the two-story ceiling. She needed a breather. But before she could get one, her mother pulled her closer and introduced someone else. Julissa pasted on a smile and held out her hand. His name ran into all the others, his promise to get in touch with her later the same. He stared at her in a way that was not at all flattering. She could almost hear coins pinging around in his head. Marrying Julissa came with a massive influx of money from her marriage trust, and this male was counting them already. She excused herself and took off for the balcony. If she were lucky, it would be empty.

She took her first deep breath of the cool night air, and the most intoxicating smell came with it. She whipped her body around, searching the large balcony for the source. Her bear wanted to lavish in that scent and roll in it. Citrus, a hint of pepper, and deep, dark, luscious vanilla laced the potent aroma.

It made her hungry…reckless.

She spotted him, or well, his silhouette, in the corner of two cement posts. His body was large and powerful. Her feet carried her closer. She didn't have a choice. Her bear was pushing her at this point. His form became clear once she entered the shadows with him, and her animal's night vision took over. His eyes glowed as he lifted his glass to sip. Intense. Julissa could think of no other word to describe his gaze. It seared through her, burning down any inhibitions she might have had.

Her mouth watered as her gaze traced his face. Strong jaw, high cheekbones, and dark, dark eyes, it was a face that would make anyone look twice. His tall, muscled body fit perfectly into a red tuxedo with an elegant, subtle, plaid pattern, the suit pants hugging his thighs. Tattoos crawled from the neck of his dress shirt right up to underneath the low-cut beard that covered his strong chin. His full lips were dark pink, begging for her to bite them. Waves covered the top of his head, faded into a taper cut on the sides.

He was…everything.

An air of danger surrounded him, her feminine instincts warning her that he may be more than she could handle, but she pushed that aside. She took a deep breath and tried to contain her racing heart. His gaze never left her as she perused his body.

Hers.

Juilssa's bear declared it, clawing at her insides for her to run to him. She was struck mute.

Where someone else would rush to fill in the silence, this male didn't. He sipped from his drink, his eyes never leaving hers. The tension rose between them, thickening the air. The years in the Motsi had made her a confident woman. Julissa had never had an issue conversing with anyone, but this man intimidated her. But simultaneously, her bear wanted to submit to him and curl under him.

She cleared her throat and fought to think of some kind of witty banter. Anything to break the weighted silence. She wanted…no needed to know who he was. Yeah, she could start with that. Before she could open her mouth to ask, he tilted his head as though listening before his lips lifted in a small taunting smile.

"They looking for you, sug."

His voice.

That deep, gravelly sound seemed to scrape over her skin, pulling goosebumps in its wake. Who was he?

"Julissa!" her mother called for her on the other side of the balcony.

Her heartbeat thundered. Fear that she would lose this man and this moment made panic flare within her.

"Go, mama. We'll meet again."

Confident. Reassuring. His words loosened her feet, and she moved to answer her mother's call. But not before one more glance at his face. Julissa burned it into her memory. Yeah, they would meet again. She would make sure of it.

♠ ♠ ♠ ♠

ROCCO WATCHED THE FEMALE, Julissa, as she left the balcony. She left behind a scent that would haunt him and his bear. It was deep, sensual amber layered on top of a bright, floral magnolia. He committed it to memory, knowing he would make well on his promise to her. It wouldn't be hard to find her. Everyone knew Julissa Crespo. Her father was a powerful man in Eastfield. One who was very protective of his daughter. Not that that would stop Rocco. His bear wanted to chase her down now, but he had other pressing matters to handle at the moment. To that end, his phone buzzed with an address.

He waited until enough time had elapsed before he left the balcony. He didn't want even the slightest hint of impropriety to hit her. He wanted her, yes, but he had no plans for anyone to know that. If he was lucky, he and his bear could get their fill of her, and she would still be eligible to be mated afterward. His bear bucked in denial, but Rocco squashed it. They couldn't keep her, no matter what part of him longed to do so. They weren't fit for her. Adina Knight spotted him the moment he re-entered the ballroom.

"Rocco," she looped her arm in his. "I have some people I want you to meet."

"Mama Di." He warned.

She waved off his protest. "I got my other boys mated off; it's your turn."

He grunted and shook his head. Mating wasn't in the cards for him. He could tell her that, but it would go in one ear and out the other. From the moment her son had brought him home, Adina Knight had been mothering him. If she had her way, Rocco would've been adopted into their family and living under their roof. Despite all the therapy she'd made him get, Rocco adamantly held himself separate from them, at least as much as they would allow.

"Silas is mated, and it's time for you to stop following him everywhere and settle down."

"I'm his security. It's my job to follow him everywhere."

She sucked her teeth. "Please. You could've been handed that over to Theo. You can work at any one of the garages you own."

He shrugged because even if he weren't protecting Silas, them people would barely see him. He spent his off time at the garage closest to his house because it specialized in vintage car restoration, and he used it to work on his own car. Adina was right. It and the others he owned made him enough money that he could quit working for Silas. But...he owed his best friend his life.

Literally.

It had been Silas who had found him on the street stealing money to feed himself. The day he met Silas, his whole life had changed.

From the corner of his eye, he spotted Julissa. She was surrounded by her friends, smiling. The brightness of that smile reached down inside of him and warmed him. His bear rumbled. What would it be like to have that sunshine aimed at him? He memorized her face, from her large doe eyes surrounded by lush lashes to her button nose and full-painted lips. Her strong jaw and high cheekbones gave her a regal appearance. Her blood-red velvet gown made her pecan brown skin glow and clung to curves that made his mouth water. She was temptation come to life. His heart thumped hard against his chest.

It wasn't for him.

"Ma, I gotta handle something tonight, so rain check on the match-making," he rumbled.

"Liar," Adina chided. "Fine. But I'm not giving up, despite your stubbornness."

"Noted," he teased and nuzzled against her cheek.

He walked away and sought out her son. He found Silas where he'd left him last, whispering in his mate's ear. The two made a striking couple. The natural and affectionate way they handled each other showcased their love to anyone who saw them. Silas was a different man than he'd been before he found his family, and Rocco loved that for him.

"I need to head out," he told his friend. "Theo is circulating and close."

Silas looked up, his eyes sharp. "What's going on?"

"A potential tenant."

"Be careful, Rock. Text me when you get home."

"I'm good."

Silas narrowed his eyes. "You going by yourself?"

"Deena's meeting me there."

"Bet. See you Sunday."

They dapped up, and Rock made his way to the exit. He felt eyes on him as he got close to the door. He turned and met Julissa's gaze. She licked her lips, and a shudder of want moved through his body. She was beautiful, and though he knew he couldn't keep her for himself, for a moment, he was tempted. He gave her a small salute and left the room before he could be put off his task.

two

He knew it would happen.

He kept his body still as his heart raced, thumping in his chest in an erratic staccato rhythm. The metallic scent of his fear filled the room, slowly dissipating as Rocco returned to himself and finally escaped the last vestiges of the nightmare. Every time he got a new tenant. Every time he saw the devastated looks on the faces of their children, the nightmares returned. It was understandable. The pain and uncertainty in the cubs' eyes were so similar to the dead look he used to have in his so many years ago.

Rocco brought his trembling hand up to his face squeezing the bridge of his nose as he calmed his breathing. His cellphone buzzed next to him on the bedside table, reminding him of what had awakened him. He squinted at the clock and sighed. It was barely six, but Deena never called him with trivial shit. She knew him too well for that.

"Yeah," he finally answered the buzzing device.

"Sorry, it's so early. I finally got 2B settled. The shelter called at five this morning." Deena hurriedly said.

"They need anything?"

His mind went to the small puma shifter he'd had to rescue last night. She had been in bad shape by the time he'd arrived at the small rundown house where the female had been staying with her abusive mate and two children. The coward had run off, and the woman had finally reached out to the women's shelter, where his friend Deena volunteered. He'd dropped the family off and let Deena handle the rest. He knew that sometimes his presence could set off the females, but he never allowed his friend to travel alone by herself that time of night. He made a small note to let Dallas's office know about the family.

"Rock?" Deena said softly.

It took his mind off the memory of the puma's children and back to the conversation at hand.

He sighed. "I'm good."

"Are you sure? I know how these cases set you off."

"Good, D." He assured her, rolling out of bed. Going back to sleep would be impossible.

"I was going to try and talk you into leasing the other vacant apartments, but last night was hard. I'll let it go for now."

He grunted. He didn't like his building too full. He never regretted helping the families, but he liked his peace.

"It's a good thing you're doing, Rocco. Let that soothe the wounds," she told him gently.

"I'll try," he lied.

She sucked her teeth, seeing through it as she always did. They'd done this dance for years. The group home where they'd spent the last years of their teenage life had made them close.

"I'll check on you later."

"I'm good, Deena. No need to mother me," He growled out.

She didn't get offended at his broken voice, only chuckling. "Fine. Later, grumpy."

He hung up the phone and headed to his shower. He turned the spray to hot, stepping in while it was still cold. It didn't take the water long to heat to scalding. He let the pain wash over him for long minutes before finally relenting and turning it down. The heat never matched the fires of hell that the dream thrust him into.

The drive over to Silas's house was done in silence. He probably should've at least turned the radio on, but the noise would just agitate his bear more. He parked in the driveway and sighed before leaving the car. He fixed his face into an affable expression that would hopefully hide his anxiety from his best friend and family. After composing himself, Rock opened the front door and was greeted with the typical cacophony of sound that now lived permanently in Silas's house.

"Uncle Rock!" Sariyah jumped into his arms, her school uniform halfway tucked.

"Morning, Poppet," he greeted, settling her down on her feet. He could tell from her mother's flustered expression that they were likely running late this morning.

"Oh, good. Hold him for a sec," Mila breathed out, thrusting her six-month-old son Carter into his arms.

He cuddled the infant, smiling as Carter grabbed his cheeks, slobbering and babbling. He growled, and Carter dive-bombed into his chest to get closer to the sound. Rock took his first easy breath of the morning as he held his nephew. Mila looked up from where she was making little swoopy things with the edges of Riyah's hair and smiled.

"He loves his Uncle Rock. Look at him," she chuckled.

"I thought y'all had to be to school early today," Silas commented, coming down the stairs.

Mila sighed and grabbed Carter out of Rock's arms. "We're getting there."

Silas leaned down and kissed his mate and daughter, nuzzling his son. "We're gone, then. I love you."

Rock smiled at his friend and the happiness he'd found. That happiness had managed to rub off on him, his best friend's family bringing him joy when he'd long thought he wouldn't have any. He walked Silas out to the blacked-out SUV Rock drove when he was guarding him. His friend studied him as he buckled into the seat.

"What's up with you?"

"Nothing," Rock said, backing out of the driveway.

And for the most part, it was now true. Just spending that little bit of time with his niece and nephew had improved his mood.

"How did last night go?" Silas asked.

Rock tensed before grunting.

"You do what you can, Rock."

He nodded, reminding himself that that had to be enough.

three

Julissa Crespo took a deep breath, staring at the imposing building that housed the Tri-council and the many other essential offices that dealt with the health and safety of the Motsi. She'd been here before, but only as the youngest child and only daughter to Councilman Micah Crespo. She'd played in those same halls that she would now walk as an adult and an employee. It had been one of the privileges of her father's position.

She was twenty-five, fresh out of law school, and ready to use that privilege to help the shifters in their town. If it were up to her mother, she'd have left college with her MRS and been married to the wealthiest, most powerful shifter her parents could arrange. But she'd wanted different.

Her new job was one she was looking forward to. Yes, her father had gotten her the job, but damn it, she would prove she deserved it. Taking a deep breath and slipping her Chanel bag over her shoulder, she headed towards the security check-in, ready to take on the day. Her designer heels clicked against the pavement, and she counted her steps, using the sound to calm her nerves. She went through security quickly, her face one they were used to seeing in the building. Pushing through the glass doors of Silas Knight's office had her hands trembling.

His staff was small, just four other shifters who did the research and work that went into crafting the bills and amendments that were eventually turned into laws protecting shifters across the country. Ever since the war with the humans, the shifters had kept themselves separate. Each state had its own governing system, but most adopted the tri-council method. The Shifter Liason's position worked with all those councils to meet the needs of all the shifters in the country. It was a huge undertaking.

She was giddy with excitement. Silas's assistant looked up, smiling at her. Julissa talked to Keisha last week when she learned that her father had successfully gotten her on the staff. She hoped Keisha's easy demeanor was the same with all the staff. She didn't know how they would treat her, knowing nepotism had gotten her the job.

"Hi, Julissa! Welcome aboard." Keisha greeted, standing. The bright jade pantsuit contrasted with the woman's beautiful light skin and re-assured Julissa that she hadn't over-dressed.

Julissa held out her hand. "I'm so happy to be here."

"Come on. I have a desk ready for you and a ton of paperwork for you to fill out. I'll get you a badge, though I'm sure you'll never have an issue getting into the building."

"You have no idea how excited I'll be to flash a badge, though." Julissa joked.

Keisha laughed, giving her a warm look. "Well, let's get you started. You have a meeting with Silas at ten. It's a simple meet and greet where he'll run down your duties. You're fresh from law school, so it'll be mostly researching."

Julissa nodded because Keisha had gone over that information with her when they spoke over the phone. Within the next few minutes, Julissa was settled into her new desk with a pile of papers to go through. She took a deep breath to settle her nerves and got down to it.

♠ ♠ ♠ ♠ ♠

Julissa flexed her fingers as she filled out yet another NDA. Keisha had said there would be forms, but good God almighty, she had under-sold it. Her bear moved through her body, and she froze, inhaling deeply, tilting her head in confusion. The animal was tense, the alert-ness warning her that something was coming.

She inhaled again, and her bear rolled over in her chest, making it flutter. She recognized that smell. Her eyes scanned the office, brushing over the employees that had been here when she'd arrived. None of the five people had elicited even a smidge of curiosity from the animal. Her bear knew the owner of that scent and was begging her to get up and find it.

He'd promised to meet her again. Was she finally getting her chance?

"You ready?" Keisha asked, stepping into Julissa's line of sight.

Clearing her face, Julissa nodded, standing and brushing her hand down the red wide-legged trousers she was wearing. She slid her arms into the matching jacket, covering the black blouse. She nervously followed Keisha, her bear getting more active the closer they got to Silas's office. Once his door was open, the elusive scent was like a hammer. There was only Silas Knight in the office, so she was confused. He was mated, so her bear dismissed the male quickly, scanning his office for the source of that heavenly smell.

The bear shifter from Sunday night stood in the corner of the room. His arms were crossed over his chest, his dark eyes intent and laser-focused on her. Her body ignited, and longing filled her. He was here! Instead of the red tux, she'd first seen him in, his muscular body was covered in all black—from the fitted slacks to the dress shirt he wore opened to the top of his chest. A whole fucking snack.

"Julissa, hi." Silas stood and extended his hand. "Long time no see."

She tore her eyes from the male and focused on her new boss. "College and then law school kept me away."

"Of course," he said, sitting back in his chair. "Do you remember my best friend, Rocco?" He indicated the male in the corner.

She frowned. This was Rocco Jamison? She'd heard of him. He was feared all over the city. His name alone kept Silas Knight safe in most instances. This was the male her bear had chosen? Even without consulting the animal, there was no mistake. She was drawn to him.

She nodded to Rocco and turned her gaze back to Silas, almost positive she would embarrass herself if she kept staring. Her palms were sweaty as the realization of what Rocco was to her rained down on her.

Her father would throw a fit if she mated with him. Her bear bucked. Ok, no if…when? But that would all be dependent on him. She was afraid to look at him. But everything in her was yearning for him.

When she finally got up the courage to look him in his face again, the heat in his eyes took her breath away. Rocco was staring at her intently. She felt like she could see her future with him. It made her feel amazing. She knew she would fight her whole family for a chance with this man.

four

Rocco stared at the door of Silas's office, his bear bucking against his skin. He'd finally sat back down, his leg bouncing as what just happened washed over him. His bear had been restless all morning, but Rocco had ignored the animal. Julissa spent a lot of time with her father in this building, so he brushed aside her distracting scent earlier. He was operating on about three hours of sleep and could ill afford another distraction. Protecting Silas would take every ounce of his waning attention span today.

At least, that's what he'd thought.

Now, he understood his bear's restlessness. The animal had probably clocked her presence hours ago. Where he was sleepy just minutes ago, nervous energy pinged through him. Just her presence had done that. What would it be like when he finally had her? His bear was talking reckless, sending out signals of her being theirs, but he'd already reconciled himself with just having a taste of her.

"When did you hire her?"

Silas smiled and inhaled, his eyebrows shooting up. "I didn't see you with a pampered princess." He ignored Rock's question.

Rocco growled. "Not too much."

Silas outright laughed. "Wait until I tell Mase. You better tell Dallas Knight before he finds out from the streets."

Rocco sucked his teeth. "What streets? You?"

His friend simply smiled and went back to his work. "You already know I'm finna tell my baby, and she gon' tell CiCi, and then…."

He groaned because the Knight family was tight as hell. They didn't keep secrets from each other, and as Silas reminded him, they considered him family, so his life was fodder for their meddling. His eyes went back to the door.

Julissa Crespo.

His bear had to be tripping. He wanted her with a need that frankly scared him. Silas was right; she was a pampered princess. A darling of the Motsi society and way too good for him. He licked his lips, inhaling deep before the bright notes of her scent faded. She was built like most sows. The female bear-shifters all had those wide, luscious hips and thick thighs. Her deep red pants accentuated her waist, giving her a coke bottle shape. His mouth watered.

"Councilman Crespo won't allow it."

He hadn't meant to say that aloud, but now that the words were out, he realized how true they were. Besides, he had no plans to mate with the woman. He wanted one…maybe ten nights with her. Surely that would be enough to get her out of his system.

"Fuck her daddy. He can't come between mates." Silas didn't even look up from his work.

"I'm not mating."

That got his friend's attention. Silas looked up with a frown. "Rock. I can feel your bear from over here. No way that girl ain't yours."

Rocco shrugged. She didn't deserve to be saddled with him.

Silas sighed. "So you plan to what, have an affair with her?" He snorted. "Yeah right."

"That's all I can offer her," he murmured.

"Bullshit." Silas snapped. "But I'll let you make it. Your animal don't give a fuck what you talking about anyway."

"She's too young."

Silas grunted but didn't answer. Rocco had to be at least ten years older than her. Would that matter to Julissa? Maybe if he intended to mate her, it would matter. But for an affair, surely it wouldn't. He debated his first steps, ignoring his animal for now.

♠ ♠ ♠ ♠ ♠

For once in his life, Rocco was glad that it was Friday. It had been the longest week of his life. All week, Julissa's presence tortured him. Silas's words had haunted him during the day as he watched her, and at night, dreams of what he would do kept him up. He was down bad. He'd never thought about what he would do if he met his mate. As far as he was concerned, he'd never get that lucky, and if he did, he'd planned to ignore it. He hadn't understood the pull the mating call would have on him.

It was foolish to think he could have sex with her and discard her when he was done.

Naïve.

He'd never really made rounds in Silas' office before, but with Julissa there, he'd left his friend's office every few minutes to get a glimpse of her. He was still unsure whether he would do something about their mating. The age thing gave him pause, as well as her position in the Motsi society. He came with a lot of baggage.

He pulled the antique Chevy Nova he drove to work into the parking lot of his building. The four-story building had been Dallas' gift to him when he finished college. Rocco hadn't wanted to go, but Adina had been insistent, and there wasn't anything he could deny the woman. She'd all but adopted him, but he wouldn't let her take that last step.

At the time when she'd asked if he wanted them to adopt him officially, he told them no. He didn't want to forget his own mother and the shit she'd suffered to make his life possible. Adina hadn't taken offense, but she still showed up to his school for conferences and to chew him out when he and Silas had gotten into trouble. It wasn't just her either. Silas and Mason had treated him like their brother. In the first two garages he'd opened, the two had been next to him, gutting the interiors and helping him flip the warehouse space he'd bought into a pristine working space.

They'd cussed and fussed about it, but it hadn't stopped them or Julian from showing up every weekend. He had meant to eventually flip this apartment building, but he hadn't been able to part with it. He'd diligently worked on it until he was able to rent out the apartments.

He and Deena worked with the local women's shelter to find tenants. He wanted a place for the women to go that would be safe for their children and allow them the space to get back on their feet. So far, he and Deena had helped many women, and he was proud of that. It enabled him to honor his mother's memory.

He frowned as he spotted the blacked-out Range Rover idling in front of his building. His doorman knew damn well better than that. He got out of his car and took in the scents of the night. He frowned at the familiar scent. He sucked his teeth when he realized why it was partially recognizable. He knew the familial scent to match very well. It was someone kin to Julissa, and if rumors were correct, more than likely her brothers.

The doors to the truck opened as he got closer, and the two bulky males exited the truck, leaning against the hood as they waited for him. Lachlan and Liam Crespo were paying him a visit. Wasn't he lucky? The two men were identical, their six-five height and heavy bodies made to intimidate. Their skin was darker than their sisters, their sharp features a mirror of their father's. They were dressed in all black, and Rock could only assume it was supposed to scare him or some shit.

He shook his head, not even bothering to let them get under his skin. "Get from in front my spot like this. Shit looks janky," he rumbled.

"We came to talk."

He didn't know which of them spoke, and he didn't give a damn. He eyed them because, from the way the twins were squeezing their hands, talking was the last thing they came to do. He crossed his arms over his chest.

"Say your speech and get the fuck on."

They growled and moved closer in tandem. Rock didn't move an inch because ain't shit he feared out here.

"Our sister has been asking around about you. We want you to leave her alone."

"No," he said calmly.

The fuck he look like letting someone scare him off his mate? He'd had no plans on claiming her, but just the thought of someone coming between him and his potential mate riled his bear and had him changing his mind. So, against his better judgment and despite a week's worth of fighting, Rocco would claim his mate. A petty way to decide, yes, he could admit that. But the animal wouldn't allow anyone between them. His bear filled his body to drive that point home.

"You know who the fuck we are, Rock."

"I can say the same." He told them, and they frowned.

Before Dallas had made his way into the Motsi, he and Silas stayed in shit and had a reputation that had preceded the family's ascension into society. While Silas had cleaned up his act to maintain his current position, Rock hadn't seen the point. Besides, he did the same stuff he'd been doing in the streets, except now for the family's protection.

"We can make this conversation more painful if necessary." One twin warned.

Rocco smirked and shook his head, walking around them. He might have taken them up on that any other night, but now that he'd decided to pursue Julissa, dragging her brothers across his parking lot would likely not endear her to him.

"Julissa is promised to someone else."

He didn't slow his pace towards the door, though the words struck him right in the chest. He would kill anyone who even thought to take her from him. Damn, it. Silas had been right. His bear didn't care about any of that shit he was talking about earlier. None of his reasonings mattered to his animal.

"She's mine. Tell him to find something safe to do with himself," he told them over his shoulder.

They growled louder as Rocco gave them his back and walked inside.

The night doorman stood abruptly. "I already tried—"

Rock waved him off. "Next time, call back up."

He nodded. "Yes, sir."

He turned and stared at her brothers, dropping his fangs in a warning. He had no problems getting active if the situation called for it. Shooting him an aggravated look, the twins got in the truck and drove off. Rock already knew he would hear about it. He went to his apartment and sighed. The last thing he wanted was beef with a tri-council member about his daughter, but Julissa was non-negotiable.

He had barely gotten out of the shower when his phone rang. He shook his head when he saw the number.

"Sup, PD."

"The councilman's daughter, Rocco?"

He chuckled at Dallas's tone. "I'm being respectful."

Dallas sighed. "What we doing?"

"She's my mate." He told Dallas. His bear finally relaxed, hearing the man claim her out loud.

"I'll handle it then."

He grunted, already knowing Dallas would have his back.

"Her brothers ain't wrapped tight, though, so they may still come at you about their baby sister," he warned.

"I ain't worried."

Dallas chuckled. "Alright then, that's all I needed to know. You remember what I told you about heat?"

Rocco grunted. He remembered the very detailed information Dallas had given them all about sex and mating when they hit puberty. Bears differed from panthers, but PD ensured Rocco had gotten information specific to his animal. It was one of many small ways the Knights had shown him that he was a part of their family.

"DiDi and Iris know, so you already know what will happen on Sunday."

Lord have mercy.

He pinched the bridge of his nose. "PD."

"My name is Bennet, and I ain't in it." Dallas laughed, hanging up the phone.

He hadn't even made moves on Julissa, and already gossip was flying around Eastfield.

five

Julissa rolled her shoulders and maneuvered around the boxes scattered across her new apartment. She'd been in the place for two months and made no moves to unpack. There were two bedrooms, and she planned to use one of them as her closet. Or at least she would when she got around to organizing all her clothes. Right now, they were carefully stored in wardrobe boxes. She finished tying off the silk scarf that covered her hair and headed for the kitchen.

She shoved boxes of kitchen stuff to the side. She didn't cook, so she hadn't seen the need to rush and unpack those. Besides, with her new job, she would barely have the time. She was in awe of Silas Knight, she'd seen him from afar and studied so many of his bills and case law, but nothing had prepared her for how hard he and his staff worked. It was exhilarating being a part of it. The Motsi was supposed to help shifters, and for so long, she'd felt like they hadn't been doing enough. She wanted to do more, help more, and now she could do that.

A month and a half in, and yes, the hours were long and the details tedious, but she was excited all the same. Now, if she could just get her hormones under control. She had to work in the same office as Rocco daily, and he had yet to approach her. Her bear insisted that he was her mate, but damn if she could work up the courage to say something to him. Just like the night she'd first seen him, he had her tongue-tied.

It hadn't stopped her from asking around about him. She wanted to know as much about him as she could. She'd hoped it would help her step to him, but she'd chickened out so far. For the last week, though, she'd noticed little gifts left on her desk, covered in his scent. She didn't know how to take that. His promise that night on the balcony had fueled many of her dreams about him. Julissa was waiting impatiently for him to ask her out. Though she appreciated having her favorite lunch delivered to her desk, she wanted to eat those lunches with him. Off him.

She shuddered at the need that slammed into her. Just thinking about the man made her hot. When was he going to make his move?

Julissa sighed in frustration and sucked her teeth at the sad state of the refrigerator. Once again, she'd forgotten to grocery shop. She slapped a sandwich together with the measly fixings she found, too tired and hungry to wait on takeout. She frowned when her phone rang. It was the front door of her building.

She sighed when she saw her mother and her detail hovering around her doorbell camera. Julissa pushed the button to let them in and waited. A few minutes later, she heard the beep of the keypad as her mother let herself in, leaving her detail in the hallway.

Therese Crespo was everything one could expect for a society maven. The graceful woman was well into her fifties, but her caramel brown skin glowed smooth and unwrinkled due to her meticulous care. Her hair was back in a low chignon, with tendrils surrounding her beautiful face. Therese was her version of 'dressed down.' Tailor-fitted cream-colored slacks hugged her ample curves, and the white silk blouse on top opened to her collar. The cashmere sweater worn on top was one her mother had owned for as long as Julissa could remember. According to Therese, it was Micah's first gift to his mate, and she cherished it.

"Mom," she greeted around the sandwich she was eating.

"Julissa, really." Therese looked around her apartment and sighed. "I could've had this all done for you. Why do you insist on living like you're still in the dorms?"

"Mom, my apartment is fine. I'll get to it eventually."

Her mother sat her purse down on the counter and looked around. "I see you managed to unpack your bookshelf and set up your reading nook," she said drolly.

"The important stuff." she joked.

Therese stared at her only daughter.

Julissa sighed. "What did they say?"

She knew that look on her mother's face. Either her father or brothers were complaining about something she'd done. She racked her mind for what kind of trouble she could've gotten into in the last month. She'd kept her head down and worked, so she couldn't imagine what sacred breach of safety she'd violated. She hadn't even attempted to lose the detail her father had put on her in that time. And she certainly hadn't had time to attend any Motsi events. Her friends had been nagging her for the last week about it.

"Liam and Lachlan are under the impression that you're mated."

Julissa frowned, though her heart thumped a little in guilt. What did she even say to that? "Mom, seriously."

Therese shrugged and opened one of the kitchen boxes. She started putting away the fancy dishes that Julissa had never had a reason to use, but Therese had insisted she needed.

"I'm just relaying."

"I'm not mated."

Therese eyed her but carried on with her task. "So, who has your brothers and father so worried?"

"What are they worried about? I go to work, and I come home. The not-so-secret detail dad has on me can attest to that."

Therese nodded, not bothering to deny that her husband kept tabs on their only daughter. "There is clearly someone, Julissa. Your father was in a screaming match with Dallas Knight a couple of weeks ago, and you know Micah never yells."

Her eyes widened. "Mom, I swear I haven't mated behind your backs."

Therese turned and put a hand on her hip. She pointed to her daughter. "See that? See how careful you are with your words. Who is he?"

She sighed and gave up on the rest of her sandwich. "I...we have barely exchanged more than a few words. Why in the world do the twins think anything is going on?"

Julissa bit her lip. Perhaps she'd not been as discreet as she thought when asking around about Rocco.

Therese huffed and moved to the next box.

"Mom, you don't have to do that. I can do it when I get ready to."

"I'm here, and you know I can't just sit around in mess."

Julissa sighed and took that gentle rebuke for what it was. "Mom," she put her head down on the counter.

"You know the plans your father had for you, sweetheart. Just spit it out so I can fix it. I need peace in my house, child."

Julissa straightened, "Mama."

"Aht-aht, don't even, Julissa Nicole, out with it."

"His name is Rocco Jamison."

Therese's eyebrows shot up. "Rocco Jamison. I see. That explains your father and Dallas. He's older than you, baby."

That didn't matter to her. She would have him. "I don't want to start anything with Daddy's allies."

Therese waved that away. "I'll talk to Adina, and the two of us will fix it. You can't leave it to men to do anything but measure their dicks."

Julissa snorted. "He's my mate, but we haven't even...."

Therese walked to her daughter, cupping her cheek. "An actual mate, Julissa? Not just a man you want to marry?"

She nodded.

Her mother gave her a happy, watery smile and backed away, returning to the boxes. "I'm happy for you, love. I prefer a mating to any match your father could make for you."

"I wouldn't be too happy yet. Rocco doesn't even talk to me. He just..." she sighed. "He leaves me gifts and buys me lunch, but he's not making a move."

Therese smiled. "Bear mates are different, sweetheart. They have to make sure you're receptive before they make a move. Have you even looked up from work to let him know?"

She frowned. "You see what happens when I show even a smidge of interest in a man."

Therese sighed. "Liam and Lachlan are worse than your father. They even went to his apartment to scare him off the other day. Probably another reason your father and Dallas got into it."

She growled, aggravated. "Mom."

Therese shrugged. "You know how they are. I rein them in where I can."

Julissa could only sigh because her mother was right. Therese had fought for her to be able to leave the state for college. Every time she needed her mother, she was there backing her up when her brothers and father ganged up on her.

"What did they say to Rocco?"

Therese gave her a droll look, and her stomach churned. Julissa needed to go over there and clean up her brothers' mess. She looked down at the t-shirt and tights she wore. She needed to change clothes first. She wondered briefly how she could speed up her mother's visit. She already knew where he lived. That had been one of the more complicated pieces of information to get, but gossip was hard to escape in the Motsi, and everything about the Knights and the people they'd brought with them to the society was fodder for it.

That included where her mate laid his head.

"Forget them for the moment. Tell me about him." Therese ordered.

"Rocco is...stoic," she searched for a better word. "How do I let him know I'm receptive, Mom?" She asked softly.

Therese smiled. "Well, sweetheart. Let me tell you about trapping a bear."

six

Rocco slid a pair of joggers up his leg, his bear still restless within his body. He'd upped time in his animal form, running for an hour, but the damned beast was pushing. He knew what his bear wanted, but he was going at his pace and wouldn't be rushed. Lowkey still didn't even think he deserved his mate, so the fact that he was making moves at all should've satisfied the animal. To that end, he picked up his phone off the bed and scrolled through the florist's website he'd been perusing before he'd gotten into the shower.

He frowned when the intercom near his door rang. Slipping his phone into his pocket, he pressed the button. The face of his doorman appeared.

"There's a Julissa Crespo here to see you."

Rocco cursed, and his bear bucked in excitement. "Send her up."

He looked around, but there was nothing to clean. He kept his apartment sparse, and now wished he'd put in more effort. The apartment details were meticulous and luxurious, from the crown molding and gold lighting fixtures to the hand-laid hardwood floors. He had done the built-ins himself, making his place look not as empty...but still. There was a sofa and his massive tv mounted on the wall. That's it. What would his mate think?

She knocked a minute later, and he took a deep breath before opening the door. He'd seen her just two hours ago as she was leaving the office, and still, her presence hit him in the chest. He drank her in. She was so beautiful and elegant. She wore a soft, thick sweater dress that hugged her frame from neck to ankle, though it left her arms exposed. It made him want to rub against her.

"Hi, Rocco," she said softly.

He inclined his head, and she entered his space. His bear rumbled his chest triumphantly, but he squashed the animal before it got carried away. She was only here for…whatever she had come for. He inhaled, indulging in her scent.

"Have you eaten?"

Where the fuck had that come from?

She shook her head. "Whatever you're making smells amazing." She turned from her perusal of his space, giving him a small smile.

The fish he'd put in the oven before he jumped in the shower should be near done. There was enough for him to share, but even if it weren't, he'd have given it all to her. He didn't say anything, simply pointing to the stool at the kitchen island. He turned off the rice cooker and pulled down plates for them.

"Do you need any help?" She broke the silence.

He shook his head. He didn't speak much on most days, but the people who knew him were used to it. He'd always been subconscious about his rough voice. His tattoos easily covered the scars on his neck, but that gravelly rumbling had never healed, which was odd for shifters, but he'd been injured prior to getting his animal, so he was stuck with the damage his father had caused. He shook the morbid thoughts from his head and focused his attention back on Julissa. He didn't want to scare her off with his brooding.

He plated their food and placed hers in front of her.

She smiled up at him. "This smells amazing. Thank you for sharing. I know I dropped by unexpectedly."

He nodded and sat down next to her. She grabbed his hand, praying over their food. That small act settled his whole body. It was like everything he'd been missing in his life clicked into place with her presence in his den. She finished and dug in, moaning at the first taste. He closed his eyes to keep his bear from showing its ass. He already loved feeding her, but to know she enjoyed food directly from his hand was an experience he didn't realize would mean so much.

"This is amazing," she gushed. "Do you cook like this all the time?"

He cleared the lump from his throat and carefully modulated his voice. "Not all the time."

"Don't do that," she said, touching his shoulder. "You don't have to adjust your voice for me."

He stared at her, and she squirmed, pulling her bottom lip between her teeth.

"I'm sorry. Did I overstep?"

He shook his head and went back to his food. She pushed her green beans around on her plate, and what was once a comfortable silence shifted. She pushed out a breath and straightened her shoulders.

"So...I came over to apologize.

He frowned in question.

"About my brothers," she rushed out.

He tilted his head for her to go on, and she sighed.

"They're massively overprotective and don't have any home train-ing."

A small chuckle escaped him, and she smiled. His chest tightened at her beauty. They stared at each other, the tension thickening between them for long moments. She licked her lips and cleared her throat.

"So, yeah. I'm sorry."

"You good. They did what they were supposed to do."

She squinted her eyes. "You're one of those overprotective shifters, too?" She sighed dramatically. "Just my luck. Gonna spend my life like my mom with a cadre of security."

She seemed to realize what she had said, and her eyes widened in horror. Multiple expressions flitted across her face, easy to read. She was amusing, her sweetness and light filling him, relaxing him and his bear.

"I mean...I didn't mean...like, I was just..." she blinked, her face shocked and unsure.

JULISSA WANTED TO sink through the floor. She shared one dinner with the man and was already envisioning her life with him. What was wrong with her?

She tried again. "Rocco, I…"

The corner of his lip tilted up in what she assumed was a small smile. "You good, Liss."

He returned to his food, and she waited, but he didn't say anything else. She let out a relieved breath when he didn't fill the silence. Stoic. That's what she'd told her mother about him, which was clearly true. He was a man of few words.

She hid her smile as she took another bite of food. Liss. She liked that. It sounded even more remarkable coming out of his mouth. She'd never had a nickname before. Even her friends of years called her Julissa. No one had shortened her name.

"You must've just moved into your apartment," she prodded, taking another look around the empty place.

It would be a great space once he decorated it. The sizeable airy apartment was calling for lush plants and wild splashes of color, at least if she lived here. Lord, Julissa shook her head. She was already moving into his place, and the man had yet to ask her out on a date.

"At least you don't have boxes everywhere like me. My mom was just fussing at me about the state of my apartment."

He hummed, which said nothing.

"The building is nice. I wonder if they have any apartments available." Not one to take silence, she rushed to fill it, which explained why she kept her foot in her mouth around this man. "I don't mean I'm going to move down the hallway from you. Like, I'm not gonna run down to the leasing office. Just…"

She shoved food in her mouth, hoping that would keep her from saying something else goofy.

Rocco grunted. "I own the building."

Her eyes widened. "Oh, that's so cool! How many apartments…" she trailed off because she was finna sound full-on unhinged if she kept going.

Why did he make her so nervous!?

He chuckled. "Six."

"Oh."

She was scared to say anything else after that. They ate in silence for a few minutes, but the way her mouth was set up…

"Thank you for the lunches and the flowers." She said.

He nodded. "I like feeding you. Spoiling you."

Her stomach fluttered, her bear melting with her. She waited for Rocco to expand his sweet words, but he didn't, which made his succinct statement that much more potent. Her body flushed. They ate dinner not quite in silence because she would never be what someone would call quiet. He didn't seem to mind, though, simply humming to show he was listening, answering any questions she asked in one-word sentences when required. When they finished eating, Julissa sought a reason to prolong her visit. But she probably wore out her welcome, especially since she hadn't asked to come over. So, she stood and gathered their dishes.

"I can clean up."

He stopped her with a hand on her arm. She put the plates back down. He turned on the stool and pulled her between his legs.

"I'll handle it."

"It's the least I can do since I made you share your dinner. We can go out for dessert. I'm sure your bear is still hungry," she rambled.

He smiled, a full one that lit his face, and Julissa's world tilted. She had never seen him smile this big. It relaxed his face and made him approachable. Her hand skimmed his cheek before she realized what she was doing.

"You have a beautiful smile," she said softly.

He licked his lips and nuzzled into her hand. "Thank you for coming over."

"Are you kicking me out?" she teased.

He chuckled softly. "I'm trying to behave and starting to lose my resolve."

Her stomach clenched, moisture gathering at her center. Rocco hissed and inhaled, his eyes darkening.

"See..." He shook his head and dropped his hands from her hips. "We finna get in trouble if you stay. Did you drive?"

She nodded, nervous and heated at his closeness. She was damn near salivating at his words. Why couldn't she stay? She would love to get in trouble with him. Her bear was fully with it. He seemed to read her mind, chuckling, grabbing her hips, and bringing her back into him.

"At first...I thought I could separate what my bear wanted from what I wanted." His gaze traced her face slowly.

She held her breath, unsure what that meant. She wanted to ask, but he so rarely talked that she was afraid to break the moment.

His lips quirked up into a slight smirk. "In this, I think I'll listen to my animal."

"What does that mean?" she whispered.

"It means I could never be satisfied with having you once or twice." His other hand spanned her hip, bringing her closer to him. "We'll do this right. Can't have your daddy crying foul," he said softly, cupping her cheek.

He stood to his full height, and she looked up, swallowing the moan that wanted to escape at his touch. Her stomach clenched, and her heart raced. He effortlessly put her under his spell. She held her breath as his head descended, closing the distance between their faces.

"Good night, sug." He kissed her softly.

She closed her eyes to savor it, whimpering when he pulled back. "Good night, Rocco."

He separated from her and went to the coat rack at his door, pulling a hoodie over his t-shirt. Rocco walked her all the way downstairs and to her car. He nodded to the security her father had on her. It reminded her of his words about her daddy crying foul. He was right; her father would want a marriage contract before the two of them mated. For the first time in Julissa's life, her family's position in society felt stifling, especially since it was keeping her from her mate.

He held her door open until she buckled in, leaning down into her car.

"Gimme your phone, Liss." He ordered softly. She did, and he put in his number. "Text me as soon as you get home. Not in the parking lot, but inside your apartment safe."

She sucked her teeth in amusement. Yeah, Rocco would be overprotective. "Yes, daddy."

"Now see," he growled, closing the distance between them. He kissed her hard before pulling back and nipping her bottom lip. He stepped back and closed her door. "Behave."

She heard him through the closed window. Her heart was racing, and her panties soaked. Would she be able to wait until he worked out a marriage contract with her father before she jumped him? Time would tell. Either way, her visit had been a success. Rocco had made his intentions for her clear. Satisfaction filled her. From the moment she'd entered society as a teenager, she understood that whom she married would be outside her control. But now, she would be mated and to someone she and her animal had chosen. Julissa squealed in happiness.

seven

Julissa squirmed in her seat and fought not to check her phone for the fiftieth time since she'd arrived. It was Sunday brunch, and she was supposed to use this time to catch up with her friends. It was the first one she'd attended in months. Her friends were eager to see her. She was back from law school, and they wanted her to return to the social scene immediately. She loved Motsi events but was serious about her career; not all her old friends understood that. They were spoiled, all of them, her included, so most of them hadn't planned on working.

They would go straight from their father's homes to their husband or mate's, whichever came first.

"You've missed so much while you were gone," Keara started as soon as they were seated.

Julissa gave up her inner battle and took her phone out of her purse, setting it on the table in case Rocco texted her. They had been communicating and flirting a little since the dinner at his place. She followed her mother's advice and let him know she was open to their relationship, which seemed to work.

"Can you believe mousy little Celine Harris is mated and had a baby?" Keara whined.

Julissa rolled her eyes behind the menu. She'd been friends with all of these women since they were in diapers. It was the way the Motsi operated. One had to socialize with the right kind of people in order to keep their traditions alive. She didn't know what Keara had against Celine, but it was tired. The woman never bothered anyone when she attended events.

"You still mad that he didn't choose you?" Amber asked, snickering.

Keara glowered at her best friend, but Amber ignored her. Julissa was relieved when the waitress arrived with their pitcher. Bottomless mimosas were just what she needed.

"So, how do you like your new job?" Erica asked.

"It's great! Working with Silas Knight is a lot of hard work, but it's fulfilling," she answered with a smile.

"Well, good for you," Erica said, sharing a look with Keara.

Julissa heard the shade in the woman's tone. It reminded her that she was out of practice dealing with the undercurrents of society conversations. There was a rhythm and balance to the shade. Julissa could read with the best of them, but she had better things on her mind. Julissa looked at Amber. Her friend rolled her eyes and texted on her phone. A second later, Julissa's rang.

Amber: *Why did we invite these hoes again?*

Julissa coughed to cover her laugh. She didn't have a definitive answer to that. They'd all been together since school, and technically Keara was the one who organized the brunch. But Amber was right. They should've done this on their own. The table was full, the eight 'friends' all ready to get reacquainted since some of them were finally back in town after college. She'd been halfway dreading it, but only because she'd wanted to sleep in. Some of the ladies she was happy to reconnect with.

Julissa: *Behave.*

She shuddered. That reminded her of Rocco on Friday night. She picked up her phone and sighed. No text yet from Rocco. He said he was going over to his family's house today. She assumed that meant the Knights since she knew that Rocco had grown up in the group home Adina Knight's family ran. She'd been able to extract that tiny bit of information out of him when they talked on the phone yesterday.

"Are you going to be on your phone all lunch?" Keara asked.

"You must be waiting on a call from someone," one of her friends teased.

"A man, even." Another one said.

Keara narrowed her eyes. "You're with someone?"

"I met my mate," she admitted, happy to finally get that out, though there was a little trepidation.

Was Rocco going around claiming her? According to her brothers, he was. She'd cursed them out yesterday about once again interfering with her life.

"Oh my God, who?"

"So it's true? Rocco Jamison is your mate?" Erica asked.

Of course, she knew. The sow had been trying to trap Julissa's brother Liam for years. Ain't no telling how much of her business her brother spilled. Some of her friends frowned.

"Silas Knight's guard?" Keara asked, snickering in disbelief.

Julissa was never one to lose her temper, and not much shook her confidence; she had her mother to thank for that. Because of that, she ignored the scorn in Keara's words, instead sharing a knowing look with Amber. Keara was a joke, her jealousy well known and ignored amongst them. Her best friend rolled her eyes. Julissa had already confided in Amber on Saturday night. The two had talked extensively about how Julissa could push her mate along.

"Have you seen that man? Good for you, Julissa. I, for one, am glad they brought new blood to the Motsi." Amber said.

"Here, here," they cheered, and Julissa snickered.

She knew that some of the crowd she hung with were snooty, but she would not allow that to get in between her and her mate.

Despite her initial misgivings, she enjoyed brunch. She'd had one too many of the bottomless mimosas, so she caught a ride back with her security. She was stopped in the lobby of her building by the concierge. The woman handed her a floral arrangement that made her gasp. It was beautiful, the buds fragrant, and it would fit perfectly on her dining room table. She ripped open the envelope and couldn't contain the smile that covered her face.

I can't wait until you're mine.

She bit her bottom lip and debated heading to his apartment in a trench coat and nothing else. Would that be enough to push him into giving her the dick? Knowing him, he'd tell her no since she was drunk.

Boooo.

She snort-laughed at the silliness of her thoughts and reached for the second padded envelope. She opened it and smiled at all the gift cards. They were for various restaurants around the area that delivered to her building. Rocco had said he wanted to both feed and spoil her. Her heart thudded against her chest. She'd been worried that her rambling when they talked would be off-putting to him; meanwhile, he'd been listening. The restaurant gift cards were proof of that. She didn't like to cook, and his gesture ensured she would still eat.

She pulled out her phone as she stepped into the elevator, tucking the phone between her ear and shoulder as she clutched the flowers to her stomach. He answered quickly.

"Thank you, Rocco."

"You're welcome, Liss."

She didn't know what else to say. "I just wanted to hear your voice."

He growled, and her hands trembled.

"Will you be with your family all day?"

"Just about," he said.

"Text me when you get home safe," she said softly, giving him the same words he'd given her on Friday night.

He chuckled darkly. "Will do, sug."

She ended the call, smiling from ear to ear. *My mate, my mate.*

Rocco smiled down at his phone. Julissa was incredibly sweet, and he loved that. She had grown up spoiled; anyone who interacted with her for more than a second would know that, but keeping her in that lifestyle would give him great pleasure. He wasn't hurting for money, but he had worried that she would see him only as a bodyguard and nothing more. It didn't seem like she cared one way or the other. He liked that.

Iris had always told them that 'spoiled' never meant one specific thing. He'd quickly discovered that Julissa was a foodie, so he would cater to that. It seemed to be working because, from Silas' office, he could observe her soft smile and giddiness when the lunch he ordered for her every day hit her desk. Rock had scoured the web for the top restaurants in the area, checking reviews to ascertain if she would like them. He took note of her favorites, and the gift cards he'd sent over today were from those places.

Tucking his phone away, he entered the Knight's residence, his spirit light. The home of Dallas and Adina was large but still inviting. He could smell the food Iris was making for their Sunday dinner and hear the chatter from his family as he went further into the house.

His family.

It had taken him years to get used to that. But the Knights had been patient with him. His godson whined the minute he rounded the corner into the large kitchen. Mila sat around the enormous marble island in the middle while Iris stood at the six-burner range, laughing with Adina.

Mila sucked her teeth. "I feed you. Why are you betraying me for your uncle?" She asked her son as his hand reached for him.

Rocco laughed and lifted Carter high, enjoying his happy squeal. He pulled the baby into his chest and chuckled as his godson immediately reached for his tattoos. They fascinated the baby. He greeted Adina, nuzzling her cheek and doing the same to Iris.

"Tell me about Julissa," Adina ordered straight away.

"Mama Di," he sighed. "I'm barely in the door."

She looked behind him. "Alone too. You should've brought her."

He winced as all three women turned their attention to him, tuning in. "She had plans."

"Dallas and Micah had a very animated conversation about it the other night," Adina said, waggling her eyebrows.

He chuckled at the meddling woman. "She's my mate."

Mila laughed. "Slow down, Rocco. You're giving us too much information."

The women busted out laughing. "Leave my baby alone," Adina teased.

Iris sighed. "We'll never get grandkids out of him, Adina."

He laughed at their dramatics. Mason entered the kitchen with Cici on his heels and Antonio on her hip.

"Perfect timing," he breathed, causing them to laugh again.

"Carter, my man," Mason greeted his nephew and reached for him. Carter whined and curled tighter into Rock.

"Do you see what I'm saying about this traitor," Mila told Mason.

"Nephew, that's how you do me?" Mason grabbed the baby, loudly kissing his cheeks until he stopped whining.

Now that Rocco's arms were free, Antonio started babbling and damn near jumped out of his mother's arms, reaching for him. Rock grabbed him, growling at his nephew, who laughed and grabbed his cheeks.

"I already know y'all are going to make my baby rough," Celine fussed, smiling.

Dallas came into the kitchen and waved for him. The male's power was potent, filling the space and making Rocco's animal alert. Despite how long Dallas Knight had been in high society, that feral energy still accompanied him. The strength of the man's panther should've made a young Rocco wary, but it had given him a sense of security that still carried over into adulthood.

He tried to give Toni back to his mama, but the kiddo gripped his shirt tightly.

"Okay then, nephew. Let's go talk business with Poppa." He'd long ago stopped worrying about how his voice sounded with the Knight children. Neither of them seemed to mind his rough timbre.

"Dinner in fifteen," Adina called after them.

"We won't take that long, love," Dallas assured her.

Rocco had been in Dallas' office many times before. The whole room fit the man to a tee. The dark green walls contrasted the oak bookshelves that held more awards than books. An entire unit housed his humidor and liquor, situated in the corner of the room behind a deep leather chair where Dallas spent much of his time. To this day, the smell of cigars and leather reminded Rocco of the man. He spotted the plants Adina had snuck into the place to 'give it more life.'

He settled into the leather chair in front of Dallas' heavy desk, sitting Antonio on his lap. Dallas slid into the one behind his desk, passing a stack of papers to Rocco.

"We're still working out details, but your mating contract is nearly done."

That surprised him. The contracts were reserved for higher-ranking families. That Dallas had required it for him proclaimed him a part of the Knight family.

Rocco frowned down at the list of his assets. "You're negotiating with Councilman Crespo?"

"Why wouldn't I? You're a member of my family." Dallas sucked his teeth. "You got me fucked up if you think I'm finna let them hose you in a contract."

His heart thundered. "PD."

Dallas held up his hand. "I just need you to mark out the hard 'no's, and I will handle the rest. I'm proud of the way you've grown the assets I gifted you with. I took great pleasure in rubbing Micah's face in the fact that my son is bringing more to the table than he thought."

Rocco couldn't help the smile that tilted his lips. "You been giving him hell?"

"You already know how I operate."

He leaned down and studied the outline of his assets, marveling how far he'd come from the boy thrown in the group home when his mother had been murdered. He owed Dallas more than the money he'd invested in him. He owed the man his life. He marked out what he wouldn't part with and passed the papers back to Dallas.

Dallas frowned at the single line. "That's it."

"It's just money, and she's my mate. I trust you." It felt good to say and mean.

Dallas' eyes softened, and he cleared his throat. "I got you. Always, I promised you that."

He nodded and stood. "Thank you. For this...for everything you've ever done for me."

The two men stared at each other, all the things unsaid showing in their eyes. Dallas nodded, understanding all that Rocco couldn't articulate.

eight

"Let's talk sanctuary cities," Silas announced Monday morning.

They were all gathered in chairs scattered across his office. Their office's current project was drafting a bill to protect the last sanctuary cities across this country. There were twenty left, and they were all under threat because an energy company wanted land rights for just one.

The cities had been established to protect smaller shifter packs and their rarer animals. After the war with humans, laws were put into place to leave the cities as they were, shifters only under their own individual rule. The new law would rip that independence from them. Julissa spent the first two months in her new job researching the town charters and coming up with possible solutions to close up any exploitable loopholes.

She worked to keep her eyes off her mate and focus on the meeting, but that was near impossible. She made a note to herself to find out Rock's thoughts on public displays of affection. She didn't want to cross over any of his boundaries. Julissa had been keeping her hands to herself all day, but she wondered how he would feel about that if they weren't at work. He was sitting on the sofa in Silas's office. His gaze concentrated on the laptop in front of him. She wanted to know what he was doing, but Silas' following words snagged her attention.

"Congressman Stuart is halfway to the support he needs for his new bill dismantling the Sanctuary cities in this country. That means we need to work on our counter proposal fast. But we don't want to move too fast where we leave out their needs and wants. To that end, I need a volunteer."

Julissa's arm shot up quickly. "I'll do it."

Silas sat back and narrowed his eyes. "You haven't even heard what I needed."

She adjusted in her seat and straightened. "Well, if we're drafting laws that further protect sanctuary cities, then we'll need to make sure it covers their needs and any benefits Congressman Stuart promised them to sway their vote. That means talking to the city council members and getting it directly from their mouths. I can do that. I've been studying the town charters for two months now."

Silas nodded for her to keep going.

Julissa licked her lips in nervousness. All eyes were on her, and while she was used to it, it still unnerved her. But she pushed past it. She wanted to do a great job and, most of all, for people to see her differently than just her daddy's princess.

"I'm new, I get that, but I've been in politics my whole life, and I don't mean that as hyperbole. I've shadowed my father for as long as I can remember, attending tri-council meetings and sitting in on his meetings with the bears of the city. I know how to determine the needs of the shifters we serve."

Despite her age, she had some experience parsing needs from the requests of the shifters her father ruled. Micah had never had an issue breaking down what he did to his only daughter. He may have wanted to keep her celibate her whole life, but he took pride in crafting her mind. Micah had been ecstatic about her decision to go to law school.

Silas studied her, tapping his pencil against his desk. "It's not just talking on the phone with them. You'll need to visit each city. We can set up meetings with their individual city councils from here and coordinate with the mayors. That's twenty cities in less than a month. Can you handle that?"

She nodded eagerly, fighting to keep still in her chair because, besides Silas's stare, she could now feel Rocco's prodding gaze. Julissa stood firm in her argument and swallowed down the need to fill in the silence straining the room.

"Let's get the meetings scheduled and all the information on the town charters that we can find so we can arm Julissa with the most up-to-date information," Silas ordered. "Everyone else is dismissed."

She expected jealous glances or even resentment, but the four other team members sent her thumbs up on their way to do their assigned jobs. She wanted to slouch in relief but would wait until she left Silas's office to celebrate.

Silas spoke the moment the door closed behind the last person. "It's too dangerous, Julissa."

She opened her mouth to protest, but he held up his hand.

"I understand having to prove yourself, in any case. So, I'll send you, but Rock will go with you as protection."

A thrill went through her, and she tucked her lips to hide her smile. "You think that's necessary?"

Julissa didn't look in Rocco's direction. She'd fold if she did.

"Very much so. Keisha will book all your travel arrangements. Most of the cities are concentrated in the center of the country, so it shouldn't be too taxing. Go home and pack."

"Oh…now?"

"The sooner you bring back the assessments, the sooner we can get the jump on the senator."

She nodded, but indecision froze her. Had she bitten off more than she could chew? "I…"

"Now, Julissa," Silas chided her gently, waving towards the door.

"Ok. Thank you. I won't let you down," she said, quickly getting out of her seat.

She rushed from his office, celebration forgotten. There would be no time for that.

Rocco watched her leave, his bear rumbling in his chest in anticipation. A road trip with his mate would break his resolve to keep his hands off her. That was a given. He was okay with that. It was the danger to her that he didn't like. But he would never stop her from doing the job she obviously loved. The hours she'd put in the past two months had proven that. Julissa rarely left the office before Silas did.

"You good with that?" Silas asked him.

His bear protested because even if his naive mate didn't understand the danger she was putting herself in, they did.

"Micah?"

"Pop already dealing with him for you. You just keep her alive. But also, quit pussyfooting around and mate that girl. Y'all got the whole office full of pheromones."

Rock growled, and Silas laughed. "Don't get mad at me. I already called Theo, so you're good to go home and pack. And heads up, Mom's looking for you."

He frowned and gave his best friend his full attention.

"Your niece let slip last night that your apartment 'was naked,' Ya-Ya's words, not mine."

Rock sighed. He'd let Riyah ride with him yesterday to pick up something from home, and she'd been on his ass the whole ride back to the Knight's. That little girl was determined to drag him out of his self-imposed isolation whether he liked it or not. He groaned when his phone rang, punctuating Silas' point. The only other people who called him were in this office, so he already knew who it was.

"Mama Di," he greeted.

"I didn't want to invade your privacy by entering your den. Come let Sariyah and me in," she gently ordered. "We'll meet you there."

He groaned, and she laughed. "It'll be painless," she promised.

He looked at Silas, who laughed.

"That's what you get for spoiling her," Silas said, shaking his head and returning to his paperwork.

The 'her' could've been either one of the ladies. Yes, he spoiled his niece, but he could admit he treated Adina and Iris the same. Either of the women knew that they only had to call, and he would drop what he was doing for them. Luckily for him, they didn't take advantage of that. It was one of the things he loved about them both.

"I'm on the way," he said.

She ended the call, and he lowered his head. A naked apartment. He had to chuckle. He could only imagine how the eight-year-old had described it. His mind went to Julissa; decorating his apartment would be good. He wondered what she would like and what her tastes were. He hadn't yet visited her apartment to see. He'd be out of town for who knew how long, so in reality, he didn't have to go through every step of the redecorating process.

That was tolerable.

He headed to his apartment to pack and deal with his niece and her grandmother. They were there when he pulled up to his building. Sariyah quickly jumped from Adina's Bentley, rushing towards him. Her kinky hair was spilling from the bottom of the pink beret she wore that matched her sweater and boots. Her brown skin was flushed with excitement.

"Uncle Rock, we're going to get stuff for your house," she said excitedly. "Aren't you excited?"

He grunted his answer to that. "My place is fine," he said gruffly.

She smiled at him, her missing teeth making her extra adorable. "Sure, sure."

She grabbed his hand and dragged him towards Adina. The Knight matriarch was dressed identically to her granddaughter, except her grey and black hair was straight and flowing around her shoulders. She was a beautiful woman. Graceful and powerful, the energy from her panther was always at the forefront. Adina carried her panther well and had never tried to conform with the humans.

"Mama Di."

Adina smiled and cupped his cheek. Her power soothed him. "You know I would leave it be, but your niece is insistent."

"I'll be gone."

Adina's face creased with worry. "With Silas?"

He nodded to their security. "Inside."

She hummed in understanding, and they all marched towards the secured building. He greeted the doorman and headed to the elevator.

Ya-Ya prattled on with her grandmother as they rode up. Sariyah stepped off the elevator, but she didn't approach his door. He smiled. The little girl learned fast. They didn't play about keeping Sariyah safe. Before opening his door, he checked to ensure his security measures were still in place. He swept the area, using his senses before giving them the all-clear.

He sighed, knowing what would happen the moment Adina realized how he was living. It wasn't that he couldn't afford better. It was just that growing up the way he had, nothing was permanent, least of all a home, so he planned accordingly. He kept his prized possessions in his bedroom, hidden in his closet. Outside of the bedroom furniture and sofa, there was nothing else in the apartment.

Adina narrowed her eyes at him before dropping her purse on the small kitchen counter. She took out her phone and started taking notes. He thought about how Julissa would feel knowing he'd been in the building for nearly a decade. He hadn't corrected her on Friday night when she'd rightfully assumed he'd just moved in. The place was sparse, and it was the first time he'd been embarrassed by that. He didn't allow people into his house, so he'd never had to worry about it before.

Knowing there was nothing he could do, he headed to his room to pack. He was nearly done but tensed when he felt Adina's presence.

"How long will you be gone?"

He shrugged.

"Alone?"

"With Julissa."

Adina's eyes widened in happiness.

"Protection." He warned her.

"Sure, sure. I talked to Therese. Dallas and Micah have nearly finished negotiating the mating contract, but it's handled."

He nodded again.

"Be careful, my love."

"I will," he promised, zipping his wardrobe bag and small suitcase.

She waited until he left the walk-in closet to hug him. Adina understood that being in an enclosed space with him could set him off. He loved that about her. She read him like no other person. She held him tight, her panther sending out soothing energy.

"Call me when you get where you're going and if you need anything."

He inclined his head towards the living room.

She sighed. "If I didn't understand why, I would be so mad at you, Rocco. It's okay to settle in. You own the building. No one can take this place from you."

He grunted.

"I'm moving you to the penthouse where you belong. You have the whole fourth floor you could be in."

He raised an eyebrow.

Adina chuckled. "That's not the same. I am not taking away your home. I'm attempting to nudge you into making one for yourself and your soon-to-be mate."

He didn't bother arguing, but she seemed to sense his reluctance.

"You're never going to allow more than three or four tenants in this dang gone building, so don't act like you'll have an influx of renters vying for that condo. I'll make sure that the place is aired out so that no extra scents linger when the movers finish."

He nuzzled her cheek and grabbed his suitcase.

"I'll keep your mate in mind too." She said to his back.

He stopped walking and debated turning. Adina wiped away the smug smile as he gave in and turned around.

"I'll ask Therese for her likes and dislikes…discreetly, of course." He stared, and she laughed. "I can be discreet, Rocco Jamison. You'll bring her by the house for dinner when you're back."

Adina held up her hands when he said nothing to that. "She's beautiful. I won't rush you, but I can't speak for Iris."

He grunted in amusement.

She walked closer to him and cupped his cheek. "You understand that your parent's mating has no bearing on what you'll have with Julissa?"

"Ma," he said softly.

"I know you fear that you'll be like him. I took over raising you when your mother could no longer. I don't raise cowards, and I for damn sure don't raise men who put their hands on women. You're nothing like him." She insisted, her animal's power filling him.

He nuzzled into her hand, his throat tight. Adina had always been able to read him and his fears. Despite her words, apprehension about the mating trapped him. He kept that to himself.

"Go, be careful, and keep in touch." She said softly, letting him off the hook.

He nodded and headed out. Sariyah was waiting for him when he reached his living room. Instead of making notes, she watched his TV and ate the fruit from his refrigerator. It seemed her grandmother would be doing all the redecorating herself. He chuckled.

She jumped up when she saw him. "Bye, Uncle Rock. Be careful on your trip. Bring me back something."

"Just something?" he asked.

Sariyah gave him a sly look. He smiled and lifted her, nuzzling her cheek. The little minx. Her tight hug soothed the anxiety brought on by her grandmother's words. She wrapped her arms around his neck, the charms on her bracelet jingling. He bought her one from every city he and her dad visited.

"Be good for your parents." He finally said.

"You know me," she said instead, and he huffed out a small laugh.

He loved the busybody and was happy his friend had found her and his mate. Rocco checked his email as he rode down the elevator. Keisha had already sent over the itinerary. He raised his eyebrows at how much driving they would be doing but pushed it aside. His only priority would be keeping Julissa safe.

nine

Rock drove his personal car, parking his vintage Lincoln Continental into the spot reserved for the passengers of private jets. Silas would pick it up on his way home this evening, so he didn't have to worry about it while he was gone. He didn't like the idea of anyone driving his baby, but Silas would be careful. Julissa was already on the tarmac waiting when he walked up. A bear was beside her, his all-black uniform and alert demeanor screaming security. His mate had changed out of her work suit and wore a skin-tight black jumpsuit and a camel-colored trench coat on top. The coat did nothing to hide the curves underneath, and Rock's mouth watered, his bear rising enough to push out his claws. He took a deep calming breath before approaching her.

"My father insisted on a guard," she grumbled as he walked up. "Never mind that I'm trying to do my job. I don't need two of you."

He grunted at her tone, and she sighed.

"I'm not trying to sound ungrateful."

He held out his hand, and the other bear shook. "Byron. I've heard a lot about you around town. You'll have point, but Councilman Crespo thought another pair of hands couldn't hurt."

He nodded because the more eyes on his mate, the better. She was fussing about him and Byron, but another guard was already on the plane. Julian had sent him ahead like he did anytime Silas and Rock traveled. He inclined his head towards the private plane, and the bear got the hint, moving quickly towards the jet with Julissa's luggage. She had packed for a solid month, it seemed.

Rocco's gaze never left Julissa, cataloging her irritation. He lifted her chin. It wasn't his first touch with his mate, and still, his hands shook. She was pouting, and damn if it didn't do things to his bear.

"Will we have a problem with the extra security?"

She shook her head and dropped her gaze. She shuddered, and he wondered if the timbre of his voice was too much for her. No fear laced her divine scent, so that was a no.

"Itinerary?"

She nodded. "Keisha sent it and all the other details we need for the first town."

He didn't move, simply soaking her in. He lost his fight with temptation and skimmed his hands down her waist, bringing her into his body. She sighed and relaxed in his embrace.

"You ready?"

She nodded and put her forehead into his chest. "I'm looking forward to alone time with you."

"Won't be alone." He reminded her.

She sucked her teeth, which made him chuckle. She joined him, sliding her arms into his jacket and around his waist.

"What you want, sug?"

"You," she whispered, and he shuddered, tightening his fingers on her waist.

"I'm yours, Liss."

She looked up, surprise coloring her face. He threw caution to the wind and kissed her. He needed it like his next breath. Julissa melted into the kiss, her bear reaching out to his. The two animals sent out magic, brushing against each other, and Rock was ready to drag her back to his car. He pulled back and groaned.

"Daddy says our contract is done," she said softly.

He growled as his phone rang. He whipped it from his pocket.

"Yeah, PD."

"Contract done," Dallas announced, confirming her words.

He stared down at his mate, his bear bucking because nothing was stopping him from claiming Julissa. All of a sudden, the trip looked better and better. Julissa nuzzled into him, her hands making slow circles on his back in a soothing motion.

"Bet."

"How long y'all gon' be gone?"

"Not sure. A few weeks."

"Be careful. Julian sent extra guards?" Dallas asked.

"He did."

"Ok. Then keep us posted. Love you, kid."

"You too." He ended the call, thinking about everything he could do to his mate when he got her alone.

"Let's go, sug," he ordered.

He escorted her onto the plane. His eyes raked the interior, and he got the all-okay signal from the guards already posted in their seats towards the back. That left him and Julissa in the front alone. The jet was big enough to hold Silas's entire staff, so there was enough space between Rocco and Julissa that they would have a small semblance of privacy. He settled her into a chair before taking the one next to her. Julissa tensed as the flight attendant went through her checks. Her leg started bouncing, and her bear's energy was erratic. He placed a hand on her knee to still it.

"What's wrong?"

"Nervous flyer," she admitted. "Talk to me to distract me."

He snorted, and she laughed, knowing how that request would go. But he could think of another way to distract her.

JULISSA KNEW ASKING Rocco to talk to her as a distraction was a ridiculous ask. The man only spoke when necessary. She turned in her seat to face him.

"Why do you call Councilman Knight 'PD'?"

He stared at her for a moment, and she didn't think he would answer.

"Buckle, sug." He ordered as the flight attendant signaled they would take off soon.

She did what he ordered, still waiting on his answer. She gripped the sides of the chair as the plane taxied. He pulled her hand into his lap.

"Papa D. I shortened it to just PD after a while. It stuck." His gravelly voice calmed her fear, and she gripped his hand tightly.

The small plane was bumping across the runway, and she was working on regulating her breathing. Her nerves had her animal frazzled. Rock leaned over and nuzzled into her neck, huffing against her skin. She froze in shock and pleasure, her nervousness momentarily forgotten.

"Smell good," he rumbled.

She tilted her head to give him more space, and he scraped his teeth against her skin, sucking on her neck. She swallowed and squirmed in her seat as moisture gathered at the apex of her thighs. His hand traced her thighs, and her breath shorted in anticipation.

"What are you doing?" she whispered.

She cursed her idea to wear the full bodysuit. She would give anything to be in a skirt right now. Rocco tilted her chin towards him and kissed her gently, licking her bottom lip.

"Distracting you," was his answer.

He kissed her again, and she opened her mouth, and he slid his tongue inside. She lost herself in the kiss, her body flushing in pleasure. He couldn't get inside her pants, but it didn't stop him from pressing his thumb against her pussy, expertly finding her clit. *Fuck*, she was going to come all over herself. He didn't move his finger; instead, he exerted just enough pressure that her stomach clenched.

"Is it working?"

She rocked her hips forward and nodded. Oh, it was definitely fucking working. He pinched her nipple, and Julissa sucked in a sharp breath. She couldn't help the whimper that escaped. She bit down on her lip to keep herself from moaning.

"Nah, let me hear that shit. Tell me how good I'm making you feel."

The rumble of his voice raised the hair on the back of her neck. Her stomach dipped as the plane took off. He pressed a little harder against her clit, and Julissa moved her hips in a circle to ride that feeling.

"Rocco," she whispered, mindful that there were not alone on this plane.

"Feel good, mama?"

"Yes," she hissed as he circled her nipple slowly.

She reached down and held his hand in place, writhing her hips. She could feel an orgasm on the horizon.

"Breathe, baby," he whispered, nipping her ear lobe.

She let out a shuddering breath. "So close."

He nuzzled his cheek against her neck, the hair of his beard scraping against her skin. The added sensation sent electricity tingling across her skin. Her body tightened, and Rock lifted his head. He gripped her chin and turned her to face him. His gaze was dark…hungry. His animal stared from his eyes, a feral look that made her pussy clench in need.

"I want to see your face when you come." He kissed her softly. "I'm gon' memorize that shit."

Julissa closed her eyes, but he nipped her chin hard, the pain spiking her pleasure. It forced her lids open, and she could only stare at him in helpless wonder as her body went up in flames. Rocco kissed her hard, his tongue spearing her mouth as she rode out her orgasm.

He pulled back. "Claws, baby." He whispered against her lips.

She looked down and noticed the scratches on his arm. "Oh my God, I'm so sorry, Rocco."

She hadn't even been aware her animal was that close to the surface. Her cheeks flamed in embarrassment. There was no pain on his face, just satisfaction as he chuckled and inspected his arm.

"I'll never stop you from marking your shit, sug." He hovered over her mouth, not kissing her, just inhaling. "You smell amazing. I can't wait to have you in my mouth."

Julissa squeezed her thighs together at that thought. For a man who said few words, he definitely knew the right ones to use. She took a deep breath as her body calmed. She was utterly relaxed and euphoric. She lifted his arm and snuggled into his chest. His heartbeat was steady, and the sound soothed her like nothing she'd ever experienced.

He curled his arm around her waist and kissed the top of her head. "Try to sleep. We got a long night ahead."

She hummed in answer, already halfway there.

ten

Julissa had been happy for the nap that she'd been able to snag on the plane. Seven hours of traveling was no joke. It was well into the evening when they'd arrived at the small Montana airport, and it was colder than a bitch outside too. She let her bear off its leash to warm her as she waited for the SUV they'd rented to drive up. It didn't take long, but she had felt every second of the wait. Rocco escorted her into the running truck and helped the others get the bags inside. She looked down at the reservations Keisha sent over.

"There weren't any hotels in town, just a bed and breakfast." She informed Rocco as he got inside with her.

"What does that mean?" He gruffly asked.

"There were only two rooms. The two of them should share the larger one, which leaves the one with only one bed for us." She fought not to smile at Rocco's hungry look.

The guards in front of her snickered.

"It's just two nights; we'll survive." She teased them.

Rocco simply grunted and tapped Byron on the shoulder to get him to move along. The bear was driving while Harold took the passenger seat. They had another hour in the car before they reached their destination. The sanctuary towns were small and, luckily, clustered not too far from each other. After this town, instead of another flight, they just had a four-hour drive to the next one. She would see more Middle America than she wanted but was over-excited about her task.

Julissa gasped an hour later when they pulled up to the white-washed building that was their bed and breakfast. She saw small glimpses of cottages towards the back that were all white and adobe style, the stone beautifully kept. It was quaint and beautiful. She didn't know what she was expecting, but this romantic place had not been it. She wanted to squeal in pleasure.

She waited until Rocco let her out of the car, but she gripped his hand, rushing inside to see the rest of the place. The stone floors were meticulously maintained, and she could smell the wood burning from the giant fireplace that was the focal point in the room. Leather chairs and sofas were scattered across the room, with colorful pillows covering them. A few guests were having drinks, but the place was empty otherwise.

The owner struck up a conversation with Rocco while he checked them in or, well, attempted to. He gave her a polite smile and filled out the required paperwork, sliding the woman his credit card. Julissa shrugged when the woman looked at her.

"Is there a place that serves dinner here?"

"We have a diner that's still open for a couple of more hours," she answered with a smile, handing Rocco their keys. "The only other foxes in town run it. Just tell them you're staying here, and they'll send the tab here if you want."

Julissa nodded. "Thank you so much."

She was anxious to see their room first. Rocco handed off the keys to Harold and Byron, gripping Julissa's hand as they walked out the back door of the main building. She gasped. Lights were strung across the desert setting, and despite the snow that covered everything, it looked magical. Rocco walked her to their small cabin, and she was happy to be out of the cold. The queen-sized bed was inviting. There was a small bathroom off to their left, but a bathtub sat directly in front of the bed and the wall-to-wall window that looked out towards the snowy landscape. It was breathtaking.

"I can sleep on the sofa for tonight. You need to concentrate on the meetings ahead," Rocco's voice rumbled.

She sucked her teeth. "I can control myself if you sleep beside me, Rocco."

Maybe.

She'd see, wouldn't she?

THE ANSWER WAS YES, she could control herself, but she was grumpy as hell and horny to boot. Not a good way to start her first meeting of the trip, but there was nothing to be done about it. She looked out into the gathering crowd of the school gym that doubled as their town hall, her stomach fluttering with nervousness. Rocco stood at her back while Byron and Harold were scattered throughout the crowd at the exit points.

She politely waited her turn as the town alpha and mayor introduced her and her purpose for visiting. There were murmurs and questions scoffing at her age, but she ignored them, focusing on the speech Silas had sent ahead. Taking a deep breath, she took the podium.

The speech took twenty minutes, which wasn't long enough to cover all the ways their new bill would help, but it gave the bullet points. The mayor and his council would get the full breakdown tomorrow. For now, it was more about opening the floor up for inquiries. Her eyes widened when she realized how many people had questions when she was done.

"Why does this Knight want to help us all of a sudden?" One of the townspeople asked.

She took a deep breath and considered her answer. "Mr. Knight just wants to ensure he's representing your true needs and wants without you giving up any of your independence. It's not all of a sudden. His position as Liaison to this county's shifters requires that he certifies we're all represented."

"Councilman Stuart promised more money coming into this town."

She nodded. "I'm sure that's true. But he doesn't tell you that federal money comes at a cost. Your independence is its first toll. You'll have to answer and account for every penny the government gives to this town. And again, I'm not here to talk you out of voting. If that's what you want, then Mr. Knight can add you as an exception to our bill. You'll get the federal money, and your town will be disbanded. What our bill does is stop the blanket dismantling of sanctuary cities. It may not mean anything to your town, but there are smaller towns still counting on the protections sanctuary status provides for them."

The murmuring from the crowd picked up at her words.

"How do we know he's not feeding us false information?"

She smiled. It was a fair question. "Mr. Knight's website lists all the bills he's passed and how they've assisted this country's shifters. There are resources there for you to research for yourself. You don't have to take my word on anything."

That seemed to pacify the crowd, and they settled. Julissa stepped back from the podium and allowed their alpha to take control.

ROCCO'S GAZE SPLIT TIME between his mate and the restless crowd. There were a couple of specific males he was keeping his eyes on. They didn't look interested in the proceedings; instead, their gaze was on Julissa. He could understand that, though. It was fascinating watching her speak. He'd seen how she controlled a room when he attended Motsi events; this town hall was no different. She was confident in her manner and charming in her words. He watched her settle the fears of the townspeople without losing her temper. Empathy and compassion coated her every word, and though many of the shifters had given her a hard time, she seemed to be winning over some of them. It was a huge turn-on.

Though, it seemed everything she did was a turn-on for him. The alpha dismissed the meeting, and some people swarmed toward Julissa to ask more questions.

He stepped in front of her, "Two feet." he ordered them, and they stopped and formed a line.

He dodged questions some of the women in town aimed his way, keeping vigilant at Julissa's side. His mate was damn near growling by the time another female walked up to him. Her bear became agitated and more aggravated as the questions kept coming, so he cut it all short.

"Time to go," he ordered her.

She sighed in relief and smiled. "Thank you all for your questions. I'll make sure Mr. Knight understands all of your concerns."

He guided her to the SUV and helped her inside. The heels she wore were not necessarily practical for snow. Instead of closing the door, he turned her legs so that they buffered his waist. He leaned over into her space. She sucked in a sharp breath, her bear reaching for his as she wrapped her arms around his shoulders. He allowed his animal off the leash to soothe her.

"You got a jealous streak," he said softly.

She sighed. "How would you like it if males were all over me?"

He chuckled, "That tells me you ain't paying no attention to your surroundings, sug."

The men in town had been eyeing her from the moment she walked her fine ass into that school gymnasium. The yellow suit she wore beneath the trench accentuated her every curve and made her stand out like a ray of sunshine. He hadn't been the only one to notice.

He lifted her chin. "What do you need from me?"

Her pulse raced beneath his thumb as he gripped her neck loosely.

"I...what do you mean?"

"I got this thing with jealousy. It sets off my bear and not in a good way. Tell me why you worried about other women."

Though her jealousy didn't feel toxic, it, unfortunately, triggered way too many memories, and he wanted to nip it in the bud asap. She searched his eyes, debating what to tell him.

"You haven't tried to claim me even though our contracts are finished. It makes my bear insecure." She whispered.

"I'm moving too slow for her?" He nuzzled into her neck, and the animal in her flared and wrapped around him.

She nodded in response.

"I'm sorry, love. I...got a few hang-ups. I don't know if you should tie yourself to someone like me."

She growled. "Don't talk about my mate like that."

He smiled, a slight tilt of his lips. He kissed Julissa gently before pulling away. "Buckle, sug."

He closed the door carefully and walked around the truck. He needed to sit with what she was telling him. He didn't want to acerbate her insecurity, but he was having difficulty with his own where she was concerned. He had better examples of matings that worked, so he knew they wouldn't all end like his parents' had. But he was still wary.

"Do you have any idea what you want for lunch, Liss?" he asked to break the silence.

She groaned. "I don't even want to think about it. I want a nap."

He chuckled, knowing the work she still had to do before she could relax. "I'll take care of it."

She gave him a smile that warmed his whole body. "Thank you, Rocco."

He loved the way she said his name. He gripped her chin and brought her closer, kissing her firmly. He pulled back when they pulled into the driveway of the bed and breakfast. The woman made him lose his head.

eleven

Lunch was a thing of the past, and by the darkening skies, it was time for dinner. Julissa happily ended the Zoom call with her coworkers, happy to be done for the day. They'd reviewed the townspeople's concerns and devised a strategy for tomorrow's meeting with the mayor. Rocco had long ago left her alone in the room. She stood, stretched, and debated whether or not she should shower before hunting down her mate and something for dinner. Instead of doing either, she checked in with her parents.

Her mother had been sending her messages and pictures all day. She went through them now that she had time and shook her head. Why was Therese sending her furniture pictures? She dialed her mother.

"Lady, you better not be trying to redecorate my place," was how she greeted her mother.

Therese laughed. "Girl. I just wanted your opinion. My life does not revolve around you."

"Since when?" Julissa joked.

"Which one of the sofas did you like?" Therese prodded.

"Mama, I don't even know where you're putting it. How am I supposed to answer that?" She unbuttoned her pants and slipped out of the tight trousers, sighing in relief.

"Pick, Julissa. Why are you so argumentative?" Her mother grumbled.

Julissa snorted in amusement. "Fine. You know I love velvet, so the green one."

"Now, was that so hard?" Therese asked.

"What are you up to?"

Julissa put the phone on speaker and changed into something comfortable but appropriate for dinner if Rocco decided they would go out. Though, she was hoping he wouldn't want to.

"None of your business."

Julissa laughed outright. Oh yeah, her mother was definitely up to something.

"How was your first day?" Therese changed the subject.

"It was good. I felt like they were receptive, but we won't really know until the result of the vote comes out."

She looked up as Rocco came into the room. He was carrying a load of takeout trays. The smell wafted over to her, and her stomach rumbled on cue. She inhaled and closed her eyes as the scent of barbecue filled her senses. Julissa could even smell the chocolate cake hiding somewhere in those containers. She did a little dance that caught Rocco's attention. He smiled and shook his head. He cleared the small table where she had been working all day and set it for their dinner.

"Julissa," Therese called, bringing her attention back to the conversation she'd been having with her mother.

"Sorry, Mom. What did you say?"

Therese sighed dramatically. "Never mind. Just answer my texts when I send them. In a timely fashion if you please."

"Mama, do not rearrange my apartment. I mean it. I'll get to those boxes in my own time."

"I love you. Keep me posted when you can, love." Therese quickly ended the call.

Julissa sucked her teeth and tossed her phone to the bed. Ain't no telling what that woman was doing to her apartment. She would probably have to change it all back around when she returned home. She moved closer to the table her mate was setting. Instead of just putting the food down, he'd arranged it into place settings, even going so far as to add a small flower as a centerpiece. She smiled.

God, this man.

"Where did you get these plates and stuff?" she asked, peeking at the array of food.

"Downstairs." Was all he said in that rumbly tone of his.

The man wouldn't talk, but obviously, he missed nothing. The food he'd laid out was some of her favorite barbecue choices— sausage, ribs, even down the corn and potato salad. There was no chicken on her side of the table at all. She only ate chicken when it was fried, and even that was sporadic. He'd remembered.

"You got my favorites." She said it aloud just to confirm her thoughts.

"Come," he ordered, pointing to the chair he held out.

She settled into the chair. "How did you know what to order me?"

"I listen when you talk, Liss."

"Rocco," she whispered, her cheeks heated.

She knew that was all she was getting out of him. They ate in silence. She didn't have the energy to talk, and Rocco never felt the need to fill in quiet. She thought it would make her nervous, but it didn't. Her bear was settling, and that was so puzzling to her. She didn't see a mate like Rocco for herself. She thought she would mate with someone like her father, ambitious and slick, but her bear was adamant about this indomitable man sitting across from them.

She put the first bite of chocolate cake in her mouth and moaned. Rock stilled across from her. She closed her eyes on the next taste, and when she opened them, he was staring at her, his eyes dark, dark, onyx. She stared at his bear, the feral animal watching her. She licked her lips, and he mirrored that. He sucked in a sharp breath and pulled back, his animal retreating.

He stood. "I need to…" he didn't finish the sentence.

He rushed from their room, leaving her flustered in her chair. So he wasn't entirely unaffected by her. She smiled. She could work with that.

ROCK MADE ANOTHER ROUND around the small bed and breakfast. The foxes who owned it had well-marked their territory. They were well known in the small city, so he wasn't worried about the town's residents bothering them, but he didn't slow his steps as he lumbered across the property. He'd spotted unfamiliar tracks a little too close to their cabin for his comfort, so he'd loosened the leash on his animal as he circled the property. It reminded him that he needed to stay vigilant. He couldn't have his head messed up by mating with Julissa just yet.

Satisfied that all the scents outside matched those inside, he returned to their cabin.

His bear was slamming against him to shift, but he refused to give the bear any more leeway. He already knew what the damned animal wanted, or rather who. He didn't understand how his mate could make the simple act of eating so sensual, but he had been seconds from snatching her across the table and devouring her the way she had done that cake. He was hard as stone, and it was uncomfortable at this point. Something needed to give.

The contracts were completed, and nothing stopped him from claiming Julissa...except his fear. He wasn't sure if he could be gentle with her at first. He wanted her with a ferocity that scared him. He would do anything not to hurt his mate. He let himself into their room and wished he'd insisted they find a regular hotel with separate rooms. Staying with her was going to be the death of him. He heard the shower going and *swear to God* he would break.

She came out in a robe, her face dewy from her night cream and her hair wrapped and pinned. Some of it escaped her scarf, moist and sticking to the sides of her face and temple. His feet moved. Maybe he could've stopped himself had he let his bear run off the energy, but he didn't think so. He walked to her and grabbed her into his arms. Julissa released a whoosh of air, surprise written all over her face.

He lowered his head and kissed her. A small kiss, just a little one to satisfy him and his animal. Except...Julissa went up on her toes and opened her mouth, her tongue tracing his closed mouth, asking for entrance. He obliged her—as if he could ever deny this woman. At the first taste of her, his knees went weak, and every cell in his body tuned itself to her. His bear even paused its fight with him.

She sighed, and her arms went around his waist as she kissed him deeper. Her hands trailed up and down his back, her body going soft and pliant in his arms. How could a kiss both soothe and rile him up at the same time? He lifted her and planted her on the small chest of drawers. Her legs parted, and she pulled him between them. She drew back from the kiss and buried her face between his neck and shoulder.

"Are you done fighting, my love?"

He shuddered at the longing in her voice and the feel of her breathing along his neck. Was he done? They were from two different worlds. Yeah, he moved along the periphery of hers, but still. He didn't belong, no matter that the Knights didn't seem to get that memo. She kissed his neck and clutched him tight, sighing.

"You're going to make me beg, aren't you?"

"Never, sug." He gripped her chin and brought her up for another kiss.

This time, he savored her kiss, eating at her mouth. She returned the energy, and the scent of her arousal rose between them. She gripped his dick and squeezed, and Rock pulled back.

"You're fighting me and your bear, Rocco. Put us out of our misery," she pouted, and God, his chest hurt.

She was so fucking beautiful.

"I'm not fit for you, Liss." He whispered, nuzzling against her cheek.

"Bullshit. Our animals don't make mistakes. You're mine, which means I'm made for you. Next excuse."

He studied her eyes and saw the look that he'd come to recognize. His mate was stubborn and determined. The shit that made her good at her new job was making it hard to keep his distance.

"I can't protect you if my head is fucked, Liss."

"I want my mate," she whispered.

Rock tried to swallow past the lump in his throat. She rubbed against him, the heat from her pussy scorching him through his clothes. It made him realize that she wore nothing under that robe.

"Liss," he groaned.

"Rocco," she mocked.

He kissed her to shut her up. She grabbed his hand and brought it to her wet center, and his hands shook as he gently slid his finger across her clit. She moaned in his mouth. She pulled back and kissed down his neck, her hands going to his pants. She unbuttoned them. He should stop them. If he went past this line, there was no coming back. All the reasons he'd made up for them to wait flew out the window. He wanted her. She hummed in appreciation when she finally got his pants down his waist. His chest swelled.

He tried one more time to make her see reason. "We still have work to do. You don't want to wait until after the meeting tomorrow?"

"Fuck work." She muttered, nipping the skin of his shoulder.

Her eyes were focused as though she was already picking out a place to put her mark. He didn't know how it was possible to get harder, but his dick jumped in anticipation. Her soft hand wrapped around his erection, and every thought in his brain scattered.

"I need a shower."

She growled, her bear making its displeasure known.

He laughed at the insistent animal.

"Was that a full-on laugh?" She leaned back and smiled at him. "I might just be breaking you down, Rocco Jamison."

He snorted and lifted her, walking her to their bed. He laid her down and took his time parting the robe, opening it like a long-awaited present. He kissed her chest.

"Stay."

"I'm not going anywhere," she told him.

He smiled, and her eyes softened. He was done fighting this woman.

twelve

Julissa took a shaky breath when she heard the shower stop. Her body was a mass of neediness, and she couldn't wait until he touched her. She wanted to know if he matched all the daydreams she'd spun about him. He came out of the bathroom with just a towel swung around his hips, and her pulse raced. He was gorgeous, his body inkstained, mapped with muscles and dewy skin. Her mouth watered.

His eyes were on hers, intense, dark, and flashing with his animal. Her bear answered, heating Julissa's body, making her skin sensitive to the sheets she lay on.

"You moved." his voice rumbled.

She swallowed, unable to say anything. All she'd done was move up the bed to lean against the headboard. Her heartbeat thumped in her chest, her bear roiling inside. Rocco growled and closed his eyes, inhaling deeply. When he opened them, her breath caught at the molten darkness in his gaze. He looked at her as if she was the most important thing in his life.

"Rocco," she whispered.

He dragged her legs roughly, pulling until her ass was perched right on the edge of the bed. That aggressiveness should've given her pause, but her clit pulsed, and pussy quivered in yearning. His hands were tight on her thighs, but he took a shuddering breath and gentled his touch. She gasped when he went to his knees, parting her thighs and growling. Longing and lust infused the sound, and she'd never felt as wanted as he made her feel.

"In my life, I never imagined I would have anything as beautiful as you." He kissed the top of her mound, his gaze spearing her for a hot moment before his finger grazed the lips of her pussy gently. He kissed her there softly, hissing when he found her wet. "Are you mine, Julissa?"

"Yes," she rushed out.

He shuddered, his tongue sliding against her sex. It sent shivers of desperate need down her spine.

"One last time to save yourself, sug, because once I have you, I'm not letting another soul take you from me." The intensity of his gaze brought tears to her eyes.

She ran her hand over his head, guiding him where she needed him. "You're mine, and I'll fight the world to keep you," she swore. The fire that lit his eyes warmed her from the inside. "Now, quit teasing me, Rocco."

He took that as his go signal, devouring her. With his tongue and fingers, he explored her pussy, mapping every pleasure point. His nails dug into her thighs, sometimes scraping against a spot she didn't even know was that sensitive. Every time he sucked her clit into his mouth, Julissa's back left the bed in a high arch.

"So fucking good," he murmured, his eyes on her pussy as though he'd been waiting forever to taste her.

"Rocco," she whispered his name.

He undid her, sucking, biting, and scratching until she screamed with the force of her orgasm. He gentled his sucking until her tensed muscles loosened. He licked his lips and moaned.

"Your taste is something I'll be addicted to."

"Let me see," she whispered, gripping his arms and bringing him close.

The feral growl that rumbled his chest brought her bear forward, the wanton animal wanting her to get straight to the marking. Her claws dropped, and it spurred Rocco forward. He dropped his towel and slid up her body. She licked against his lips before kissing him.

Their tongues lazily tangled, and her mind floated along a wave of bliss. Her body was limp with satiation.

Julissa found herself further under his spell. He pulled back and lifted her legs and settled them into the crook of his arms, holding her legs wide.

"Please."

"You ready, sug?" He probed the entrance of her sex with his dick, waiting on her answer.

She eagerly nodded, wanting every last bit of him. She hadn't been prepared for so much of him, though. She whimpered as he stretched her, her clenching muscles fighting against the sweet invasion.

"So tight," Rocco murmured. He nuzzled into her neck. "Let me in, sug."

His words worked, and her pussy relaxed, her stomach fluttering at the rough pleading.

"That's right, baby, relax and take me," he encouraged, his strokes leisurely and shallow until her body adjusted.

She held him tightly against her as sensations bombarded her. Feral and dominating power rushed over her as his bear pushed forward. Rocco hissed as he slid out, cursing and plunging back inside, deeper now that she'd adjusted to his size. Julissa arched her hips, taking more of him.

"This…" he paused and shook his head. "This pussy finna have me wildin', I can tell."

He released one of her legs and leaned down into her. He made love to her, his strokes gentle and deep, igniting a fire within her that threatened to burn her to ash. He was careful with her, and her bear wasn't having it. She swirled her hips and tightened down on his dick.

"More," she whispered.

He cursed. "Why you rushing me, sug? I'm trying to enjoy my pussy."

She scraped her nails down his back, allowing her bear to fill her body. The resulting power surge sped his hips, and Rocco drove into her with fiery strokes that made her frantic. Even her dreams couldn't touch the almost desperate and carnal need between them.

She screamed as he hit a spot inside that had her stomach contracting tightly.

"That's the sound I want to hear," he told her, nipping the skin of her neck.

Her bear stilled within her. His nips turned into small bites as he worked his way down to her shoulder. Julissa tilted her head, nearly begging for him to mark her and make her his. He chuckled, lifting her leg to fuck her deeper.

"Waiting on my bite, Liss?"

She whimpered. "Please, Rocco."

"Give me what I want first," he murmured, sliding his free hand between her legs to pluck at her clit.

"There," she whispered hoarsely, swiveling her hips, chasing her climax.

"Mhmm, that's a good girl; give me that nut."

He licked her shoulder and growled, the vibrations on her skin sending her over the edge. Julissa screamed, tightening down on his dick, and Rocco gave her what she wanted. His teeth pierced her shoulder, and his power flooded her body, prolonging her orgasm. His bear moved through her, twining with hers.

Rocco released her leg and cupped the back of her head. Instinct was already moving her. She sucked on the skin of his shoulder before biting down. He cursed, his hips frantically driving into her as she shoved her power into him, marking him deeply. She wanted no question as to whom he belonged. Rocco came with a yell. She pulled her teeth but continued to suck on that spot until his body shook on top of hers.

"Enough, sug," he husked out.

She acquiesced, licking the bite closed. Rocco pulled her into his body tightly, rolling until she was on top of him. He didn't pull out; he simply held her close.

"Even in my wildest dreams, Liss," he whispered against her temple.

She nuzzled into his sweaty chest, basking in their tight bond. Her bear was quiet and content. Her heart was whole, knowing she would know his emotions at any given moment. It would keep him from hiding his needs from her. She loved the thought of that.

"Gonna sleep," she said drowsily.

He kissed her forehead. "Shower or you won't be able to sleep well."

Unfortunately, that was true. "You gotta tote me."

He laughed and rolled over, lifting them off the bed. If she thought Rocco was done with her, she had been mistaken. Their shower had turned into sex, followed by more sex. By the time her mate let her rest, it was well past midnight, and Julissa didn't have a single complaint about it.

ROCCO JERKED UP, his heart racing, his breathing shallow as the nightmare played through his head. Sweat coated his skin, the uncomfortable sticky feeling a reminder of all the nights he'd laid in his childhood bed worried what the night, and hell, morning would bring. When his mother was alive, he'd feared the heavy footfalls of his father coming home drunk. After she'd died, insecurity with his various living situations had kept him up many nights. He took a deep breath and slid from the bed.

He walked into the bathroom and splashed water on his face. He scented Julissa before her arms slid around his waist.

"What's wrong?" She slid her cheek against his back, nuzzling his skin.

"Nightmare." He tensed, not wanting to admit that.

"I can feel your bear. Is it safe enough to run?"

His body relaxed when she didn't pry further. Happy to have his mind on something else, he went through his memory of the town's layout before nodding. It was a shifter-only town, so theoretically, it would be safe to shift, but that didn't mean they would be safe. His thoughts went to the tracks he hadn't recognized, but he pushed them aside. Rocco was confident he could take care of his mate.

"Let's let him out for a while. Plus, mine is anxious to meet her mate." She kissed his shoulder and walked out of the bathroom.

They threw on robes and walked out of the French doors of their room. It led to the back of the property and would have the privacy they needed to shift. Julissa dropped her robe and shifted first. He waited, giving her bear time to meet him. The sow rushed to him, butting against his chest with her head. He smiled and ran his hands through her fur. His bear pushed against his skin, impatient. Still, he took his time, allowing her to rub her scent along his skin. He dropped his forehead against hers, closing his eyes as the comfort from the animal flooded his body. She chuffed, and he chuckled at the impatient sound.

"Fine," he conceded and backed up.

He shifted, and his bear quickly changed his body, eager to meet its mate. The two animals butted heads, rubbing their sides together. He inclined his head towards the surrounding area, and Julissa ambled off at a leisurely pace. He followed suit, allowing his bear to take over entirely. The animal would keep them safe, of that he had no doubt.

JULISSA STRETCHED HER body as their bears gave them back control. She watched him as he shifted back. Rocco could feel her probes at their bond as she tried to figure out what was happening. His body was relaxed, and he was sure his face showed nothing, but she was privy to all that roiling emotion he hid beneath the surface. Their bond was tight; hiding from his mate would be a fool's errand. She stepped back while he inspected their room before he allowed her inside. It was close to two in the morning, but she ran the bath instead of showering.

Rocco smiled absently as she added the bath beads she'd found in the bathroom to the water. He made no moves to stop her. He could feel her determination to care for him, and after his nightmare, he would take the luxury his mate offered.

"Get in," she ordered him.

He snorted. "Sug, that tub ain't big enough."

"We'll fit." She assured him.

He chuckled softly but followed her orders. She let him get settled before she slid in on top of him. He grunted as she settled between his legs. His knees were high on either side of her, but for the most part, they fit. He closed her eyes as the hot water enveloped them. He luxuriated in the press of Julissa's heated skin, the touch more healing than sexual. Rocco kissed her shoulder.

"Tell me, my love." She prodded.

He sighed, knowing what she was asking. "My parent's mating was full of turmoil—fighting, jealousy, anger. I didn't want to even think about relationships for a long time, never mind mating. She left him, and we moved from place to place for a while, running from him. When I was ten, he found and killed her during one of their fights."

"I'm so sorry, Rocco," she whispered, her voice thick with unshed tears.

He laid his cheek against the back of her neck, seeking comfort. Her bear filled her skin with power despite the animal being exhausted from their run.

He took a shuddering breath. "I don't want to fuck this up, Liss."

She grabbed his hand and kissed his fingertips, rubbing her cheek against his palm.

"There is no part of me that fears you, Rocco. Our mating would never be toxic so long as we communicate and set boundaries that we're both secure with." She paused... "Is that how you ended up at Winnie's house?"

"Not at first. There were so many other homes before then. I can't do chaos, so I would run at the first opportunity. I spent many nights on the streets of Eastfield before Silas found me."

"How old were you?"

"Twelve."

Two long years he'd been on the street. He hated thinking about that time, but he'd long since dealt with the trauma from it. There were counselors that worked with the young shifters at Winnie's House, but Adina had personally taken him to therapy concerned with the anger that used to ride him. Julissa lowered her head.

"Don't sug," he ordered, butting against her shoulder. "I came out of it fine."

"The Knights adopted you?"

He chuckled. "Tried. It took me a while to settle into Winnie's house. But when I did, it felt safer there than risking another situation like my parents. The place was clean. The other shifters there kept to themselves for the most part. There was never all the yelling and fighting I had encountered at the other places. Adina..." he sighed, "I don't know. She took one look at me, and it was like she refused to let me go. I just...replacing my mother with her felt like a betrayal. Silas and Mason would hang out at the house when their mother volunteered. Silas and I clicked immediately, and we all started hanging out." He shrugged. "The rest is history."

"But you've satisfied yourself on the outskirts of their family."

"I'm more comfortable there. Adina fought it at first, but eventually, she understood."

Julissa slid her cheek against his chest. "Will it set you off if I ask about your voice?"

He shook his head. "In one of his drunken states, my father lifted me by my neck with his claws. It punctured my vocal cords. It was before I got my bear, so the healing took forever. It was the last straw for my mother."

She turned as much as she could and traced the tattoos on his neck. He'd gotten them to cover the scars from his childhood. She kissed his neck softly.

"Ain't no space in this tub for all that, mama," he said huskily.

"Out then." She said.

She grabbed a towel and wrapped it around her body. She turned and did the same for him.

He lifted her chin, "Taking care of me, sug?"

"Always," she swore to him softly. "You're mine to protect now. No more outskirts, Rocco Jamison. I'm showing you off."

He chuckled, lifting her. She wrapped her legs around his waist.

"Showing me off, huh?"

"That's fucking right." She declared, kissing him.

thirteen

Before the sun sent its rays across the sky, Rocco's bear was waking him. Heat poured from Julissa, her body hot to the touch as she nuzzled closer to him. He cursed and rolled over quickly, his heart pounding. Panic confused him momentarily, and he could only stare down at his mate. Heat. He should've been ready for it; it wasn't like he hadn't been warned about what happened when sows mated. But he wasn't prepared for his own savage response. The enticing scent and warmth emanating from her body called to him, beckoning his bear. He needed…

He needed space first.

Fresh air to clear his mind before he did what his body was begging for. He quickly dressed, scrawled a hasty note, and vacated their cabin, taking his first easy breath once he reached a safe distance. Rocco stared back at the room and debated his next move. Julissa had one more meeting before they could leave town. Their next trip was a four-hour drive to the next sanctuary town. No way would either of them make it. They would be stuck here, so his first phone call should be to Silas to give him the schedule change. Except, it wasn't Silas' number he dialed.

Dallas answered on the second ring. "What's wrong?"

"PD," he said desperately.

"Talk to me, Rocco."

"Mating heat."

Dallas laughed. "I reminded you about this the other day. You good?"

"I don't know, PD."

"I don't know shit about bears except what I've learned from you. But we already talked with that elder bear. Everything will be fine." Dallas assured him with a chuckle.

"What if I hurt her, Pop?"

All his childhood memories threatened to rear up and drown him. The fights between his parents—the jealousy-led drinking binges that resulted in him and his mother being knocked around. All of it would take him under. He wasn't good enough for Julissa, despite her faith in him.

"She's yours, Rocco." The amusement left Dallas' voice. "That means she was built for you."

He nodded though Dallas couldn't see him.

"You are nothing like your sperm donor," Dallas continued.

Rocco heard him, but he looked in the mirror and saw his father's face daily. Dallas seemed to sense what he was thinking.

"Just think… which of my boys looks exactly like me, and which one acts just like me."

He had to chuckle because Mason was Dallas through and through, but Silas was his twin. That…strangely made him feel worlds better.

"Thank you, PD."

"Anytime, son. You need anything else from me?"

"No. I can handle it."

"Good. Then let me tell DiDi we may get more grandkids sooner than she thought."

Rock let out a rough laugh, his chest constricting with both longing and fear. The thought of a family of his own was as daunting as it was exciting.

"Good luck," Dallas told him before ending the call.

He took a deep breath and made his next call.

"The fuck, Rock?" Silas asked, his voice distracted.

"Need Keisha to push the next few meetings back a couple of days. Three at the most."

"Man," his best friend complained.

Rock heard him move around before his voice was clearer.

"What now?"

"Liss is going into heat."

Silas laughed. "Fuck. I forgot bears are different. You straight?"

He wanted to fuck his mate clear into the mattress, but he didn't tell his best friend that. He just grunted, to which Silas chuckled again.

"You need extra guards since you'll be down a few days."

He sighed and rubbed the back of his neck. That would probably be a good idea. "Yeah."

"I'll get Julian on it. Bears go into heat to make it easier for them to get pregnant, right? Her brothers finna be on your ass. That's good. We ain't been in a good fight in a while."

He laughed, his hands shaking as he wiped his face. "The fuck is wrong with you?"

"Just saying. You know how bears get down about their females."

Shit, he knew firsthand. He was already ready to die behind that woman. "You got me?"

"Always, Rock. Handle your business, and I'll take care of the rest. Congratulations, man."

"Thank you," he ended the call and went to get the things he would need to get him and his mate through the next few days.

He was glad that he had called both PD and Silas. They'd managed to calm the panic that had been taking him over. Now he could at least think clearly. He needed to talk to the guards on duty with him to give them a heads-up, and then he would take care of his mate. However, he would have to stay away from her for the duration of the meeting because he didn't think they'd get anything done if they were within touching distance. Even now, his bear thrashed against him, begging for release.

It would be a long morning.

JULISSA WAS CALLING Rock every curse word she could think of as she wrapped her meeting with the town alpha. She'd woken up alone and yearning for her mate, and he'd been nowhere to be found. If she'd followed her bear's instincts, she would've used his scent and hunted him down, but the note he'd left bedside had cautioned her against the action. God, mating heat. It wasn't as though Julissa hadn't extensively talked with her mother about it. Even with those conversations, nothing could have prepared her for the searing urgency that overtook her body.

Rocco had warned her last night. He'd rightfully asked her to put it off at least until they'd completed the meetings, and now she understood why. She wanted to rail and curse, but there was no time for that. Not when the urge to fight and then fuck with her mate was riding her hard. Byron had taken one inhale and told her that he couldn't drive with her today. He'd sent Harold, a cougar shifter who wouldn't be affected by her heat. Luckily for her, the alpha of their town was a wolf, so he didn't have an issue with it, though he'd been visibly uncomfortable.

She was shocked that she'd been able to get through the meeting. Julissa had gone over the points she and Silas had discussed, her leg bouncing the entire time. She was flushed and irritable as she got into the back seat of the SUV they'd rented. Rock had made himself scarce the whole meeting, which pissed her off. Maybe if he had been in the room, she could've concentrated a little bit more. Luckily for her, she'd attended many of her law school classes on scant hours of sleep, partially hung over, so she hadn't missed anything important during the meeting. Still…

It was nearing midafternoon when Julissa reached their cabin, and she was starving in more ways than one. She growled when she entered the room, and it was empty. Where in the hell was he? She stripped out of her clothes, unable to take the cloth against her skin. She was down to her panties and bra when she heard the door beep. She swung around when it opened, and her body went up in flames. Rock entered the room in all black, and she realized that had he been at that meeting, it wouldn't have happened.

She would've fucked him right in the middle of the whole city council. She growled, her bear riled at the sight of him. He came in with a bag of food, his hands up.

"Food first, sug, then I'll take care of all that heat," he promised softly, moving slowly.

Her eyes tracked him like prey across the room to her. She was afraid to move. Afraid she would attack him if he got too close. He must have sensed it because he hastily dropped her food on the table. The scent of the salmon rose, and her stomach growled. He set out their food, and still, she stood there, rooted to the spot, her body overheated and overwrought. He finally finished and walked over to her. She shuddered the moment his hand grazed down her shoulders.

"Easy, mama," he whispered.

Her body shook in need, her womb clenching, and her clit throbbing as the heat exploded with his nearness. He made a choked sound before his claws dropped. She could smell the wildness of his bear as it fought him. He scraped his teeth down her neck.

"You left me," she managed to choke out.

"I had to, Liss. The heat had my mind gone," he whispered against her skin.

"Need you," she whispered.

"Food, then fuck."

"Fuck. Now," she hissed.

His body shuddered. "Baby, if we start, you won't eat until tomorrow, on my life." He swore.

A tear slid down her cheek as her pussy contracted. He hummed and pulled her into his body. Her bear filled her, reaching for him, their magic intertwining. She would explode if he didn't touch her now. Instead of pleading with the man, she bypassed him entirely, her power rubbing against the bear inside him, roiling to the surface, turning his eyes darker. His pupils lit, and she smiled. Yeah, that was how she would get what she wanted.

fourteen

Her heated skin scorched him. His baby was hurting, and Rocco could barely think straight. He woke this morning, his dick hard and his mind on nothing but fucking her until neither of them could walk straight. What must she be going through? He left their bed to give his bear release. It hadn't worked. And now his mate was using the animal to get what she wanted. That turned him on even more. He would never have to worry about running over this woman. Her bear called to him, broadcasting its wants across their bond.

Rocco's knees damn near went weak in need. Dallas had reminded him that they'd had the mating talk when he was a teenager, but nothing could have prepared him for the fire raging through his body. Rock had extended their stay another three days and gathered supplies for him and Julissa. He made sure that they remained separated while she got her work done, but they both paid for the distance. Now, his mate was in front of him halfway to naked, burning up, and his dick was hard enough to split through his pants.

Food, he reminded himself.

He could take the edge off for her and then feed her. After that, it was up. He slid his hand up her thigh, edging higher until he reached her sopping-wet panties. He begged his bear for control enough to pull back his claws. She whimpered.

"Easy, sug. I'll take care of you," he rumbled.

Rocco sighed in relief when his claws retracted. He inserted his fingers into her throbbing pussy and cursed as she squeezed down on him.

"Food," he whispered aloud this time.

He had to focus.

Fur rippled up and down his back as the bear pushed him for more. Julissa's claws pierced his shoulders as she rode his fingers. She threw her head back in ecstasy, and he bit the front of her neck. She screamed as she came, and he reluctantly pulled his fingers from her. He licked them clean, pulling her head down and kissing her. She sucked on his tongue, moaning. His body clenched as her anguished need transmitted across their bond. It took everything in him to pull away.

"Food, mama." He managed to say as he stepped back.

Her eyes were feverish, her bear watching him as he washed his hands. He pointed to the chair at the small table with shaking hands, unable to organize his thoughts, let alone speak. She sat obediently, which...lord, he just had to let her eat. He had to.

Otherwise...

Julissa devoured the food before her, her eyes never leaving his. Rocco got everything on the list for a sow in heat—salmon, lentils, sweet potatoes, high-energy foods, and fruit. The diner waitress had given him a smile and thumbs up when he'd ordered the disjointed foods. He was sure that bears weren't the only shifters that went into heat.

Once they were done eating, he skirted around her to the bathroom. Her eyes followed him, and he shivered in anticipation. Rocco started the shower in an attempt to wash off. She was a flame at his back as he stripped. He'd barely gotten into the shower stall before she was on him.

"Food, then fuck," she whispered, going down on her knees.

He cursed when she swallowed him down. He touched the back of her throat, and Rock saw stars. His eyes rolled back, and his body trembled. Between her hand tugging on him and the wet suction of her mouth, he wouldn't make it long. Rocco watched as his dick disappeared between her full lips. She was taking his soul and wasn't shit he could do about it. He pulled her up and pushed her against the wall.

He entered her in one stroke, swallowing her gasp as he fought through her clenching pussy.

Fuck, he wouldn't make it.

It didn't stop him from driving into her, fucking her desperately. If it was just the physical, he could maybe gentle his strokes, but the emotion down their bond had his chest tight and his animal feral. Her claws scraped his back, and from the scent of blood, those marks would be deep and brand him for weeks. His bear growled in satisfaction. Rocco lasted longer than he thought, the water going cold around them as he pounded into his mate. She moaned loud and long as she came, pulling him behind her. Fire raced down his spine as he erupted inside of her. She kissed him, her body still undulating.

He turned off the water and guided them out of the stall, but they never made it past the bathroom sink. His dick hadn't softened. His bear wasn't done with her, and the heat hadn't yet released Julissa. The hot clasp of her pussy was addictive. He slowed his frenzied strokes, savoring every pull of her tight inner muscles. She growled in complaint, and he hissed as she bit down on his shoulder.

He chuckled. "Mean ass."

Rocco shoved in deeper, biting her back. Julissa screamed and tensed, another orgasm crashing over her. He was glad he had moved their departure because there was no way they would get any sleep tonight.

fifteen

"I'm taking you out," Julissa announced.

Rocco looked up from his emails and squinted at his mate. They'd barely been back in their room for half an hour. They were in town number eight and had just wrapped their last meeting with the town alpha. So far, they had been getting next to no pushback from the towns, so he was starting to relax his guard just a bit. But complacent enough to go out on a date? He wasn't entirely sold on that.

He got a good look at Julissa as she moved closer to him. She wore a pair of leather pants painted on her curves and a Beyoncé concert tee underneath the camel trench she loved. High-top J's completed the outfit, and he smiled. He'd never seen her dressed down to go out. She had a million and one 'lounging' outfits, as she called them, but she never left their room less than done up. Her makeup was still immaculate, but a knit cap covered her long hair. She looked cute…approachable.

"Where are we going?"

"To a drive-in movie," was her answer as she shifted her stuff from her purse to a pouch around her waist.

He frowned and looked out the window. "It's the middle of the day, Liss."

"Do you want to change, or are you going to wear that?" She ignored his statement.

He looked down at the suit he'd worn to their meeting and back up at her. "I'll change."

The smile she graced him with warmed his heart. He dressed to match her fly—a pair of black jeans, Jordans, and his Tupac hoodie. He tucked his heat and texted Byron and Harold that they were leaving the room awhile. A drive-in movie during the day seemed silly, but his mate was taking him out. He would just see what the day brought. They loaded into the rented SUV, and he smiled at the bag full of snacks that Julissa pushed into the back seat.

Julissa loaded the address into the GPS, and they hit the road. He didn't mind the distraction. They had wrapped their meeting early and would head to the next town in the morning. Their itinerary kept them on a tight timeline, but he was happy for these little pockets of rest. He thought Julissa going into heat would push them back in their schedule, but it had passed quickly. The fact that it had ended with her not being pregnant was a relief. He'd been a little disappointed, but he wanted more time with the two of them.

According to the GPS, they were thirty minutes from their destination. Julissa kept up her usual chatter next to him. He assumed that his bear would tire of the noise, but the animal loved the cadence of her voice and that soft tone she used when thinking aloud. He didn't think she really needed anyone to answer her musings. He was charmed by what he learned about her on the trip.

He pulled up to the theater and bought their tickets. He smiled as he realized it wasn't only a movie but also a car show. There were vintage cars scattered across the grass lot. He turned to her, and a smile took over her whole face.

"Surprise!"

He was touched. Excited. How in the world had she known this was happening? But then, he shouldn't be surprised. Julissa talked to everyone. The woman could find something to discuss with anyone she encountered everywhere they went. From a security standpoint, it had been frustrating, to say the least. But she enjoyed being around people, so he sucked it up. He tapped the steering wheel, momentarily worried that he should've brought back up. His eyes roamed the grass lot filled with shifters and cars, glancing at his mate. Seeing her happy expression, he wouldn't ruin her moment with practicality.

"Get out, Rocco. We'll be safe here. As you can see, it's mostly shifters." She read his mind. "According to the waitress in the restaurant where we had breakfast this morning, they meet once a month."

He didn't bother asking when she'd had time to find all that out from their short breakfast run. She amazed him. He grabbed his gun from the glove compartment and put it in his holster. He walked around and helped her from the car. She gripped his hand immediately, tugging him towards the crowd. Though he'd probably not admit it aloud, he was excited. He loved vintage cars, and the fact that Julissa had pulled that from him and gone out of her way to find this event warmed his heart.

She made him fall in love with her every day. He had expected a wave of love to overcome them the moment they bonded, but it was the little interactions that had sank him. He understood why she was so popular with the Motsi. Julissa paid attention to people and remembered details that most overlooked. He didn't talk much—he could admit that—but his mate treasured every word he spoke and noted the important things he'd slipped in their casual conversation. It was hard not to be charmed by that.

He lifted her hand and kissed her wrist. "Lead the way, sug."

Her smile both made his dick hard, and his bear settled. She was an amazing woman, and he was happy he'd put aside his insecurities and mated with her. Julissa led him around the grass lot, and Rocco relaxed so he could enjoy the time with his mate.

About an hour into their outing, his bear tensed within him. Rocco looked around, his chest rumbling as he spotted the male he'd seen in more than one of the towns they'd visited. Rock had spotted him three other times since the first town. He didn't believe in coincidences. He gripped Julissa's hand and pulled her away. Cars were parallel to each other in two lines, with food stalls and other vendors circling the show. Rocco tugged her closer to the stalls, away from the middle of the crowd gathering around the cars.

"I need you to stay put for a moment, love."

She furrowed her brows. "What's wrong?"

He cupped her chin. "Don't move from this spot, hear?"

She swallowed and nodded, her eyes darkening in lust at his tone. He kissed her, unable to help himself. He stepped away a moment later, scanning the crowd until he spotted the man. He circled the stalls, his bear protesting as they left Julissa unprotected. Predictably, the male sped his steps to get to Julissa. Rocco kept her in his peripheral as he came up behind the man. He growled as he pulled in the scent of the human. He pulled his heat and pressed it into the back of the man's head. The human's hands came up immediately.

"Talk to me," Rock said, his tone low and deadly.

"I...I work for the National Gazette." He hastily explained.

Rocco grunted.

"I wanted to ask Ms. Crespo a few questions about Mr. Knight's plans regarding Suncoast Energy's push to disband sanctuary cities."

"And it didn't occur to you to contact his office like the press is supposed to?" Rock released the safety.

His hands went higher, his body trembling. "I'm sorry. I know the protocol. I just thought..."

"You thought wrong," Rock informed him. "You've been following us."

He nodded. "Yes. Gathering information."

"Rocco," Julissa stepped closer to the male, and Rock growled. She sighed but paused her movement. "I can answer a few of his questions, and then we can get back to our day. Once his questions are answered, I imagine Mr...."

"Latimore."

"Mr. Latimore won't need to follow us anymore, right?"

Latimore nodded quickly, inhaling sharply when Rocco pressed his gun harder into his head.

"I swear."

Rocco clicked on the safety and stepped around the human. He put Julissa firmly behind him. "Ask your questions and then go. You don't get another warning."

"Understood." Latimore released a shaky breath.

♠ ♠ ♠ ♠

JULISSA FED ROCCO, another piece of cotton candy before taking a bit herself. She danced as the sugar melted on her tongue. It had taken a few hours, but her mate had finally relaxed. She thought for sure he would make them leave after the reporter, but he had allowed her to distract him. He'd walked the reporter to his car and watched him go; that had helped. That and she'd fed him every sweet snack she could find from the different vendors. Her mate was self-possessed and sometimes grumpy but a sucker for sweets. She used that knowledge to her advantage the whole afternoon.

He was relaxed, but it hadn't stopped his watchful eye from roaming the crowd. Nor had it stopped his growls when someone got overly close or familiar with her. She was happy that her surprise for him pleased him. It was fascinating to see him open up as he talked to the different car owners. Mind, he still kept his words to a minimum, but the owners showed him all the engine parts and details about their cars. She didn't understand any of it but had loved how intense Rocco got about it all. He'd even gotten information from a couple of people.

Dark was now falling, and the movie portion of the event was about to start. She walked her mate back to their rental and led them to the back instead of the front seat. Though she wore sneakers, her feet still felt the hours they had walked around, so she was happy to be sitting. She settled in her seat but looked up when she felt his eyes on her. Rocco leaned over her, his arm behind her headrest, the other sliding between her legs on the seat.

"Thank you, my love," he said softly, nuzzling against her cheek.

The dark quiet of the car pressed around them, enhancing the intimacy. The smell of his cologne surrounded her. He was addicting. Her stomach fluttered, emotion filling her at the love she saw in his expression. It flowed down their bond, and her bear rattled her chest with a purr-like sound. He chuckled, his eyes lighting with his animal. He dropped small, soft kisses to her lips.

"Did you have fun?" she asked in between.

"I did."

He nipped her chin, moving down her neck, pushing her shirt collar aside so he could lick across his mating mark. Julissa shuddered as need slammed into her.

"Rock," she whispered.

"Yes, mate?" He scraped his teeth up her neck before sucking on her skin.

She squirmed as her sex clenched, her clit throbbing.

Rocco growled. "I can smell that pretty pussy."

Julissa threw her head back and closed her eyes. The way he talked to her during sex had to be top five of her favorite things about her mate. She cursed the fact that she'd worn tight ass pants. Unless she wanted to be ass naked in this car where anyone could walk up, she would have to behave. Her bear released its own growl.

"There's a blanket in my go bag," she whispered.

"Say less, ma," he kissed her hard.

She tangled her tongue with his and gripped his chin to keep him in place. God, she loved this man. He pulled back and reached into the trunk for her bag. It didn't take him long to pull out the blanket she carried. He spread it over her lap, and Julissa hurriedly unbuckled her pants, sliding them down.

His hand snaked under the blanket. He bit his lip the moment he brushed his finger over her sex. She was wet, and his eyes lit, a rumble vibrating his chest when he realized. He kissed her neck as his fingers parted her pussy.

"Playing in this pussy is my favorite thing to do," he told her.

"You talk to me so nasty," she whispered, grabbing his head and pulling him to her for a kiss.

He chuckled and backed up, pulling her over onto his lap. She looked around, wrapping the blanket around her waist.

"Anyone can see us," Julissa hissed.

"These windows dark as hell."

He pulled his dick from his pants, and Julissa shut up because she desperately wanted to feel him inside her.

"Uh-huh. I thought that would shut you up," he laughed, bringing her down onto his erection.

She moaned, wiggling her hips to work herself fully onto him. They both sighed in pleasure once she was seated, taking him all the way in.

"Such a perfect fit," he murmured, sliding his hands under her shirt. "Ride this shit, sug."

How could she not follow that order? She was careful to keep the truck from rocking as she slowly slid up and down on his shaft.

"Feels so good," she moaned.

He gripped her ass and scraped his teeth along her neck. "You and this good ass pussy."

Julissa threw her head back, basking in the sensations. Rocco lifted his hips, and she grunted as he pushed deeper inside. He reached between them and thumbed her clit, and she jerked at the fiery jolt of pleasure. She wrapped her arms around his shoulders, kissing her mate. Darkness pressed around them; even the sounds of the movie couldn't puncture their intimate cocoon.

"I love you, Rocco," she whispered against his lips.

"I love you, Liss," he told her before devouring her mouth.

She rode him slowly, dragging out their pleasure. Soon though, between his fingers on her clit and him whispering in her ear, an orgasm built, vibrating her body.

"Almost," she whimpered, working her hips faster.

"Let me have it, Liss," he ordered, pulling her down so that he filled her completely.

He pressed down on her clit, and she shattered, gasping as he flexed inside her. Rocco cursed, filling her. Their ragged breathing was loud, their chests moving together. Julissa snuggled into his chest, humming her satisfaction. She was sated, the hours they'd spent on their feet catching up with her. His chuckle sounded against her cheek.

"You finna sleep through this whole movie," he teased.

"Fuck that movie," she slurred.

She smiled as his laugh bounced off the walls of the SUV. God, she loved that sound and especially loved the happiness she could feel from him on their bond. He tightened his hold on her, rubbing his cheek against the top of her hair. She didn't know when she lost the knit cap she'd been wearing.

"As soon as we get home, I plan to pamper the fuck out of you. You deserve it. I've been so proud of you this trip." He declared.

Julissa's heart thumped, and tears clogged her throat. She lifted her head. "Rocco."

"Come, let's go back to the hotel so you can rest." He carefully lifted her from him.

She cleaned up with the wipes she'd packed and crawled into the front seat. She couldn't help but stare at Rocco the whole way back. She'd never thought she would make a love match. Not many of the women in her position did. The matings and marriages were arranged, their family's interest the only thing that mattered. Finding Rocco, claiming him was a blessing that she was fully embracing.

sixteen

JULISSA LOST TRACK OF their movements somewhere around town number twelve. They were finally in town number twenty, and she was having hallucinations of how her bed would feel once she finally reached home. She could feel the Egyptian cotton on her skin and the weight of her linen duvet. She smothered a yawn while waiting on Rocco as he shopped at the small jewelry store attached to their current airport.

Most of their traveling had been driving. It was faster and more efficient, not to mention cost-effective, to navigate between the towns. Most of them were concentrated in the Midwest, so that was easy enough. Though, the three- and four-hour rides between them weren't entirely comfortable. Despite how hard it had been, she was glad her mate had accompanied her.

He had expressed his concern about her after she'd gone through heat, worried she would be too overtaxed. Though she had been exhausted after it, it wasn't enough to stop her. She was both happy and disappointed that she hadn't gotten pregnant. She would be more than glad to have kids with Rocco, but she wasn't quite ready. She and her bear were incredibly smug and satisfied with their choice of mate and how Rocco cared for her. She loved being mated to him.

"Julissa?"

She winced, forgetting that she was on the phone with her mother. That happened so much when Rocco was around. Her eyes followed him everywhere, a bit obsessed with him if she were being honest.

She turned and faced the rest of the airport to keep him out of her peripheral so she could concentrate.

"Sorry, I'm here, mama. Just tired. This is our last town."

"How do you feel now that you've survived your first heat?" Therese joked.

She snickered. "Happy. I don't think I understood how mating would feel." None of the books she'd read on the subject had even scratched the surface.

"I'm very happy for you. I'm sure that's partly why you're exhausted."

Julissa's cheeks heated. "I'm not talking about that with you."

Therese chuckled. "I'm meeting with Adina today to start planning your mating ceremony."

She swallowed her sigh because there was nothing she could do about that. "Fine."

"I'm glad you see things my way," her mother laughed.

"Are you finally going to tell me why I've been picking furniture for the past month?"

"Oh…yeah. We moved your stuff into Rocco's new penthouse. I like the neighborhood. Did you know he lived so close to us? I thought surely he would stay on the Southside, but—"

"Please tell me you're joking?" Julissa cut her mother off.

"I talked to Rocco, and he's fine with it. I assumed y'all had discussed it." Therese said.

She spun around and narrowed her eyes at her mate as he stood at the register. "When in the hell did y'all do all this? Did he say you could move me in?"

"We've talked a few times. I can't remember his exact words," her mother hedged.

"Mama."

"Have you seen the article about you? It ran in a few papers. Your father was worried." Therese changed the subject.

Julissa frowned. "What articles?" Her eyes scanned the airport until she found a newsstand.

She rushed over and snatched up a paper, seeing a picture of her during one of the town halls she'd held. The headline proclaimed that shifters were taking on a giant energy conglomerate to save sanctuary towns.

"Oh shit," she whispered. She needed to contact Silas.

"Your father will probably call you, but be extra careful, love. That's a lot of attention."

"Rocco has me." She said absently, skimming the article. She quickly paid the vendor.

"Ok, well, I'll leave you to it." Therese ended the call.

Julissa sucked her teeth and tucked her phone. Therese had properly distracted her, but best believe, they would be circling back over her mother's high-handedness. Of all the things she'd expected her mother to say, moving her into Rocco's place wasn't one of them. She walked back over to the jewelry store to wait on her mate.

"What's wrong?" Rocco asked, guiding her towards the airport exit and their waiting SUV as he left the store.

They had long ago loaded their luggage from the jet into the SUV. He'd wanted to visit the jewelry store before they left. She changed the subject, unsure she wanted to reveal that her mother had already moved her into his space.

"What did you get her?" She pointed to his small bag. She had noticed him buying the little charms a few towns ago.

He smiled and pulled out the small box. She opened it and laughed at the jeweled armadillo. Julissa wondered if his niece would see the humor in it. Rocco revealed little parts of himself the longer they were on this trip. She enjoyed getting to know him. She passed him the paper she bought.

"Word's out."

He frowned as he glanced at the article. He hummed after a moment. "Silas will take care of it."

"Our mothers are planning the mating ceremony already," she informed him to change the subject. There was nothing they could do about the article until they reached town.

He grunted.

"I would ask if you want it small or large, but my mother won't care what either of us wants."

"Mama Di will reel her in. She knows me," he said confidently.

She shrugged because he'd never seen Therese in full planning mode, though she was sure if anyone could rein her in, it may well be Adina Knight. Before they got into the truck, Rocco reached in the back and grabbed a small tote that he called her 'go' bag. He'd been making her carry it when they got a little trouble around town number…six…no ten. It held necessities and a change of clothes, just in case. She didn't want to find out what the just in case was, but nevertheless, she kept the tote on her with the emergency stash.

Loading them into the truck, they were off to their last town. Julissa took a deep, cleansing breath and focused—just one more town to go.

ROCK STRETCHED HIS NECK and took deep breaths to calm his fidgeting bear. The animal was on edge, and he well understood. It had been at least a week since he'd shifted. That was long for him. Plus, he could feel Julissa's exhaustion. She had been great throughout the whole trip. She'd treated each town with the same respect and diligence, though he could tell they were all running together for her. From the first town to now their last, she'd worked hard.

He couldn't wait to get her back to his den.

He had every intention of pampering her the moment they arrived. While he'd never planned to be mated, he most enjoyed being able to spoil his mate. He thought about his friend's words. He hadn't expected the match that fate had picked out for him. Like Silas, he hadn't seen himself with someone like Julissa. At most, he envisioned someone that could relate to his life, but the difference between them seemed to fill in areas of his soul that had long been missing. Fate had chosen well for him. He felt her eyes on him.

"What?"

"My mother had my stuff moved to your apartment."

He grunted, unconcerned about that. His gaze returned to the back window and the car still following them. He'd thought they would've lost them once they left the main highway.

"She said you agreed. You don't think that's something we should've discussed."

"You told me to talk to your mother." He reminded her.

She waved her hands. "About the weather, about yourself. Not to tell her where to put my stuff at your new penthouse."

He grunted again. It was all the same to him. Therese chattered the same way her daughter did. But, unlike with Julissa, he'd tuned out a good portion of her mother's conversation. Had they talked about moving his mate? Probably. He vaguely remembered telling her that Mama Di was redoing his penthouse. Once Therese had gotten the okay from him to call him whenever she had not been shy about it. She'd called him about the apartment, yes, but sometimes the woman called just to talk to him. It was…odd. For the longest time, Adina was the only person outside of his friends to call and check-in. Now Therese.

"Adina is redecorating my place. I told your mother that she could offer suggestions that would be to your liking." He murmured, distracted.

Her eyes narrowed. "You didn't tell her to move my stuff?"

Rocco shrugged because…maybe. The woman talked a lot. Plus, she liked to sandwich apartment talk with other mundane subjects to catch him off guard. He'd been noticed it, but he let her rock because he didn't mind it.

Julissa sucked her teeth.

"Faster," he ordered Byron.

The bear had been their driver for the majority of the trip. He looked up at Rocco through the rearview mirror. "I'd clocked them about ten minutes ago."

He nodded, happy her father had sent someone competent. He reached into his go bag and pulled his gun from there.

Julissa gasped. "What's wrong?"

"Be ready," He told her.

"For what?"

He didn't know yet, but he wanted her ready if they needed to run. Byron punched down on the gas, and the truck took off. The car behind them sped up, and Rock cursed. That was all the confirmation he needed that they were being followed.

"Call Silas," he ordered Julissa, handing her his phone.

"I can call from mine."

"From mine, love. And not the first contact. Dial Silas two." He ordered.

She nodded and, with shaking hands, did as he asked. He'd given her the code to his phone a couple of weeks ago. She put it on speaker, and Silas answered after the first ring.

"What do you need?"

Julissa sucked in a sharp breath and looked to him for the answer. He inclined his head, and she nodded.

"We're being followed and are still another hour away from Summerville." She told him.

Silas grunted, and they could hear him typing on the other end. "I'm tracking your phone. I anticipated trouble in Summerville once that article came out, so I sent Julian ahead. Will you be able to hold them off until he gets to you?"

"They're only following for now. I'll make it work." Rocco said.

"Summerville is where the energy company is trying to take over. It's why I saved it for last. The coverage got them desperate, it seems. Stay safe, and I'll work on my end."

Julissa tucked Rocco's phone back into his go bag. She screamed a moment later as the car behind them rammed them. He cursed and reached over her and downed the window. Knowing the drill, Julissa unbuckled her seatbelt and hit the floor as Rocco fired at the car approaching car. It hovered alongside them, swerving to avoid his shots.

Byron cursed, and the truck jerked when one of their bullets hit their tire. He fought to control the SUV and keep it from flipping. It didn't work, and Rock grabbed Julissa, tucking her tightly into him as the truck turned over. Her screams filled his head as the airbags inflated next to them, their animal's panic scenting the air as the truck slid across the icy pavement and into the ditch. Only the radio sounded in the freezing night as Rock took stock of their surroundings.

"Liss?"

She groaned in his arms, and he released her slowly until she landed on the door.

"I'm...I think I'm good." she finally answered.

He used his claw to cut through his seatbelt and grunted as he worked himself down. It took some maneuvering, but they finally got out of the turned-over vehicle and took stock. Byron limped to the back, working on getting their suitcases from the truck.

"What do you want to do?" Harold asked, reloading his guns.

"We need to move in case they come back," Rock muttered. "How far are we from Summerville?"

"On foot? At least a couple hours."

Rock cursed and turned to Julissa. She was dazed but standing upright, which was the most important part. He looked around, but they didn't have a choice. They would need to make it on foot. He walked up to Julissa and rubbed his hands down her arms to soothe her.

"We'll have to make it in our bear forms. Are you okay with that?" He asked, nuzzling into her neck.

She gripped the back of his head. "I'll follow your lead."

His bear growled in approval and pride.

"We gotta move, Rock," Harold called from the front of the SUV.

He looked up and saw the headlights cutting through the dark night. "Let's go, sug."

They rushed to the truck, and he grabbed their go bags instead of the suitcases. The car that had run them off the road had circled back. Harold and Byron fired off shots, and the car returned the favor.

"Shift, Liss," Rock ordered.

They would have to navigate the unknown terrain in the dead of winter. Fuck.

seventeen

Julissa's body was trembling as fear filled her. She'd heard his order but couldn't get her body to cooperate. They'd been shot at more than once. She knew that her job was dangerous. She got that, but to the point where they were being fired at, scary shit. At most, she'd assumed she'd get trolling and hate mail. She hadn't once expected physical violence, and now she understood the extra guards.

"Here, sug," Rock ordered, and she rushed forward on trembling legs. He gripped her chin. "Breathe, baby. I'll keep us safe; I just need you to shake off the panic." He promised.

They could've been killed. She didn't call that okay, but she didn't argue. Her bear reacted to the power in his voice, shifting quickly, tearing through the clothes she was wearing. Julissa froze when another set of headlights pierced the night, illuminating the side of the SUV. She yelped when she heard more gunshots. She didn't know how many bullets her guards had left, which unlocked a new fear. Rock shoved a tote at her. She grabbed it between her teeth and took off toward the woods.

Rock lumbered behind her, and they were off. She heard the shots behind them and flinched every time they hit the trees beside them, but she didn't stop running. Rock was behind her, his larger body nudging her forward. She vaguely heard Bryon and Harold still shooting back, but after a while, the gunshots stopped. The four of them didn't stop running, however. She was happy to know that all of them had escaped alive. So far, anyway. They still needed to find the town and survive these frozen woods.

She was exhausted, but Rock nudged her to keep going. In her bear form, Julissa was aware of everything in the forest. The sound of the animals scurrying away from them, scents of the wood's inhabitants, and even though she didn't feel the cold, the biting wind brushed through her fur.

Rocco navigated it all, expertly skirting lurking campers, howling wolves and other animals. How he knew which direction they were going, she didn't know. Instinct bade her follow her mate. She trusted him implicitly to get them to safety. She didn't know how long they ran, but soon, she could smell the scents of a nearby town.

Her mate stopped her and shifted. Julissa did the same, damn near falling out of her animal form. She shuddered as cold air assaulted her body. The tote fell at her feet, and she hurriedly dove into it, pulling out the hoodie and yoga pants that Rocco had made her pack. She'd thought he was being overly cautious, but she thanked his foresight. The thick socks would have to do since she hadn't packed shoes in the bag. She would never make that mistake again. She looked at Rocco and gasped at the blood on his side.

"You were hit," she whispered, rushing to him.

He pulled her into his chest. "I'm fine, sug, just a graze."

The phone he packed in his bag was buzzing. He pulled it out, typed furiously, and tucked it back in the bag. He winced as he bent down to put on his pants. Julissa hurriedly helped him into his shirt.

"Come. Julian was able to clear the town," he told them softly. "Byron, you and Harold in front; I'll take the rear."

She gripped his hand tightly as they left the woods and moved through the town. There were police everywhere. Rocco marched her through the confusion, ignoring the local cops and heading straight for a small motel. He knocked on a room, and it opened. Julian Chase cursed as he saw them, grabbing Rock into a hug. Rocco grunted in pain.

"Fuck," Julian spotted the blood. "I got worried when I saw the state of your car. Hurry in."

He pulled them into the room. There were more than five shifters, stern looks, in all black, armed to the teeth. The only one she recognized was Julian, which was only because she'd seen him at a distance at Motsi functions. She looked around and took a deep breath. Julissa knew she needed to call her father, but that would have to wait until she could get her feet beneath her. All the adrenaline she'd been operating on was quickly leaving her body and leaving her a trembling mess.

"You okay, Julissa?" Julian eyed her.

She nodded, unable to speak.

"Rock, call Mama Di. She losing her shit."

Rocco was watching her, his eyes taking in all the things she thought she was successfully hiding.

"Room, first. Let me settle my mate," he rumbled.

"I got you two a room right next door. I'm staying until the meetings are done," Julian informed them, walking them to their room.

Julissa had never been so happy in her life to see a motel bed. She stood in the middle of the carpet until Julian left the room. The moment he did, her legs weakened. Rocco caught her before she hit the floor.

"Shower, then sleep, baby," he murmured, lifting her into his arms.

She nuzzled into his neck, her bear reaching out for his. His power surrounded her until she was warmed from the inside. Tears ran down her face as her brain finally processed how close they'd been to being killed. Julissa had lived a sheltered life, and this night had emphasized that better than anything could have. She owed her father and brothers apologies for all that they'd kept her safe from. Rocco said nothing, just holding her tightly as she cried. He put her on the bathroom vanity and held her while she broke down.

Julissa shuddered as she gathered her tattered nerves together. She gripped her mate tightly, not yet ready to separate from him. Her bear rumbled her chest in contentment.

"Better?"

She nodded in answer. His growly voice settled her like nothing ever had. Lifting her chin, Rocco studied her face before nodding himself. He pulled back and started the shower. She didn't move until the steam filled the place, watching him as he undressed. She was next, his hands gentle as he stripped her. There was no sexual heat, just the comfort of her mate taking care of her. She traced the puckering skin where his wound was healing with trembling hands.

She broke their tense silence reluctantly. "We still have to make those meetings."

He stiffened. Though she'd only known Rocco for a couple of months, she knew he was protective of her. She could well imagine what his instincts were telling him to do. Though he disguised the anxiety on his face, she could feel it along their bond. He had a superb poker face, but Rocco was losing his shit. Julissa didn't want to push him, but she had a job to do. He stared at her for long moments, not saying anything. She lifted her chin and met his gaze.

"No town hall, just the meeting with their alpha," he demanded.

She nodded. She could make that work. She'd call Silas and review the talking points again, but she would finish this job come hell or high water.

"Come on, sug." He lifted her and stepped them into the shower. "When we get home, you'll be able to soak and forget this day happened."

That sounded like heaven.

The first blast of hot water succeeded in relaxing her the rest of the way, and sleep seemed to slam over her. Staying awake was no longer an option.

ROCK STARED DOWN AT his sleeping mate, and his heart rate finally slowed. He'd been in situations much more dangerous than the one they'd been in tonight, but nothing had scared him more. He thanked every deity looking out for him that the men sent after them were amateurs. The men had easily given up once they'd entered the woods; a professional would've kept chase. It was probably the only thing that had saved them. They'd been outnumbered and certainly out-gunned. Keeping Julissa safe had been his number one priority, and the weight of that had had fear coursing through his body the entire trip through the woods.

Being on the street for two years had prepared him to survive anywhere, but he had worried that his mate wouldn't make the trek through the forest. The two-hour impromptu hike would've been difficult for anyone. Pride filled his chest because she had navigated the miles between them and the city without falling behind. Her bear had easily submitted to his, and the animal inside of him rumbled his chest in deep satisfaction.

Rock sighed and pulled out his phone. Now that his mate was settled, he needed to settle the rest of his family. He dialed PD first, knowing Adina was hovering. The call didn't even ring before it disconnected, and a video chat call came through. He shook his head, knowing Adina would want eyes on him.

"Oh, Thank God," Adina answered her husband's phone. Her gaze raked his body as much as it could.

He made sure to keep the phone tilted up. The wound on his side was still healing. In an hour, it would be gone, but he didn't put it past Adina to notice.

"I'm good, Mama." He said immediately, his bear riled by her anxiety.

Adina started crying, though she never took her eyes off him. "Why is the phone so close?"

He cursed because nothing got past that woman, whether she was distraught or not. "Ma."

"The boy said he fine, DiDi. Cut that out," Dallas fussed, taking the phone from his mate. "Both of you are fine?"

"Yeah. We ran into some shit, but we expected them to put up a fight around Summerfield. Julian's here now, so I have backup."

"When are you coming home?" Dallas asked.

He looked at Julissa and sighed again. She'd been insistent that they carry out the meetings as scheduled. He admired the fight in her, but God, Rocco wanted her somewhere safe. He gripped the back of his neck and closed his eyes.

"After the meeting with the town alpha."

Dallas grunted. "I understand."

"Please keep yourself safe," Adina ordered.

A slight tilt of his lip and grunt was his answer.

"I love you, Rocco," Adina told him.

"You too. I'll let you guys know when we head out," he promised before ending the call.

He braced himself for the next call he had to make. He already had the number in his phone. Rocco had talked to the bear before. He'd had to in order to do the work he and Deena did with the women's shelter. Part of keeping the women safe counted on the tri-council stepping in once informed about the abuse. He'd never had any issues with Councilman Crespo doing what he could to help the shifters he ruled.

But this was a whole other set of circumstances. This was dealing with the man's only daughter—Rocco didn't know how he would react. The councilman answered quickly.

"Jamison." He growled.

"She's fine, sleeping off her adrenaline crash," Rock assured her father.

"What happened?" Micah asked, relief evident in his voice.

"We were ambushed outside of town. I'm sure Byron already reported to you."

Micah grunted. "And my daughter?"

"She's wrapping the last meeting in the morning, and we'll head home after. I'll have her call you when she wakes up."

"I…" Micah cleared his throat. "Byron told me you took care of her. I wasn't sold on your mating initially; maybe a part of me still isn't. But, thank you."

Rock gripped his phone and kept the slick comment on the tip of his tongue to himself. He wasn't a father yet but he could appreciate Micah's worry.

"She'll call you later." He ended the call, done with the conversation.

He understood he wasn't good enough for Julissa but didn't relish having her father lay it out for him. He knew they would have plans for their only daughter. He imagined it included a male who could bring more to their family, be it money or cache. The Motsi were meticulous about their matings and marriages. But Julissa was his now, and he would care for her much better than anyone Councilman Crespo could've chosen for her. Instead of crawling into bed with her, he slipped outside. Julian was in the outside hallway on the balcony overlooking the parking lot, a drink in his hand, his mind a million miles away.

"She settled?" Julian asked, passing Rock a glass.

"Just."

His friend sighed and poured Hennessy into the cup. "They shot your shit up. It fucked with my head for a few moments."

Rocco grunted. One thing about Julian, he'd never had issues expressing the way he cared for those in his circle. Rock envied him that.

"It takes a lot more than that to take me out." He reassured him.

Julian studied him before smiling. "How is it?"

Rock didn't have to ask him what he meant. Of all of them, Rock had been the last person to even consider mating. He hadn't seen it in the cards for himself.

"She's amazing."

"I already knew that. I want to know how your bear is handling it." Julian smirked.

"I..." He shook his head and sipped. "I thought it would be uncomfortable, but she has this way of soothing the animal."

"Nightmares, all that?"

He shrugged. He couldn't say they'd gone away, but having Julissa in bed with him had certainly curbed them.

"Tell me about the meeting tomorrow." Julian prodded.

"Silas canceled the town hall meeting. I don't want to risk her in a large crowd, so we just have the meeting with the Alpha in the morning."

"I'll have your back regardless."

Rocco nodded, knowing that whole-heartedly. They had all been friends for years, and he'd learned he could count on their word.

"Go tend to your mate. I'll see you in the morning." Julian told him.

He knocked back the rest of the liquor in his glass, wincing at the taste. Though he hadn't spared a prayer in years, he sent one up that his mate would come out of all this safely.

eighteen

If Rocco had to sum up the trip, he would call it successful. They'd only been attacked once, and he'd safely brought his mate home. That had been his ultimate goal. Whether or not Julissa had succeeded at her job, time would tell. He'd seen firsthand the many months it would take for any of Silas's work to pay off.

He looked down at his sleeping mate, tucked into his side. He carefully unbuckled his seat to give her just a moment more rest. Unlike him, she wasn't used to the heavy schedule. Now that they were home, all the details regarding merging their life were pushed front and center. First thing, though, she would be going home with him. That wasn't a debate. He wanted Julissa's scent in his den.

His new den.

Would she like the place? It had been years since he'd last been in the penthouse. The last time had been to install the new tub in the primary bedroom. The same bathtub he promised his mate a soak in. Just yesterday, before the attack, she was fussing about her mother moving her in without asking. Would that still be the case? He kissed the top of her head.

"Up, mama," he murmured.

It took her a moment, but she finally sighed and sat up. "Home?"

"Mmhmm."

She stretched. "I want the bath you promised me."

He gripped her chin and kissed her. "Tonight?"

"Mmhmm," she hummed. "Hot, hot."

"Done. You hungry?"

"Not just yet." She snuggled closer to him, swinging her leg over his.

He refused to laugh at this silly woman. He loved how affectionate she was. As a whole, shifters were tactile creatures, and Julissa was no exception. Touch seemed to be his mate's main love language. Were it not for the Knights, he didn't know that he would've been ready for it.

"We should probably grab something on the way. I don't know if Mama Di stocked the new fridge."

She slid her hand beneath his sweater, her warm palm resting against his heart.

"My mom did it. So at the very least, we should be able to find something for you to cook me."

He laughed. "Food delivery it is."

She smiled up at him, her eyes sparkling.

Julian stopped at their seat, breaking up their cocoon. "You got it from here, Rock?"

"Yep." He dapped his friend. "I appreciate you."

"You know how we do. Good night, Julissa."

She straightened in her seat and fixed her face into one she used for work. "Thank you, Julian."

Jules nodded and raised his brows, smiling. Rocco knew he would hear shit from his friends about his proper mate.

"Let's go, sug." He ordered.

They descended the jet, and his car was exactly where Silas said he'd dropped it off. He dismissed Byron, knowing her father had probably ordered him to follow them home. Rocco had his mate for now and would work out with Micah about her security later. He loaded his trunk and helped Julissa into the car.

They were silent on the drive to his place, which put Rocco on edge. Julissa was never quiet. In the weeks they'd traveled, he could count on one hand the number of times his mate had kept her thoughts to herself. She expressed even the small ones that most would keep to themselves.

He tapped his fingers against the steering wheel as he parked, debating his next words. Before he could offer to take her home, Julissa leaned over and kissed his cheek.

"I can feel your bear's agitation. There is nothing wrong. I am just drained. Tomorrow I'm sending Silas all my notes and spending the rest of the weekend in pajamas."

He released the breath he'd been holding. That sounded perfect to him. He helped her out of the car, and they walked around to his trunk.

She frowned. "I only need that bag." She pointed to the smallest one. "The rest can wait until tomorrow."

"I'll come back and get them." He told her, pulling out his bag as well.

"Tomorrow, love," she insisted, rubbing her cheek against his chest.

He didn't think he'd ever tire of her affections. He was tense the whole elevator ride to the fourth floor. He locked the elevator doors for his floor and guided her to the front door. Julissa paused a foot from the door and allowed him to enter first. His eyebrows winged high in surprise as he entered his apartment. The place was immaculate and tastefully decorated. Not that he doubted Adina; she had exquisite taste. The fact that the space was so…him. It was to his taste, and he didn't know how the two women had accomplished that. He could see where his mate had made her choices. It blended seamlessly into his.

He'd expected it to be full of leather, but the women had blended rich velvets in the furniture and curtains that covered the floor-to-ceiling windows. It was an open floor plan, so he could see from the door to the other end of the room, where a reading space was set up. Two full bookshelves lined the wall with a plush armchair that was probably for his mate. She read in her spare time; he knew she would love the space. He was anxious for her to see it. He inhaled and filtered through the scents finding no recent ones.

"It's safe, Liss." He called to her.

She came in and gasped. "Oh, this is beautiful!" She walked the length of the living room, her face excited. "I can't believe you were living downstairs when this was up here the whole time."

He grunted because there was nothing he could say to that. But he felt a lot more would change with her in his life. He couldn't wait.

He would give his mate an hour...hour and a half tops. No way would he spend the whole of his afternoon with her brothers staring him down across the table. Rocco adjusted the collar of his v-neck sweater and debated lowering his fangs. Liam and Lachlan had been on bullshit from minute one, and he was near his tolerance for it. Therese had invited him and Julissa out for a family dinner under the guise of them all getting to know each other. He had better things that he could be spending his Saturdays on, especially since he could still feel Julissa's exhaustion from the trip.

But she wanted to see her family; most importantly, he was cementing his place in his mate's life. The more people that saw them together, the fewer people he would have to knock over the head behind her. So, he was all for dinner at one of the most popular restaurants in Eastfield. Plus, though he would never admit it out loud, Liam's restaurant was one that he frequented. His chef was exceptional.

Liam growled again, adjusting in his seat across from Rock. Julissa sucked her teeth and hit her hand against the top of the table.

"What is your problem, Liam?" She snapped.

"I want to know how he plans to keep you safe when he's still doing street shit for Dallas Knight." Her brother crossed his arms over his chest.

"Liam," Therese chided.

But he continued. "Not to mention, his building is filled with females who are in dangerous situations. What's to stop one of their mates from attacking your building?"

His chuckle held no amusement. "I wish the fuck they would."

He didn't raise his voice or even get irritated. While her brother was being an asshole, he had a valid point. Rocco had security measures in place, but it wasn't something just anyone would know.

Julissa's mother turned a smile at him. She was sitting right next to Rocco, opposite her husband.

"Helping battered women is admirable." Therese soothed.

"Lord, mama, don't go bragging to your friends about it. It could bring undue attention to the building," Julissa reminded her.

Therese held her hands up. "I'm just saying."

Rocco warmed. His mate understood why he did what he did and supported him fully.

"My staff speaks highly of you." Micah looked impressed. "Do you just help bears?"

He shook his head. "Any shifter. I work with one of the women's shelters in the city. Despite how well run they are, it's no place for kids. I would rather they have someplace more stable."

Therese rubbed his shoulder. "I love that."

They were impressed by work that he would be doing no matter his circumstances. It just so happened that he was in a place to help the women.

"It's dangerous," Liam said stubbornly.

"That aside, will we have to worry about your hands in her trust fund?" Lachlan cut in.

"You're being ridiculous." Julissa snapped.

Rocco sat back in his chair and put his arm around Julissa's seat. He liked his mate sticking up for him. He rubbed the back of her neck, feeling her anger down their bond. His touch soothed her bear, and Julissa relaxed, though she still mugged her brothers.

Lachlan waved off his sister. "Stay out of this, Julissa. It's between males."

Julissa sat forward. "I wish I would just sit here while you disrespect my mate."

"We can go somewhere else and discuss this." Lachlan threatened.

"I ain't got shit to hide from my baby," Rocco said, not moving.

He gave her brother a taunting smile, to which Liam growled, his eyes flashing with his bear.

Micah growled from his seat. "Cut it out, both of you. You can see their bond from way over here." He grumbled. "Y'all already tried to scare the man off. Clearly, it didn't work."

"Thank you, Dad."

"It's beautiful," Therese said. "Rocco, are you still going to work for Silas?"

He turned his attention to her mother. "Until it affects Liss, I'll probably keep protecting him. It keeps him out of trouble and me busy."

Micah chuckled.

"Well, no pregnancy this heat, but—"

"For God's sake, Therese, I don't want to hear about my daughter in heat." Micah cut in.

"I just wanted to ask about kids," she fussed.

Rocco couldn't help the small smile that lifted his lips. Thinking of Liss pregnant with his baby made him and his bear happy. For the longest time, he hadn't seen it for himself.

"As far as I am concerned, their kids will be hatched from eggs. I don't want to hear otherwise." Micah sliced his hand in the air to dead the conversation. "Where in the hell is dinner?" he asked, looking around.

"I'll go check," Liam left the private room they were in.

Rocco hid his smirk as Therese sucked her teeth.

"Fine."

"I didn't know you owned the garage over on 4th until the contract negotiations started. I've taken my car there a few times." Micah changed the subject.

"Oh yeah? What kind of car?" Rocco would much rather talk about cars if he had to pick.

If it went to the place off of 4th, it had to be a classic car. They only worked on vintage ones. It was the first garage he'd opened, and he'd only done it so he would have a place he trusted to take his own car.

"It's an Aston Martin DB5."

"No shit, the '64?" He was impressed.

Micah nodded. "I said I would do the work myself, but then I get caught up with other stuff. Did you restore the Lincoln yourself?"

"I did. That's usually what I'm doing on my downtime."

Micah sat forward, bracing his elbows on the table. Both Therese and Julissa groaned, so Rocco could only assume her father was like him in his love of cars.

nineteen

The following day, Julissa rolled out of their new bed, groggy and searching for her mate. She was enjoying being back in town. She'd been looking forward to being in her own bed, but being in Rocco's was even better. She would probably still be asleep if she hadn't felt Rocco's absence. After dinner with her family last night, they'd spent the rest of the evening snuggled on the couch watching movies. Today was dinner with his family.

She wasn't worried about that too much. She'd never had any issues with the Knights, and they couldn't be anywhere near as bad as her brothers had been last night. She'd wanted to clock them both. The only thing that stopped her from getting violent was the fact that she could feel Rocco's mood the whole dinner. Not once was he anything other than content. She'd expected anger, aggravation even, but nothing had ruffled the man or his bear.

She left their bedroom. Julissa paused in the hallway, letting that sink in.

Their bedroom.

Because they had mated on the road, it hadn't quite felt real, but being in a shared space that was theirs…It brought everything into clarity. Rocco was hers. She smiled and carried on through the apartment, searching for him. She could hear the clinking sounds of weights, so she followed her ears to the home gym on the second level. He was stretched out across the bench press. Her body warmed, sleep a thing of the past. Seeing Rocco's big body laid out on the gym equipment unlocked a new fantasy she hadn't realized she had. She walked closer to him and waited.

Once he hung up the bar he was lifting, she straddled his lap. "Why are you up so early?" She whined.

He skimmed her thighs. "Habit, plus I need to get used to a new place."

She hummed and kissed his sweaty chest.

"Don't come in here starting shit," he grumbled, sitting up and gripping her ass. His dick rose beneath her. "You hungry?"

"I could eat." She slid her hand into his basketball shorts, lightly brushing the head of his dick.

He chuckled. "You finna find yourself bent over this bench, lil mama. Behave."

"Yeah, I'm trying to sign up for that," she murmured, letting her claws out and sliding them down his stomach.

He hissed, his eyes glowing, his bear rumbling his chest.

"We have plenty of time before we need to head out." She said coyly.

"Fast ass," he growled, lifting his shirt off her.

He stood with her in his arms. She thought he was taking her to their room, but he didn't. He put her down and spun her around fast enough to take her breath away. He pushed down on the middle of her back until she was braced against the bench, ass in the air.

He kicked her legs wide and ripped the seat of her panties. He left the waist, using it to hold her in place as he slammed into her. Julissa could only curse as he made good on his word. She took every stroke, throwing her hips back, moaning his name.

"This what you wanted, right?" He husked out, slowing his strokes to a torturous speed.

"Yes!" Julissa screamed as he hit her spot.

Maybe she could've lasted, but his nails dug into her waist as his dick rubbed across that spot repeatedly. It didn't help that Rocco talked her through the orgasm, tightening her body. His rough voice, combined with the sounds and scent of their lovemaking, tipped her over the edge. She screamed as she came, squeezing and tightening the walls of her pussy, determined to have him right behind her.

"Take that shit, then," he growled, his strokes speeding erratically until he shoved into her one last time, climaxing.

Julissa chuckled, her legs weak as lethargy took over her body. This was a way better way to start the day.

HOURS LATER, JULISSA was still thinking about their morning session. The noise around her was soothing, though some would find it otherwise. But, the happy squeals of the children had her smiling as she sipped her wine. From the moment they entered the Knight's house, Julissa had felt welcomed. It was a much different reception than what her mate had gotten from her brothers.

"How was your trip?" Celine asked her. "Well, outside of the trouble you guys had?"

She smiled. She'd seen Celine at several Motsi events and had never seen her this personable and open. Mostly the woman kept to herself, so Julissa had never gotten a chance to get to know her. She found the woman sweet and funny.

"It was exhausting, but I really enjoyed it." She told her. "Having Rocco with me was a bonus."

Celine's eyes sparkled. "I bet. I'm so happy for Rocco. And you, of course," she hurriedly added.

Julissa laughed. "I understand what you mean."

"Are the two of you settling into the penthouse?" Adina asked, joining them at the table.

"You did an amazing job. It managed to blend both of our tastes." She gushed.

"I helped too!" Sariyah added, coming into the kitchen to swipe a biscuit.

"Excuse you, munchkin," Ms. Iris fussed.

Sariyah gave her an unrepentant smile and rushed from the room, her stolen food in hand. Julissa smiled. The little girl was beautiful and clearly enamored with her Uncle Rock. Her heart fluttered seeing

Rocco in his element with his family. If she leaned over, she could see him outside bouncing his nephew around as he talked to his best friends. She thought his stoicism was with strangers, but he was just as quiet around the Knights, only sporadically adding to the conversation. Oddly, it was reassuring. He didn't put on airs, and was honest, no matter the situation. It added a sense of security to their mating. She would never have to worry about waking up one day and Rocco being a totally different person.

"Therese told me she was getting feedback from you," Adina said.

"She was sending me random text messages with pictures asking me to make choices. I thought I would come home to my apartment completely redecorated." She confided.

The women laughed. The conversation between them all flowed easily, and Julissa relaxed, feeling like she'd known these people for years. Soon though, Iris was done cooking.

"Julissa, can you go grab the boys and let them know it's time for dinner?" Ms. Iris asked.

She hopped from her stool and headed for the back sliding doors. They were sitting around the pool. She took a moment to admire them all. Every last one of them was fine, but something about the men, passing babies between the four of them, caught her breath. It was beautiful to witness. Rocco had a radar for her because his eyes met hers the moment she stepped outside. He waved her over.

"Dinner is ready," she told them as she reached Rocco sitting in the lounger.

He slid his hand up her leg, crooking his finger. She bent over, and he grabbed the back of her neck, bringing her closer for a kiss.

"You doing okay?" He asked her softly.

"I love your family," she assured him.

The smile he gave her was everything. Their whole relationship flashed through her mind. If she'd made any different decisions, they might not have met. What would her life look like without him in it? She didn't know, nor did she care to find out. She was riding with him forever.

From her dream job to the man currently staring at her as though she were the only person in his world, Julissa had more than she'd ever dreamed she would have.

epilogue

Rocco waved off the waiter in front of him, forgoing the champagne he offered. If he was getting through this night, he needed to be sober. Ultimately, his mate had been correct, her mother wanted a big to-do, and Therese got it. Their actual mating ceremony had been intimate, but the woman had not budged on the celebration. Five hundred or more shifters moved around the ballroom, the décor outdoing any magazine Rocco had ever seen. In another hour, there were supposed to be fireworks going off outside. He sighed and flexed his fingers, wishing for a blunt.

"You need this more than me," Silas said, holding out his hand.

Rocco gratefully took the vape. "How many people in this motherfucker?"

Silas snickered. "How you feel?"

"Good. That's my baby." He passed the vape back. "Have you given your team the news?"

He nodded. "They worked hard to get those votes. Now the challenging part starts, but getting an injunction on the energy company will give us more time to work."

"Do you think Julissa will be in any danger of blowback?"

Silas shook his head. "You know how it goes. They're pussies, and once their intimidation doesn't work, they move on to throwing money at it."

Rock grunted and hit the vape again. He met eyes with his mate across the room, and she smiled. His bear moved within him, settling at the happy look on her face. His gaze moved over the rest of the room, and he narrowed his eyes as he spotted Dallas chatting with some wolf shifters who had never attended Motsi events before. Their faces were businesslike, and it put up Rock's antenna.

"What's PD up to?" He asked his best friend.

Silas chuckled. "Best leave that for later. You have your mate now. Gotta put that Rock away."

"Never that," he murmured.

He couldn't just turn that part of him off. That beast was still lingering, waiting to come out when needed. For all the Knight family had done for him, he would go to war for them. He now added Julissa to that number. His eyebrows winged high when Julissa nodded her head towards the balcony. Heat moved through his body, his bear attuned to her every need. He gave her a subtle dip of his chin and turned to his friend. Silas cracked up.

"Gon' head, man."

He passed the vape back to Silas and headed for the balcony where he'd first met his mate. The air was damp, warming with the coming of spring. None of that touched him as he slid into the shadows, waiting. It took another five minutes before he sensed her, his body tensing in anticipation. Not unlike the first night they'd met. Those months ago, he hadn't felt good enough for her…not that it was any different now.

But, with the reassurance and love she poured into him, he was in a place of acceptance. Julissa would defend him against anyone, including himself. His mate didn't play about him. Her heels clicked as she sauntered to him, her hips swaying the red sequined dress that was poured onto her curvy body.

God damned, that woman was bad a fuck.

And all his.

The smile she gifted him with when she finally came around the column where he was hidden made his dick hard. It was confident; none of the apprehension from that other night clouded her face. She was a woman who knew she had him wrapped around her fingers.

"I missed you," she whispered, stepping into his space.

Her scent rose between them, curling around his heart, riling his bear. But the man…the man was soothed by it. He leaned into the space between her neck and shoulder, inhaling, his body relaxing despite wanting to bend her over the rail and sink into her.

"How much longer we gotta stay?"

She cupped the back of his head with one hand, using the other to slide across his waves. "Say the word, my love, and we can bounce."

"What's the word?"

She chuckled and whispered the nastiest thing he'd ever heard her say. His knees went weak. When he thought of how different his life would be had he allowed his self-doubt to win, he clutched her tight. He would still be in that lonely darkness on the outskirts of the life his friends had tried to build for him. They'd all wanted him immersed in their lives, thoroughly enjoying the family's success, but he'd been reluctant, indulging in the darkness that had been his life for so long. Instead of allowing it, Julissa had shone her light on him, dragging him from the edge. He would never take her for granted.

"I love you, Liss," he whispered, claiming her mouth before she could return the sentiment.

For her, he would be the man she believed him to be.

For
Her
Peace
A Knight Bros Novella
Dria Andersen

2

For Her Peace

For Her Peace
Dria Andersen

Author's Note

So, let me holla at y'all for just a minute. When I write a series, I tend to plan out the whole story arc across however many books there are. In the case of the Knight Brothers, I knew that I would have four books, and then two more in a spin-off. With that in mind, there is a specific plotline in this story that does not resolve until the book spins off. It doesn't end on a cliffhanger, but it is intentionally unresolved.

That being said, I want to talk about my state of mind. When I started the series, or rather this book in particular, there was a lot more violence planned. But I just... I'm not in the mood for it, to be honest, so I've kept the deaths off the page in this story. That brings me to content warnings. Deena works to help victims of domestic abuse escape their situations. There is none on-page (refer back to my state of mind) but it's mentioned enough that it could be triggering for someone who has been through it. In Deena's backstory, there is mention of death due to domestic violence that could be triggering as well. I had a hard time debating how much of it to include. It feels unfair to gloss over such a sensitive subject under the guise of escapism, but in this case, it was the best move for me mentally. I by no means take the subject lightly and hope I've written it in a way that is considerate.

As for other trigger warnings, there is cursing, explicit sex, the mention and use of guns, and violence.

one...

Tough.

Deena Hines had had to be tough her whole life, along with resilient and fearless. None of those things were helping her at the moment. With shaking hands, her eyes traced the words typed on the fan letter she was reading. Fan mail wasn't odd or even new, especially since her and Celine's online content had started blowing up. Their social media was popping, and their channel had close to a million subscribers. Every week, she was surprised by how many people tuned in to watch her and Celine cook, bake, or make whatever they were crafting for that video.

So no, fan mail wasn't out of the ordinary.

This one, though... She took a deep breath, refolded it, and slid it back into the pile with all the other mail she'd picked up from their post office box. The box had been packed with letters and packages from their sponsors. It had been at least two weeks since it had last been checked. She wouldn't have noticed the letter amid all the other items except it was addressed specifically to her. That was odd. Most fan letters came addressed to their channel or social media handle and were never personalized.

She peered down at the letter along with the three others just like it. All of a sudden, sitting in her car in the near-empty parking lot of the post office had her feeling exposed.

Deena started her car and drove off, headed to Celine's house to work on the herb farm they both tended. She'd been looking forward to work, but now anxiety had her shoulders tight and her pulse elevated. She was thankful for the twenty-minute drive as it gave her time to calm herself. Her jaguar moved through her body, raising the hair on her arms. The animal prodded her to make a phone call. One to someone she knew could help her, but...

Was she ready for what would come with that?

Just thinking about him took her back to almost two years ago and the mad escape her and Celine made from Celine's farm. Afterward, *he* had taken her home and extracted her promise to call him if she needed anything. At the time, she'd been running on adrenaline and fear, so she'd dismissed him and his words.

Now, though... The words rang in her mind, and with the memory, a compulsion to call him and take him up on his offering of help. But one thing about Julian Chase was that he didn't hide what he wanted, and he wanted *her*. And Deena wasn't ready for his unspoken promises.

Besides, none of the letters had been signed, and by their words, they weren't threatening. So, calling Julian would be an overreaction. It just felt a little weird to be under the level of scrutiny the letters implied.

The writer observed the way she dressed, her mannerisms on camera, and even down to the lipstick color she wore to ascertain how she was feeling. It was eerie to have the writer use those things to imply a bond with her. They didn't know her, and she for damn sure didn't know them. How in the world could they tell on the days she wore red lipstick, she was feeling unsure of herself?

What gave them the right to even speculate on that?

By the time she pulled into Celine's farm, she'd worked herself into being mad about the whole thing. Tough. Yeah, she was tough and would not allow herself to be scared by innocuous letters from a coward too scared to name themselves. Having settled on that conclusion, Deena pushed it from her mind and exited the car.

Gathering the boxes, she headed into the house. Celine's main security guard, Lance, opened the door for her. Her best friend was married to Mason Knight, a businessman who took his mate's safety very seriously. Celine's father-in-law was also one of the three men who ruled the shifters in Eastfield. All of that meant that Lance was her friend's new shadow, and while he mainly remained unobtrusive, Deena was glad she didn't have to live like that.

She'd spent the majority of her childhood in youth homes. She valued her privacy above all.

"Let me." Lance held his hands out for the packages in Deena's arms.

"Thank you!" She gladly handed him the bulky items. "She up?"

"In the kitchen," he answered, leading the way.

She followed him through Celine's spacious living room and around the corner to the kitchen. Deena found her best friend at the kitchen island, her son in his high chair, food decorating his very cute face. Celine smiled in greeting and continued wiping Antonio down. CeCe's curly hair was braided down into two braids, her rounded caramel face bare of makeup like it usually was. Her friend was beautiful in a natural, effortless way. Deena waited until Celine was done before lifting the chunky fifteen-month-old.

"Hey, man-man," Deena cooed, rubbing their cheeks together.

He let out a string of garbled baby talk, reaching immediately for her hoop earrings.

"Thanks for stopping at the post office. I hadn't realized how out of control it had gotten," Celine said.

"You've been dealing with Antonio; I don't know why I didn't think to go get it myself."

Celine cocked her head to the side. "What's wrong?"

"With what?" Deena deflected immediately.

"Now, I already told you Mama Di is on me about using my panther's instincts, so that lie ain't flying," Celine told her.

Deena tensed as her friend reached for the letters, ignoring the bigger boxes. She picked up the opened letter and shot Deena a look.

"This the third one."

Deena didn't bother correcting her friend. It was the eighth one, but she'd managed to hide the others on her previous visits to the post office. The only reason she wasn't hiding these letters was because a part of her knew that it was getting scarier with each new one.

She let out a breath, dread coating her stomach. "And it's just as silly as the first. Harmless."

"It reads like a stalker. We should tell Mason so he can get Julian on it. It won't hurt to see who they're from."

She shook her head, removing Toni's hand from her earring. "It's fine. The PO box keeps them from knowing where we live, so they can't stalk us."

Celine bit her lip. "I don't know, Deena, these could escalate more."

"And if they do, then we'll tell your mate."

"Tell her mate what?" Mason asked, coming into the kitchen and kissing his mate.

His panther was powerful, filling the kitchen with its presence. Mason Knight was fine as hell, and Deena smiled because she loved him and Celine together. Her friend had changed so much since she'd mated, all in good ways. His frame dwarfed his wife's, his muscular body lean the way most male cat shifters were.

Celine nuzzled her mate's cheek before speaking. "Deena is getting threatening notes."

"They are not threatening," she protested immediately.

Invasive, creepy, and presumptuous, yes, but they hadn't reached the level of threatening yet.

Mason frowned and picked up the letter Celine pointed out. He read it, his frown deepening as Celine handed him the others she'd received last month from the post office.

"It's nothing, Mason. People see me on our sites and think that they know us," she rushed to assure him.

He grunted but said nothing until he'd gone through them all. "You've been on camera lately, lovebug. Any of these with your name on them?"

Celine shook her head. "I haven't gone through them all, but not so far as I can tell."

"I'll get Julian on them."

"That's not necessary, Mason," Deena protested, her heart thumping.

He raised a brow at her tone. "We'll be the judge of that."

She shrugged and let it go. It wasn't worth the argument.

"In the meantime, don't go pick up from the PO box anymore. They could be waiting to follow you home," he ordered. His tone let it be known he wasn't budging on it.

She hadn't thought of that, and it did give her pause.

"That's fine with me," Celine said.

"What is Julian going to do?" She bounced Toni, trying to keep her voice as nonchalant as possible.

Mason saw right through her and smirked. "He'll more than likely try and trace these."

She nodded, avoiding his gaze. "Would he need to talk to me?"

"You want him to talk to you, lil mama?"

"Just asking." Her cheeks heated, and she hid her face behind Toni.

Just thinking about Julian had her temperature up. Ever since they'd parted almost two years ago, she'd only seen him in passing as he picked up Mason or came to visit the couple as she was leaving. Sometimes they were in the same place when there were gatherings at Celine's, but they'd both kept their distance. Still, every glimpse of him had left an impression. Mason had caught her drooling once and wouldn't let her forget it.

"Keep your eyes on your surroundings from now on, but you're right. These could be nothing." He held up a hand to stop her next words. "Still, I'll let Julian deal with it."

She nodded because there wasn't anything to say after that. Besides, it would give her a good reason to get up the courage to talk to Julian finally.

two...

Julian cranked the handle of his bike, speeding up the machine as he raced after the black Escalade tearing down Highway 95. The Ducati was matte black like all his other toys, customized just for him. Even the chrome parts had been swapped for black with hints of bronze. He zipped through traffic, Rocco on his tail as they spotted their target getting off the exit. It was perfect, really. What he wanted to do shouldn't be done in a whole crowd of people anyway. He flew behind them, signaling Rock to take their right side. The car slowed to match the speed limit, and Julian rode up to the left side, revving his engine to get the attention of the driver. He lifted his visor and lowered his incisors, mugging the male. The fear in the male's eyes had a smile tilting his lips.

Julian glanced quickly into the back seat and saw their target and the wolf in there with him. He growled and gave Rock another signal. Rock lifted his bike up on its back tire and sped ahead of the car. He then swerved in front of it, forcing the SUV to stop. It came within an inch of Rock.

"Cutting that shit close," Julian told his friend over their in-helmet radio.

Rock grunted. Julian nodded as a truck came behind the car, boxing it in. He tapped the driver's window with his Glock, and the driver was shaking as he lowered it.

"Keep your composure, and this won't have to involve you."

The man nodded, holding his hand up.

"Unlock the doors," Julian ordered, switching his aim to the back seat and its occupants.

The wolf had reached for his weapon, and Julian cocked his gun in warning. The wolf froze. Rock reached into the back seat and grabbed the lion they'd come for, snatching him out. He watched with his gun trained on the Escalade until Rock dumped him into the truck that had come behind them. Once that was done, the truck swerved around them and took off. He waited until Rock got back onto his motorcycle before addressing the wolf.

Julian smirked at the angry male. "We'll be seeing you, pussy ass hoe." He tucked his gun back into his holster and dropped his visor.

They sped off, heading back to the South side. He and Rock pulled up to the Greenridge neighborhood where they had grown up and the Eastfield boxing club where his father and Dallas would be waiting. He parked his bike and got off, heading inside. A couple of his security team members were dragging in the lion, dropping him into a chair in the middle of the boxing ring.

His father, Julian Sr., was standing next to the ring, watching the lion with a sneer on his face.

"Easy?" his dad asked.

"Caught him red-handed with the wolf."

Senior cursed. "Dallas finna split his dome."

Julian nodded. If there was one thing he knew about his uncle, it was that he didn't take betrayal easy. Dallas came up, his panther lighting his eyes, his power evident despite his age.

"Cyrus?"

"It was one of his lower staff members." Julian hated to admit that because he knew it could lead to war between the cats and wolves.

Dallas growled. "I knew that motherfucker knew too much of my business. Good job, nephew."

"Of course," he said.

His father tapped his shoulder. He nodded at his pops. His phone rang, and he answered it. It was Mason.

"Yeah, Mase?"

"Aye, I need you at the house."

"What's up?"

"If you finish that shit with Pops, then you can handle this with your mate."

His lion tensed. "On the way. I'll get up, Pops." He nodded goodbye to Dallas.

"What's up?" His father asked.

"Some shit with Deena," he told them.

Dallas smiled knowingly, and Julian shook his head because the man knew too much. He sped off and headed to Celine's.

His best friend lived with his mate out of the city limits on an herb farm that Celine owned. It took him nearly an hour with traffic to get there. He was hungry as hell by the time he arrived, but if he knew CeCe, she would have something he could eat there. He'd been up well before the sun taking care of shit for Dallas. Even though he had his own entry code, he rang the doorbell when he arrived.

Celine answered the door with a smile. "Why you ain't use your key?"

Their toddler peeked from around her legs, his face lighting up as soon as he spotted Julian. "Juuu," he babbled, holding his hands up.

"I stay out of mated folks' business," he answered Celine as he picked up his nephew.

Toni squealed, his laughter ringing out as Julian held him upside down.

"He just ate, Julian," Celine warned him as she turned and headed toward the kitchen.

He righted the toddler and nuzzled his cheeks, laughing at Antonio's tiny growl. "Oh, you bucking on Unc, huh?"

He returned the sound, and the little boy's joyous giggle melted his heart. Julian loved his godson. Rounding the corner to the kitchen, he spotted Mason cleaning up Antonio's high chair. He had to laugh at the rough-ass shifter in his father role. Compared to the shit they used to get into, it was a blessing to see.

"What up, Mase?"

"How that shit with Pops go?" Mason asked, washing his hands.

"Caught him red-handed with the wolf."

Mason shook his head. "Pops finna be on one."

"Indeed," Julian agreed. "What's up with Deena?" He saw no point in beating around the bush.

Celine grabbed Antonio from him — or at least she tried. Her son clung tight to Julian's shirt.

"No, mama. Ju. Juuu," the toddler whined.

Celine sighed and shook her head. "Fine. I'll be out in the greenhouse if you need me."

Mason nodded, his gaze following his mate's exit. Julian shook his head. His boy was fully whipped. Once Celine was gone, Mason slid him a box full of open letters.

"Deena is getting some weird fan mail. Like stalker type shit."

Julian frowned. "Since when?"

"I suspect she's hiding more, but so far, I've just seen these," Mason answered. "They were at the post office when she checked this morning."

He growled, and Toni grabbed his chin, mushing his face into Julian's chest. His anger rose as he looked through the mail, reading small parts of the letters.

"She know?" Mason asked.

"That she's my mate?" Julian clarified before shrugging. "I been dealing with this shit with Unc. Now that that's over, I'll get on it."

Mason chuckled. "What you wanna do?"

"About this shit, or her?"

"Both…either," Mason said.

That was the question of the hour.

"I'll put someone on her to be on the safe side. Celine is covered by Lance, so she straight."

"And the mating?" Mason asked with a smirk. "Deena hardheaded than a mug."

Julian smiled at his friend. "It'll be fun."

three...

Deena's heart was thudding hard in her chest, and Mason's words swirled through her mind as she watched the car behind her make the same turn she had. It had been following her for the past two miles. She'd spotted it when she was leaving the craft store, and so far, the driver had been on her tail. It was discreet, but unfortunately for them, she'd been hyperaware of her surroundings ever since the last couple letters. It had been nearly two weeks since she'd seen the last one when she picked up the mail, but she'd been on pins and needles regardless.

She tapped the steering wheel at the red light and debated her next move. The best thing to do would be to lose them. But anger was starting to rile her animal. Why should she live in a constant state of fear because of this asshole? She glanced over at her glove compartment and made her decision. When the light turned green, she led the car following her on a small chase before pulling into an empty building's parking lot. Getting out, she took her gun from the glove compartment and waited until the car pulled up.

Gun hidden at her side, she made quick steps to the other car and held her Sig Sauer up to the window. It was completely reckless and probably not the best course of action, but she was committed at this point, so Deena took a deep breath, keeping her hand steady. Caught off guard, the fine ass man inside lifted his hands, a tiny smirk on his face. She wound her finger in a circle for him to lower the window.

"Okay, now, lil mama, we ain't got to take it there," he told her in a calm, deep voice.

"Why are you following me?"

His smile was not in the least bit reassuring. He didn't answer her question because he clearly thought it was a game. She released the safety and lifted it, using both hands to brace the weapon.

He laughed. "A'ight, you got that. Julian put me on you for protection."

She frowned and lowered her gun. "Julian?"

Her stomach dipped when she realized who he meant. God almighty. Her cat was excited, roiling through her body. She'd been avoiding the man for some months, making sure they were never at Celine's house at the same time. What she'd chalked up to a crush her jaguar was telling her was more, and she wasn't ready. Who did he think he was to put "protection" on her without telling her? Damn that man.

"Where is he?"

The man eyed her carefully before answering. "Likely his office."

Bet.

She knew where that was, and despite her trepidation, she rushed back to her car and sped off. The Knights' headquarters wasn't far from where she was, and she knew the building also housed Julian's security company. Though she'd been avoiding him, it hadn't stopped her from ear hustling and collecting information about him from her friend. Her adrenaline was still high when she reached the building, and instead of parking, she headed for valet.

The guy who had been following her was right on her tail as she entered the building.

"I'm Noah, by the way," he said, matching his steps to hers.

She cut him a side-eye and received a chuckle in response. The department store that took up the bottom two floors of the building was bustling. She headed for the escalator, but Noah guided her toward a side corridor that housed the elevators. Swiping a card to open one, he held his hand out for her to precede him.

She narrowed her eyes and muttered a hasty thank you. It wasn't his fault his boss was overstepping himself. "Why are you helping me?"

Noah smiled but didn't answer. She sucked her teeth and turned her attention to the ascending floor numbers. When the doors opened, she marched out of the car, where she was greeted by a receptionist with a smile. The walls of this floor were black and behind the concrete desk were the words *Julian Chase Security* in black glass. Brass fixtures hung from the ceiling, giving the space an understated and elegant look while also feeling badass.

To the receptionist's left were a pair of glass doors that led to the offices of his headquarters. Noah marched Deena past the desk and once again let her in the door and allowed her to go first.

The office was bigger than she'd anticipated. She could see the employee's breakroom and a conference room, with more glass walls lending the space an open feel. Julian's office was directly in front of them, with whom Deena assumed was his assistant keeping guard in front of it. The office door opened, and Rock exited with Julian on his heels. Rocco looked dressed for work, his all-black suit tailored to fit his massive body. She paused at the sight of her friend, fixing the scowl on her face.

"Rocco," she greeted him.

He grabbed her into a hug and kissed the top of her head. "You good?"

She nodded, stepping back. "I just have to talk to Julian."

Rocco frowned and looked between her and his friend, cocking his head. He gave her a careful look before nodding toward Julian. The bear shifter didn't use a lot of words, but he never failed to get his point across. She knew what he was asking.

"I just need to talk to him about something."

He simply raised an eyebrow. "You good?"

It was the same question he'd asked before, but the inflection was different, the ask a whole separate tone. She shuffled her feet nervously. He lifted her chin and stared into her eyes in that quiet way he always had. It assessed her, determining for himself if there was something he needed to help her with. She was used to him and his gruff voice, so she relaxed her face.

She and Rocco had grown up in the same group home, but their friendship had gotten tighter over the past few years. Their shared passion for helping women in untenable situations had brought them closer. The two of them spent many nights together rescuing domestic abuse victims, working in tandem with the women's shelters all around Eastfield. What Deena did was dangerous and Rock was there to protect her.

Sometimes, that protection extended even outside of their self-appointed missions.

With that in mind, Deena squared her shoulders and forced a smile onto her face. "I'll be fine, Rock."

He looked behind her at Noah, his brows dipping lower. "What's happened?"

Julian turned his attention to her, and Deena's skin flushed, heated from the lustful stare he had given her. He was also in all black, his suit slim and tailored just for his muscular body. The black shirt beneath his suit jacket was open to the top of his chest, and tattoos littered his light caramel skin. The dark ink was painted across him all the way up to his neck, giving him a dangerous air even in the midst of the corporate setting.

"From the look on shortcake's face, she came to argue about the guard she's finally spotted," Julian answered, smirking at Deena.

Julian's voice was nowhere near as deep as Rocco's, yet it moved through her body, lighting nerve endings. Wait... Where in the heck had that nickname come from?

Rock frowned at his friend. "You got it?"

Julian nodded. "I got her, don't worry." Rock stared, and Julian sighed. "Fine. I'll call you if it gets out of hand, but you know how I handle shit."

"Your way of handling it was to put someone on me without my knowledge. I almost shot him," she snapped, irritated all over again.

"Good girl," Rock growled, his shoulders relaxing.

Knowing that Deena was active in her safety seemed to appease her friend. Rocco nodded, giving her one last pat on the shoulder before leaving. Someone behind Julian snickered, and Deena's eyes widened as she remembered they were in the middle of his headquarters. She spotted an older male at the door with enough of Julian's features to mark him as his father. The man was just as fine, leaning against Julian's doorjamb with his arms crossed over his broad chest, a pleased smirk on his face. She didn't even have to scent the air to recognize the older man's lion. He wore his animal on his sleeve, a powerful aura that raised the hair on her neck as her jaguar tensed in caution.

"We love a woman that'll bust with us," he said, his voice rumbly…amused.

Deena's cheeks heated.

"Pops," Julian said with a shake of his head. "I got her, Noah. Come into my office if you finna cuss me out, shortcake."

"I'm not…" she growled, not even bothering to argue with him, instead following him inside his office.

His father watched her with amusement and interest as she passed him.

"Pops, this is my mate, Deena. Shortcake, my father, Julian Senior."

"I'm Julian, the first and best," his father said in introduction.

She couldn't suppress the tilt of her lips at his charming smile, but then she straightened her face. Wait… Her heart thumped. Did Jullian call her his mate…in front of his father?

four...

Julian kept his smile tucked as his mate marched into his office. She was *mad* mad, her eyes flashing between gold and the dark brown of her natural irises. Noah had called and given him a heads-up that they were coming, for which he was thankful. It had given him time to compose himself and get ready for her presence.

Right now, her animal was riled, the jaguar very much making its presence known. He liked that his mate was in tune with her cat. His father chuckled at the door, stopping Deena's movement by grabbing her hand.

"It's a pleasure to meet you, lil mama." He pulled her closer and nuzzled the top of her head, inhaling deeply. "Strong ass cat. Perfect." Senior stepped back and shot a mischievous smile at his son before saying, "Get in his ass, baby girl. Junior too spoiled."

Julian could only growl at his father's instigating ass.

"I'll get up with you later, Junior," Senior said on his way out the door.

He shook his head and headed behind his desk. Deena was still standing in front of it, her perturbed countenance a lot more enticing than he was sure she realized.

"Did you hear what I said out there? I almost shot your man."

"But you didn't. I got good people, Deena. I'm not worried about Noah," he told her as he settled into his chair.

She huffed before sitting in the chair in front of his desk. "Why did you introduce me as your mate?"

"Were you not expecting me to claim you?"

"You can't just say you're my mate like it's a done deal."

He smiled then, allowing his animal off its leash a bit. His teeth lengthened, and Julian knew his eyes would be flashing gold. "Let your jaguar out, and we'll see what she has to say about it."

The pulse at her neck raced as her body shuddered. Leaning back in his chair, Julian licked his lips before running his tongue over the tips of his fangs. Deena adjusted in her seat.

"Tell me what has you upset, shortcake."

He was soaking her up, taking in all her beautiful features. Her makeup was well done, accentuating her beautiful cat-like eyes and emphasizing her high cheekbones. Her full lips were painted and glossy, and he wanted to taste them. The last time he'd seen her, her hair had been pulled up into a messy bun, but today, it was straightened and parted down the middle, reaching well past the middle of her back. She wore a long black and white cardigan that reached her knees, but it didn't hide her curves one bit. It had been weeks since he'd last gotten a glimpse of her. But he'd had spies to root out of Dallas's office, so he hadn't time to dedicate to pursuing his mate. All that was different now, though. He was done, and it was time for him to apply pressure.

She eyed him, her gaze raking over him, studying. "When did you know?"

The question surprised him, though it shouldn't have. The limited information he knew about Deena told him she was upfront.

"Remember the shootout at Celine's farm?"

Her eyes widened. That was a chaotic time. Celine's family had tried to kill her and Mason so they could gain access to her inheritance. Julian's first glimpse of Deena had been as she and Celine were escaping. Both women had every reason to be panicked, but they'd handled themselves well. Even before his lion had asserted itself, that small glimpse of her strength had caught his attention. He'd dropped her off at her apartment, making her promise to contact him if needed. Clearly, that didn't happen, but he would let her slide this once. He knew that, at the time, he wasn't ready for her. Now, though…

She cleared her throat. "Why didn't you say anything?"

"I had some shit to handle, this" — he indicated his office — "to build. I wanted to wait until we had time to get to know each other."

Deena kept quiet, lowering her eyes a moment. He stood and moved to stand in front of her. Perching on the edge of his desk, he leaned into her space.

"You gon' run from me, love?"

Her soft gasp of surprise did something to him. It gave away a hint of her vulnerability. But no sooner than she showed it, she gathered her composure and shrugged. So that's how she would play it?

He chuckled and leaned back. "So, you spotted your guard."

Her eyes flashed, and she sighed. "It's not necessary. I already told Celine that those letters were nonsense."

He nodded as though he agreed and smiled as she settled more comfortably in the chair, her face relaxing.

"It's not that I don't appreciate the sentiment, though I wish either of you had consulted with me. I would've told you all of this before accidentally shooting Noah."

"Have you read the letters?"

She nodded. "I saw the ones from the post office."

"For the past two weeks, my men have been picking up your mail."

He reached behind and grabbed the file where he kept the letters that'd been gradually getting more unhinged. They'd received six in just the weeks they had been checking. He passed the folder to Deena, observing her as she read over some of it. She closed the file with shaking hands and gave it back. His lion whined at her cat's distress.

"I understand your need to be independent, but I need you to understand that I won't allow anything to happen to you. Even if I have to fight you to protect you."

She took a shaky breath. "I'll be more careful."

He nodded. "Okay."

Her face lit, and she smiled. "Okay?"

"Yes, okay. Please be more careful. The guard stays. If these letters get more disturbing, I'll order Noah to watch closer."

She growled in irritation. "I don't want people in my space like that, Julian. I've worked very hard to get where I am right now."

He pulled her chair closer and put his hands on the arms, caging her in. "Shortcake."

"Why are you calling me that? I am not short," she muttered.

He snorted at that lie.

"I'm not ready for a mate," she said softly.

"That's fine, mama," he said, cupping her chin. "But I don't plan on pretending that you won't be everything to me, which means I'm going to protect you with everything I have. You understand?"

She nodded, her face softening.

"Now, outside of Noah, are you doing okay?"

"I'm fine. Since I'm not seeing the letters, I can almost pretend it's not happening."

He hummed. "And the guard is reminding you."

"Yes," she breathed out, happy he understood.

His phone rang on his desk, and he ignored it, knowing he had a meeting in a little bit.

She stood. "You're busy. I'm sorry for busting in like I did."

He pulled her in between his legs, wrapping his arms around her waist. "How long you gon' make me wait, shortcake?"

She sucked her teeth at the nickname.

He chuckled, lifted her chin, and dropped a light kiss on her lips. "Answer the question, Deena."

She sighed. "I like my freedom."

He grunted.

She wrapped her arms around his waist, and the feeling of home she gave him soothed his animal.

"I just bought my own house," she whined.

He tightened his grip on her, chuckling. "I see you gon' be stubborn as hell. Don't be mad at me when I start applying pressure to get past that."

Deena shuddered at the promise in his voice. She was officially on notice.

Julian kissed the top of her head and inhaled his mate's scent. He could sense she was going to give him shit, but he'd spent his entire adult life searching for his mate. He had no plans to play games about it.

five...

Now she knew good and damn well her neighbors were not up cutting the grass this early in the morning. She squinted at the clock on her bedside table and growled. It was barely after eight. She probably wouldn't be as mad about it if she'd gotten more than four hours of sleep the night before. All night, she'd tossed and turned, dreams of Julian making her jaguar restless and hard to settle.

So, being that those little handful of hours were all she'd gotten, she was ready to fight. She flung the sheet off her body and snatched her robe off the chair, stomping to the front of her townhouse.

Somebody was finna get cussed out.

She sucked in a surprised breath when she looked out her window and saw Julian's father leaning against a blacked-out pickup truck on wheels that were ridiculously large. His arms were crossed, a thermos in his hand as he watched whoever was cutting her yard. *What in the hell?*

A sane person would've reevaluated her nearly naked state under the robe and changed, but Deena valued her sleep, and being awoken was one of the top two ways to get her hot. She rushed out the front door and approached the older man. Her steps faltered slightly when she spotted Julian pushing a lawnmower over her small patch of yard.

God, she was not in the mood for this.

"Good morning, daughter," Julian Senior called out.

She groaned because it was entirely too early in the morning for their charm. He met her on the driveway, pulling her into his arms. He nuzzled against the side of her face, and her jaguar immediately reacted. An overwhelming sense of security overtook her, his animal welcoming and greeting her. She swallowed down the lump in her throat and stepped back.

Deena cleared her throat. "Why, pray tell, are y'all out here so damn early?"

The question didn't have the bite it would've had a few minutes ago, his hug effectively calming her. She would ignore for now the fact that he'd called her "daughter."

"It's Florida, lil mama. It'll be hot as hell here in another hour. You want your mate to faint out here cutting your grass?"

Even though it was the end of October, he was right. It would warm up as soon as the sun fully ascended the sky. She didn't so much as twitch her eyes toward Julian because if she did, after the dreams she'd had last night...ain't no telling what Senior would be able sense from her. Lord have mercy, why was she being tested?

"Why is he cutting my grass?"

"Your mate is doing what he's supposed to do," was his answer.

Which... She sighed. Wasn't no use in arguing with this man. It seemed like Julian had gotten his arrogance directly from his father. From calling her "daughter" to outright proclaiming Julian as her mate, the two men were obviously of one accord regarding her.

"Would you like something to drink?" she offered.

He smiled, and she shook her head. It was clear where Julian had gotten his charming manner as well.

"Thank you so kindly, lil mama."

She let him in and went straight to her kitchen to fix ice water. "Make yourself comfortable," she told Senior.

Everything in her wanted to stay and ensure he didn't disturb her space, but she quashed her usual distrust. She walked back outside and waved Julian down. He'd traded his lawnmower for a weed whacker. Her mouth watered the moment she took time to observe him. He was sweating in the sleeveless shirt he wore, his black joggers hanging on his waist in a way that had heat flushing her body. Once again, she cursed the fact that her temper had her outside in just a robe.

He stopped in front of her, smiling.

"I brought you some water," she murmured.

"Morning, shortcake," he greeted, taking the glass.

He chugged it down and handed it back. He leaned into her space, and knowing what he was asking for, she pecked his lips. His smile made her body warmer than the sun was doing.

"What you got on under that robe?" he asked, feral golden eyes raking her body.

She closed the lapels over her chest tighter and changed the subject. "Why are you cutting my grass, Julian? I've managed all this time on my own."

"That's just it, shortcake. You're no longer on your own. The faster you understand that, the easier this all gets."

She sucked her teeth. "And you brought your daddy."

Julian scoffed. "You'll soon learn that Senior does whatever he wants. He wanted to see you, so here he is. He would've come over without me if I hadn't put my foot down."

She frowned, and he chuckled.

"I've been an only child for damn near forty years, my baby. It's your turn."

What in the world did that mean? Instead of asking, she turned around and headed back inside.

His father was walking around her living room. Even though Halloween hadn't even passed, she already had her house decorated for Christmas. She'd done it to perk up her mood. Her tree was up, fresh pine garlands were strung up across the room, and there were lights everywhere. A small Christmas village adorned her wooden coffee table, and her TV was mounted on the wall over the faux fireplace she used for aesthetic purposes only.

Senior was glancing over the artwork she had on her walls. They were pieces she'd found at the many flea markets she frequented.

"I don't know how long Julian will take. Would you like some breakfast?" she asked to get his attention.

He smiled at her and walked back over to her small kitchen island. It could only fit two stools, but he took one and settled at the counter. His presence seemed to swallow up the space in her kitchen.

"Junior told me you liked to cook."

She nodded. "I have a cooking channel with my best friend."

Though her relationship with Celine had started as them going into business together, they'd fast become friends, and now the two of them were as close as sisters.

He snapped his fingers. "On the internet, with Celine, right?"

"Yep."

He looked into her eyes, his lion momentarily taking over his gaze as he studied her. "Tell me about yourself."

She raised her eyebrows. "Umm, I'll need coffee first for that."

He laughed. "Gon' and put on some clothes. I'll take care of it for you."

She nodded and did what he ordered, not even questioning it. By the time she'd brushed her teeth and washed her face, throwing on some biker shorts and a t-shirt, she felt marginally better. He was sitting back at the island, two steaming cups of coffee in front of him.

"Thank you."

"Why you got everything in your cabinets labeled with your name?" His eyes were shrewd. She had a feeling he knew the answer, but she gave him one anyway.

"I grew up at Winnie's House; it's still a habit to label my stuff."

He nodded. "Who your people?"

She sighed. "I don't have people. I lost my mother when I was eight and never knew my father. I bounced around foster homes until I landed at Winnie's."

"That's why you do what you do with Rock?"

She tilted her head in assent and smiled wistfully, touched he knew that much about her. She was incredibly proud of the work she and her friend did.

"Are waffles okay?"

"Of course."

They made conversation while she cooked, and she found herself relaxing. Julian the First was charming, and it was hard not to fall into an easy rhythm with him. Senior asked her so many questions about what her work was like, how she was feeling, about her childhood. For a moment, it was easy to imagine what having a father would've been like.

After a while, Deena realized it was quiet outside. Moments later, Julian knocked on the door before entering with a bag slung over his shoulder. She tried to keep the lust to herself as he sauntered over. He was careful to keep his sweaty body off of her as he leaned over her.

"I'm taking a shower."

Something about his voice made her shiver in need. "I think you mean 'may you,'" she corrected.

Senior laughed, and she shook her head at the mischievous man.

Julian kissed her, and her body was pliant once he swept his tongue across her lips. She opened for him, and he took full advantage, deepening the kiss until her knees went weak.

"Towels are in the hallway closet outside of my room," she whispered.

The smile he gave her was cocky. The man knew well his effect on her. Deena sucked her teeth and stepped back. If she weren't careful, he and his daddy would take over her life. And to be honest, her jaguar had no problems with that. It was the woman that was being stubborn about the whole thing. By the time Julian returned, smelling good as hell, she was setting their plates at her small glass dining room table.

Nothing about spending time with the two men felt strange to her. It was as though she'd known them both for years. She learned a lot about Julian from his father without half the pressure a first date would've entailed, and she was able to relax and get to know them both. Julian helped her clean up when they were finished, and she walked him to the door, half the day already gone.

Julian grabbed her into a hug at her door. "Noah told me you still been trying to lose him when he follows you."

She rolled her eyes, even though guilt niggled at her. "He's unnecessary, Julian."

"Shortcake." He sighed and shook his head. "I'ma plant him in your front yard if you can't cooperate."

"Fine." She couldn't help the pout that turned down her lips.

"Pouting makes me think of clever ways to occupy your mouth, ma. You might want to be careful with that," he muttered, nipping her bottom lip.

She shivered, and her stomach clenched. She licked her lips, already knowing what she wanted to do with her mouth.

Julian chuckled. "You better be glad your father-in-law is waiting in the truck."

"You and your daddy think if y'all claim me enough times, I'm just gonna give in?"

"Wait 'til Michelle finds out she has a daughter. There will be no escaping me," he teased.

She hated that she laughed because she knew it would encourage the ass. "Go. I got shit to do."

"Don't be dodging Noah, shortcake," he warned.

"Fine, I'll be on my best behavior."

A devastating smile was his answer. He kissed her lightly and left, his scent lingering in the air. She wanted to call him back to her. That man was dangerous.

six...

Julian lifted the box out of his truck and shook his head. He'd had no idea the amount of mail Celine and Deena got from their fans. Or even that people still wrote letters. Shit, he'd expected a note here and there, but besides the free shit they got to their mailbox, they got a lot of personal letters. They ranged from recipes the fans wanted them to try to "helpful" suggestions. He didn't know how either of them did it.

He and his team read through everything.

The threatening letters had escalated to gifts, and now his mate was mad at him because he'd told Noah to stick closer to her. Deena wasn't the only person chafing at her extra security. The letters began mentioning the male around her. It was starting to get sinister...taunting even. So, though she was upset, Julian wasn't budging on Noah sticking closer to her.

He knocked on the door once before entering. Mila's car was in Celine's driveway, so he figured it would be okay to just go in. Both women were in the kitchen sitting at the table, drinking hot chocolate. Julian only knew it was hot chocolate because their kids had rings around their mouths. Carter and Antonio were in high chairs, their shirts a mess. He could only assume Mila and Silas's daughter was in school.

"What's going on in here?" he asked, carefully dropping the box of mail on the counter.

"I came to hang out with my sister," Mila answered, lifting her cheek for his greeting.

He nuzzled her cheek, their animals greeting each other.

"My Ju," Antonio whined.

"Boy, don't nobody want your uncle," Mila laughed.

Celine snickered. "I'm finna pack a bag and send him right home with his godfather."

"Say less," he joked, nuzzling Celine. "That's my baby."

Antonio lifted his arms.

"Nah, man-man, you too messy for Unc." Julian looked down at his white dress shirt and shook his head. He was heading into meetings once he left here, and picking up a toddler covered in chocolate was not the move.

"Up!" Toni insisted.

"What brings you by?" Celine asked, getting out of her seat. She cleaned up her son and released him from the high chair.

The toddler rushed right over to Julian. He chuckled and shook his head. He would never tell his baby no. He had a change of clothes in his office, so he lifted the toddler. "I brought your mail by. I already filtered the mess out."

She winced. "How is it going with Deena?"

"You need to talk to your stubborn friend," he answered.

Deena was still chafing at the guard, especially now that Noah was full-on following behind her.

"What's going on?" Mila asked.

"Deena was getting threatening letters." Celine sighed. "I'll talk to her when she comes by today."

Julian didn't think that would make a difference, but he shrugged all the same. "Where's your mate?"

"In his office." Celine pointed down the hall.

He toted Toni to Mason's home office. His best friend was behind his desk, his fingers flying over his keyboard.

"Why you working from home?" Julian asked, setting Toni on the floor.

The toddler took off for his father's side of the desk, climbing into Mason's lap.

"I've been working late the past couple of weeks, and you know how lovebug gets when I work too much."

Julian smiled. His friend was a changed man, and he could admit to loving the way he was around Celine.

"What did you want to talk to me about that couldn't be done in the office?" Julian asked, settling into the chair across from Mason.

"Man." Mason wiped a hand down his face. "You talk to Unc lately?"

Julian frowned. "I saw Dad the other day when I went by Deena's. What's wrong?"

"I was on the West side at some kind of flower market for CeCe. I caught sight of Dad's detail."

He sat forward. "The fuck they doing in wolf territory? Was your dad with them?"

Mason gave him a droll stare as Antonio slobbered over his cheek. Julian sighed because Dallas didn't go anywhere without his detail, and if they were somewhere without him, then chances were that he'd sent them.

"You know if Pop's up to something, then Senior is right behind him."

"What in the world could the two of them be plotting?" Julian murmured. "Dallas hates Cyrus."

Mason nodded. "Especially since he's been interfering with dad's business. After that spy shit, I thought Pop was finna drive through the West side hanging out the window."

Julian snickered at the visual, but he straightened. Dallas openly being in wolf territory was bold, and disdainful. He didn't even want to imagine what their fathers were getting into. He cursed.

"Let me handle this shit with Deena, and then we can see what's what," he promised his friend.

"Pop's been dodging my questions," Mason admitted.

The two friends shared a look, knowing what that could mean.

"Handle your mate, man. Until we know something, ain't shit to do," Mason told him. "Did you tell Deena about the packages?"

He shook his head. "She cussed me out because I told Noah to start following her into places instead of staying in the car."

Mason smirked. "I told you that woman was stubborn."

"Not too much on my baby," Julian laughed.

"You got that. Let me know when you talk to Senior," Mason said.

Julian nodded, standing. "I'll get up with you later."

He waved to the women as he left, smiling as he exited the door. His mate was pulling up. Now he could scratch hunting her down off his list. She parked and got out, a pair of faux leather leggings painted on her body. Her cropped hoodie showed off a sliver of her toned stomach, and his lion raised to attention.

He licked his lips and descended the steps, anxious to be in her space. Deena looked up as he headed to her car. She closed the door but stood there with a box in her hand.

"Morning, shortcake."

"Hi. I thought you didn't guard Mason anymore. What are you here for?"

"Visiting my best friend. I can't do that?" he teased.

She huffed out a breath, rolling her eyes.

"You need help with that?"

Deena shook her head, keeping the box between them. It made him smile. Like a box would keep him from her. Her hair was slicked back into a ponytail, the end of it hanging to her shoulders. Her pecan brown face was free of makeup, her large dark eyes luminous and beautiful.

She was gorgeous.

"You busy tonight?"

That wasn't what he meant to ask, but the woman distracted him. He had a whole security talk planned for her, but all he could think about was getting alone time with her. He'd caught her off guard; he could tell by the way she shuffled in front of him.

"Umm…"

"Okay. I'll pick you up at eight."

She frowned. "You're supposed to ask for a date."

"I done told you I'm applying pressure, my baby." He cupped her chin just to feel her soft skin against his fingers. "So be ready, and wear something short." His eyes trailed down. "I like looking at your legs."

Her eyes widened, and her pupils changed color as her cat showed itself. He let his lion off its leash just a little bit, enough to show her animal what they were about. She gasped and stepped back. She was flustered, clearly, and if her scent was anything to go by, she was intrigued.

"Don't be late, shortcake," he told her, walking away before he pushed her too far.

Likely, she would remember she was mad at him and tell him no, so he chuckled and hustled to his truck before she got the chance.

seven...

Deena was nervous.

Duh. Julian was fine as hell, and he was looking and smelling good on her doorstep. Who wouldn't be nervous? She didn't want him to know that, so she played it cool. From the smirk on his face, it wasn't working. His amorous gaze surveyed her body, and she couldn't stop the shudder that wracked her. She felt the caress as though it were his hands, not his eyes skimming her.

At first, the part of her that was naturally petty had her ironing out a pair of slacks to wear tonight. Instead, at the last minute, she'd dug into the back of her closet for a dress she'd not worn in years. The black dress reached her ankles, but the slit in it was nearly to the top of her hip, leaving most of her right leg exposed. It fit her like a second skin, the demi cups pushing her breasts up nicely, with tiny straps holding the whole thing together.

It was worth it to see the look on his face. For a moment, he stared at her, speechless, the lust in his eyes burning across her skin.

"You look fucking phenomenal, shortcake." His voice was another weapon in his arsenal.

"Thank you," she managed.

He held out a thin gift box. She questioned him with her eyes, but he simply smiled, waiting for her to take it.

"You didn't have to get me anything." She stepped back from the door and let him in.

Deena walked the gift over to her kitchen counter, curiosity burning her up inside, but she set it down. She'd open it later when he

153

wasn't staring at her. She was almost scared to show him how much his gesture meant. Clearing her throat, she turned back to face him. Julian dominated any space he was in, and being this close to him in her darkened house was a temptation.

"Where are we going?" she asked, stepping into her heels at the door.

The shoes put her at his neck, finally within comfortable kissing distance. Lord, where did that thought come from? His eyes heated and glowed as he raked his gaze across her body.

"I'm taking you out to dinner."

She smiled. "Perfect, I like to eat."

Julian laughed and guided her outside, helping her into a matte black Mercedes. He closed the door once she was settled into the seat. Deena looked around, impressed. The only vehicle she'd seen him driving was his pickup truck. His cologne filled the space as he entered the car. The compulsion to lean closer to that scent was almost too much to resist.

The drive through town was quick, and within fifteen minutes they arrived at a swanky restaurant. It was a place that Deena had never envisioned visiting. He was not playing. Julian pulled up to the valet, coming around to open her door.

She was nervous, pulling the wrap at her shoulders around her tightly. He chuckled darkly as he helped her from the car.

"Shortcake, this dress got your ass sitting, my God," he murmured in her ear, his hand brushing down her back.

Goosebumps erupted along the skin of her arms. The fact that he said whatever came to his mind would be her undoing. Something about it made her feel secure and on solid ground. She would never have to worry about where she stood with him. That was appealing.

Julian guided her into the restaurant. The hostess spotted him and didn't ask questions, simply showing them toward the back. Deena's eyes ballooned when they were led to their table, which held a gold box filled with white and red roses. Her gaze darted across the crowded restaurant, but their table was the only one with flowers. Her breath caught at the beautiful display.

Okay. Pressure.

"Julian," she whispered.

He gripped her waist from behind her, rubbing his cheek against her neck. "Light work, mama. I already told you how I'm coming." He kissed her shoulder and helped her into her chair.

She shivered when his hand brushed her shoulder, her heart racing as she sat. She could barely see the other side of the table around the flowers. The hostess grabbed them, a wide smile on her face.

"We'll hold these in the front for you. The tasting menu comes paired with select wines, but a waiter will be with you shortly if you want anything else."

Deena nodded, too stunned to speak. She was being wooed. She'd had game run on her before, not to mention more first dates than she liked to think about, but this felt different. Yes, they were mates; she wouldn't dispute that, but it went back to Julian saying what he meant. He told her he would apply pressure, and so far, he was a man of his word. The part of her that had learned never to depend on anyone was soothed in his presence.

"The tasting menu? Fancy," she said after clearing her throat.

"I thought you'd appreciate it." Julian smiled at her as he took his seat.

"I can't wait." Excitement added to the butterflies in her stomach.

"How was your day?" he asked.

"We were in the field all day, but it was fine."

"The amount of fan mail the two of y'all get is wild," he commented.

She nodded. "Trust, we were just as surprised. We started the channel to show the different things we do with the herbs and spices we harvest. I don't think either of us expected it to take off like it did."

"I'm proud of you."

Her face heated. "Thank you." She lowered her head, unable to meet his intense stare.

"So, tell me about Deena." It was an order.

She noticed Julian didn't ask many questions. He used declarative statements and issued commands. His questions were reserved for things he was truly curious about. She wished it didn't turn her on so much. Deena adjusted in her seat.

"What do you want to know?"

He licked his lips. "Everything, ma."

"Umm, I told you how I grew up." She shrugged. "I've spent the last few years focusing on getting me and Celine's business up and running."

The dedicated time had paid off, and Deena was proud of everything she and Celine were accomplishing.

"It's allowed me a lot of freedom, and I bought my townhouse six months ago. That was a huge milestone for me," she told him.

"Ah, your need for your own space," he posited. His fingers drummed against the table. "That's why you gave Noah such a hard time."

She shrugged.

"Tell me your hopes and dreams."

Deena rolled her eyes at the corny question, and he laughed in response. She smiled wistfully. "I just want peace. It's all I've ever wanted out of life. I've learned that nothing is promised or permanent, but if I can just carve out a little peace and comfort for myself, I'll be happy."

He nodded, taking in her answer. "Then I'll make sure you have it. No matter what it takes."

Her stomach fluttered, and she blinked away the tears threatening to form. When had she become such an emotional woman? "And you?"

"Shit, peace sounds perfect. I tend to be a people pleaser. It comes from juggling between my parents. Sometimes, I forget to factor in myself."

"You take care of everyone else, so your mate will need to take care of you." She nodded. "I can do that."

She didn't know what possessed her to say that, but Julian's eyes lit with his lion as his hand fisted on the table.

"Shortcake, we won't get through dinner if you talk to me like that," he rumbled.

She reached out her hand, and he grabbed it, squeezing tight. "If we do this—"

"Ain't no *if*, my baby," he cut in.

She chuckled. "You can't even help yourself. Bossing me around is the quickest way to make me dig in my heels, just so you know."

He lifted her hand and kissed her wrist. "You may as well get used to it. I'm not one to beat around the bush."

"Fine, Julian. *When,*" she conceded. "I can give you a list of things that are important to me, but more than anything, I just need you to know I don't like false promises. Mean what you say, and don't play with me."

She knew it stemmed from everything she dealt with as a child being shuffled around between foster families. There had been so many adults promising her permanence and safety, and so few had been able to deliver.

Deena hated promises for that reason.

"I can't be nothing but real, shortcake. If I tell you some shit, I'ma stand ten toes in it."

She believed him, and that was a first for her. Her jaguar trusted him and his animal wholly. There was none of the nervousness the woman had about their mating. Still, it didn't mean they wouldn't make him work for it.

She sat back in her chair. "So now you tell me about Julian."

"I've been doing the same as you. Building. I had to stop guarding Mason personally once my business started growing. I was content for a while to have a small operation, know what I mean? But then, I met you. That shit put a battery in my back."

She cocked her head to the side, unsure of what he meant. "I'm a simple woman."

"Maybe so. But that won't stop me from making sure I can provide you with anything you'd ever want. I got money and have never had a problem getting it. I want a legacy. For you and any jits we have."

Deena reminded herself that she hated when people promised her things, but the sincerity in his words... She wanted the dream he spun. She could only nod at him, too overwhelmed to speak.

Dinner was amazing, and despite her nervousness, their conversation flowed nicely. They talked until the place closed. Julian drove her home and walked her to the front door.

She fidgeted with her purse. "Thank you. I had a great time."

"Good. What do you want to do for our second date?" he whispered, closing the distance between them.

"Oh, I get a choice?" she teased. "Do I also get to pick what I wear?"

He traced a finger across her collarbone. "Don't act like you follow directions anyway, brat."

She shivered at the dominance in his tone. "I'm showing leg."

Julian growled and slid his hand up her thigh. The contrast of his tattooed hand against her brown skin was fantasy fuel. He gripped her leg, nuzzling into her neck.

"Your defiance gon' get you fucked, shortcake. Keep playing with me."

God damn this man. She was heading straight for her room and her vibrator the moment he left.

"Next time you got orders for how I dress, I expect cash to come with that request," she told him breathlessly.

He lifted his head and smiled. "Say less then, shortcake." Leaning forward, he kissed her softly, sweetly. But before they deepened it, he stepped back, biting his bottom lip. "Go inside and lock up."

She nodded, debating whether or not to kiss him again. "Text me when you get home."

Julian smiled bigger. "Of course, mama." He inclined his head, and she understood his unspoken order.

She hid her smile. He couldn't help himself. His dominance should be setting off all types of alarms within her, but her jaguar was reveling in it. Deena slipped inside and locked the door behind her. Her gaze strayed to the gift box she'd left on her counter, and she smiled, finally able to assuage that curiosity. Kicking off her heels, she padded over to it. She lifted the top and gasped. It was a leather-bound book with *Deena's Favorite Recipes* etched on the cover. It was an heirloom cookbook!

Tears gathered in her eyes. She thought about what he said about building a legacy, and her throat got tight. This book was meant to be passed down, and it touched her that legacy meant more than money to him. It raised her respect for him a bit more. She lifted the book with shaking hands, her heart melting, then laughed as she opened it. *My Mate's Favorite Dishes* was the title of the first blank page. It listed his favorite foods.

This man. Pressure indeed.

eight...

His phone ringing in the middle of the night was nothing new to Julian. He often got late night calls. Only half of them were what he'd consider emergencies, but being the boss came with the aggravation of dealing with people. So, he rolled over and grabbed his phone from the bedside table, swallowing his growl of irritation when he realized who it was. He lamented the sleep he would lose. Rocco only called for emergencies.

Though he'd only been sleeping a few hours, he prepared his body to get up.

"Yeah?"

"Your mate on her way out the house this time of night," was Rock's gruff greeting.

Julian sighed at the teasing tone, even though he knew his friend wasn't joking. "Shelter business?"

"If you busy, I got her, but I thought you'd want to know."

He shuffled from his bed to get dressed. "Nah, I got shortcake. Thanks, man."

"Always."

He ended the call and slid on a jogging suit, hoping to catch her before she left the house. It had been a week since their date, and even though the circumstances weren't ideal, he would be happy to see his mate. Squinting at the time, Julian prayed Noah was already at his post. He'd rented one of the townhouses in Deena's complex so her guards would be nearby.

Noah answered on the first ring.

"You got eyes on my baby yet?"

"Just posted up. She ain't left the house at all, according to Champ."

"A'ight. She getting ready to, so be on the lookout. I'm on my way to her."

"Bet."

They hung up, and no sooner than he got into his truck, his phone rang again. It connected to the Bluetooth as he started the engine.

"Morning, shortcake."

His mate's voice filled the truck. "Don't 'morning' me. Why did Noah say I had to wait on you? I have shit to do, Junior. I can't be waiting on you to come all the way from wherever you are."

He sucked his teeth at her calling him Junior. That woman stayed trying him. "I understand what you do, lil mama. If it's time-sensitive, then go ahead with Noah and send me your location."

She was quiet for a moment before sighing. "Fine, thank you. I'll share my location with you now."

"Shortcake, if you get in some shit, I'ma be on your ass, hear?"

"I hear you," she grumbled. "Stop for coffee on your way. Sometimes this takes a while."

Julian smiled, picturing the pout on her face. "Okay, love."

Plugging her location into his GPS, the coffee she'd asked for was his first stop. Twenty minutes later, he pulled up on her in a neighborhood that wasn't the best, especially while it was still dark out. He jumped from the truck, tucking his heat just in case. Deena was guiding a woman into Noah's car, the woman's face battered, her fear easy to read. It was no surprise when she reared back as Julian approached. Not wanting to make the situation worse, he stopped, holding his hands up.

"What do you need from me?" he asked Deena, suppressing his anger.

"We need to hurry before he gets home. Can you and Noah follow me? She won't want him in the car with us." Deena's voice was calm, her face patient.

Following her instructions, he nodded, backing toward his vehicle. He and Noah watched them from inside the cab of his truck as the two women got into the car. Julian kept his eyes out in case the mate arrived, almost wishing the male would show up. Noah muttered his thanks as he passed him his coffee.

"We should wait on him here and get rid of the problem for her," Noah commented.

Julian nodded, feeling the same, but they both knew killing the woman's mate could adversely affect her. It varied with shifters, so they could end up making the volatile situation that much worse.

"She do this a lot?" Noah asked.

He nodded as he followed Deena into the sparse early morning traffic. She was phenomenal, and pride swelled his chest for the work his mate did. It was dangerous, but he knew Rock had been taking care of her ever since he'd found out what she'd been doing. Julian followed Deena to a women's shelter on the north side of town, deep in bear territory. His eyes took in all the weak spots in the safety of the shelter. He would be fixing that.

He exited the truck, keeping enough distance between the women but close enough to appease his whining animal. The director came out when Deena knocked on the door, which was perfect. He would talk to her while Deena settled the female bear.

The sun was peeking over the horizon when Deena finally stepped out of the shelter. Julian had sent Noah back home hours ago, reassuring the male that he would take care of his mate this morning. Her eyes swept the parking lot, her face relaxing once she spotted him. Getting out of the truck, Julian rushed to meet her halfway, pulled in by her very presence. Even in a simple pair of joggers and a cropped hoodie, Deena was sexy as hell as always.

She paused halfway to him, squinting her eyes. His hand automatically went to his holster as he looked around. Julian didn't relax until she was standing in front of him. He grabbed her and tucked her into him. Her body relaxed in his arms and she sighed, her jaguar rubbing against his lion before settling. Cuddling her cheek against his chest, Deena tightened her arms around him.

"What were you looking at?"

"I thought I saw someone I knew from way back." She hummed and rubbed his back. "Rock is always with me, so I feel safe, but this…" She sighed. "This feels so healing."

Fuck, the woman undid him. He kissed the top of her head, moved by her words. He nuzzled her hair before doing the same to her neck, his lion pushing him to scent mark her.

She chuckled. "I can feel your cat's worry."

He couldn't even dispute her words. "I don't like you out in the open like this." His lion wouldn't settle until he knew Deena was somewhere safer. "Want something to eat?"

"I could eat." She followed him to his truck.

He looked around one final time, his hand pausing over the ignition as he noticed a male sitting in his car and watching them. He reached for the door, but the male drove off. The car didn't have plates, which raised his hackles.

"What's wrong?" she asked.

He shook his head, not wanting to alarm her. It could be nothing. He drove them to a small diner she guided him to. It wasn't full, so he was able to breathe easier. There was a relaxed silence between them as they ordered and got comfortable across from each other in the booth.

"What made you start helping the shelters?"

She sighed. "I had a friend…Dana." She shook her head and sighed. "I didn't see any of the signs of her being in an abusive relationship until it was too late. I found her behind the house, beaten to death. The police said there had been old bruises all over her body. All I could think about was how incredibly isolated she must have been, and as one of her good friends, I missed it. I blamed myself for a long time after her death. I couldn't help her, but I can help others."

"That's admirable. I'm glad my kids will have such a badass mother."

She busted out laughing. "Sir! You just don't filter shit, do you?"

The darkness in her eyes was lightening, and he smiled and relaxed. A presence loomed over his shoulder and Julian reached for the gun on his back. He sucked his teeth when Rocco slid into the booth next to him.

"How in the hell did you find us?"

Rocco grunted and nodded toward Deena. "Got her chipped."

He snorted and moved his hand off his Glock. "Announce yourself next time."

Deena rolled her eyes. "I knew you had a tracker on my phone."

Julissa slid into the booth next to his mate and settled her head on Deena's shoulder. "I told you he be doing too much."

"How did he get you up this early?" Deena asked, laughing.

"She nosy as hell," Rock answered without looking up from the menu.

He and Deena cracked up as Julissa threw a balled-up napkin at her mate.

Their impromptu breakfast was fun and went a long way to dissipate the anger and worry from their early morning errand. They waved at Rocco and Julissa a couple of hours later as they drove off.

"Where to, mama?"

She sighed and laid her head on the door. "Got orders to prep with CeCe today."

"I'll drop you off and have Noah meet you there."

She sucked her teeth. "Fine. I'm gonna sneak in a nap first."

He turned his music down and let her sleep. Celine lived on the other side of Eastfield, way out past the city limits, so it would take them a solid hour with traffic. Julian knew it would be hours before he could rest himself, but being there for Deena would always be his priority.

nine...

"It smells good in here!"

Deena walked into Celine's house after a cursory knock. She found her best friend in the kitchen, the dried herbs they needed for their orders spread out along all the surfaces of her countertops. Glass containers were in neat rows on the dining room table waiting to be filled. Lance was sitting on one of the stools at the island, a book in hand. He waved as Deena walked in.

Celine snickered as she pulled down the scale from a cabinet. "Says you."

"I like the smell of anise," Deena told her, dropping her purse on the sofa.

"You look tired, what's wrong?" Celine squinted at her when Deena fully entered the kitchen.

"Long night into the morning," she told her friend. "Julian dropped me off today and told me not to leave Lance's eyesight until Noah arrives."

Lance snorted and continued his reading.

Celine's face brightened. "Why did he drop you off? Did you spend the night?"

"On that note, I'll be in the living room." Lance stood and left.

The women laughed and got to work. Celine said nothing about Deena not answering her question. She was used to her tight-lipped friend. Preparing the herbal blends was tedious, but Deena loved the process. They had all of their dried herbs laid out; all they had to do was chop them and measure them out.

"You didn't answer my question," Celine reminded her after they'd been working in silence for a few minutes.

Deena rolled her eyes. She should've known the woman would circle back. "I didn't stay the night, but he replaced Rocco last night on one of my runs."

"Are you okay?"

Deena shrugged. "It was routine, so it wasn't as bad as it could've been."

"How is it going with you and Julian?"

"Nosy," Deena complained.

Celine snickered. "I want to know!"

"Fine. We had our first date last week," she admitted.

"And...?"

"And it was amazing. He was damn near perfect."

Celine squealed in happiness. "Yes, my bestie has a mate!"

"Ma'am, you're dragging it." Deena bit her bottom lip. "I don't know if I trust it just yet."

"What are you worried about?"

Deena opened her mouth and then closed it. What was her worry? She wasn't opposed to the mating at all. Was it fear? She wasn't an easy person to be with. As Julian had called her before, she was hyper-independent to the point where it had scared off other men. She didn't see that being a problem with Julian. He was self-assured, bordering right on arrogant. She actually found that attractive.

"It feels too good to be true," she finally answered.

"You felt the same way about our partnership and friendship," Celine reminded her.

She paused her scooping, struck by that truth. For a long time, she'd kept herself apart from Celine, afraid that the partnership they'd been building would collapse. So far, it had been nothing but blessings.

"He's moving as though the mating is a forgone conclusion. It almost makes me feel silly for resisting," she confided.

Celine hummed. "What are you going to do?"

Deena shrugged. "Let him woo me?"

"Right answer," Celine said with an impish tilt of her lips.

Hours into their orders, her phone rang, and she already knew who it was. She excused herself and stepped outside to answer.

"Mr. Chase."

He chuckled, the smooth sound of his voice making her giddy. He hung up but called right back, this time a video call. For a moment, she panicked. Her hair was still in the messy bun from the morning, and spices and herbs probably covered her shirt and dotted her skin. She looked a mess. She answered, rolling her eyes. He didn't seem to mind her appearance, his gaze taking her in, dark and intense.

"Alright now, you being flippant, but I like that Mister shit."

Why was he so fine? In between the time he'd dropped her off and now, he'd changed into a navy-colored suit, his button-up shirt opened to the top of his chest. She could see the fine details of the large lion tattooed on his neck from this close. He licked his lips, and she followed suit. Clearing her throat, she shook off the lust he elicited in her.

"Anyway, I'm glad you called. I wanted to invite you out for our second date."

"This will be our third date, shortcake. Breakfast counts."

She chuckled. "Fine, third then. This time I'm taking you out."

He smiled in surprise. "Do tell."

"Washington Park, do you know it?"

"Downtown Eastfield?" He looked intrigued.

She nodded. "They've made a bunch of improvements and additions to the park, so now it's a little hangout spot. I want to take you."

"Okay." He smiled again.

Butterflies took flight in her chest. "I'll pack a picnic."

He chuckled. "A picnic? I've never done that."

"Good. I'll be your first." She grinned. "Are you available Saturday?"

"I'll always make time for you," he told her.

Her cheeks heated, giddiness taking over. She worked to compose herself. "Then I'll pick you up at ten-thirty."

"Oh, I'm getting the whole treatment," he teased. "It's a date, my baby."

"Okay, then. Goodbye, Mr. Chase."

He shook his head. "Keep playing with me, shortcake."

Deena smiled and ended the call, clutching the phone against her chest. She fixed her face and walked back inside. Or at least she thought. Lance chuckled the moment she walked back in.

"You down bad, Dee," he teased her.

"Leave me alone, Lance," she fussed, laughing.

Celine laughed from the kitchen. "Deena's got a maaate," she sang.

They all froze when the proximity alarm rang. Even though she was used to the sound, it always took her back to the time they'd been attacked while on the farm. Lance pulled out his phone, checking the cameras.

"Councilman Knight," he told them, relaxing.

Both women released their pent-up breaths and went back to the packaging they were putting together. The front door opened a few minutes later, and Deena could hear Antonio babbling. Dallas Knight swaggered in holding the happy toddler, Julian's father walking in behind him. Power preceded both men, the animals beneath their skin prominent and unmistakable. It was intimidating, only softened by the fact that Senior was toting a small baby bag. They were both wearing golf polos and khakis. Had they taken the toddler golfing? The thought of that tickled her, and she smiled as Senior spotted her.

He rounded the counter, nuzzling against her cheek. "Well, hello, daughter."

The man was incorrigible.

"Good morning, Senior."

"I need to get your number. I can't be bothering Junior every time I want to talk to you," he told her, moving back to stand beside Councilman Knight.

She remembered Julian's words about stopping his father from coming over to her house by himself. He'd warned her that Senior considered her family and would treat her as such.

"You needed to talk to me?" She handed him her phone, intrigued.

"We're a part of the Motsi, and as Junior's mate, you'll need to start attending events." He added his information, using her phone to call his own.

She frowned, not having thought of that. Celine snickered next to her, and she shot her friend a glare.

"There's a fundraiser for Winnie's House coming up. That's a good one to start with," Senior continued with no input from her.

She nodded, dazed. She would confirm with Julian, but she had a feeling he would back his father.

"Ju said you grew up there?" Councilman Knight turned his attention to her.

She squirmed under his intense stare. "Yes. I spent my teenage years there."

"Oh, so you're acquainted with Declan Edwards."

He didn't state it as a question, and Deena had a feeling he already knew the answer. "I grew up with him and his brother, technically."

"You still talk to either of them?" Dallas questioned.

"Well, I really didn't know Devon like that. I occasionally see Declan when I'm on that side of town."

"Interesting," Senior said, sharing a look with Dallas. "When's the last time you spoke with him?"

She frowned. Silence dropped between them, only disturbed by the happy babbling of Antonio as he bounced in his grandfather's arms. The two shifters were up to something, but Deena would not be prying. For one, she was intimidated, and for two, it was really not her business. A part of growing up where she did was learning how to keep out of business that didn't have anything to do with her. It was ingrained in her, part of the code they all lived by. That included telling someone else's business. It was damn near akin to snitching.

She debated how to answer his question without giving too much of Declan's information away. She had no way of knowing what either man wanted with her friend. She'd just talked to Declan a few weeks ago when he called to check on her. He was an asset manager and his company had a mortgage division. He'd helped her get into her townhouse a few months ago, and he was making sure that everything was fine. She could go into detail and tell them that, but she answered the question he asked.

"Not too long ago."

Dallas hummed. "He good people, you think?"

She gave him a small nod, understanding what he was asking. Layered in the subtext was the question of whether her friend could be trusted for whatever Dallas's purpose was. She trusted Declan to take care of himself and certainly wouldn't want him to miss out on any opportunity the councilman could have for him.

"Declan's a good dude," was her answer.

Dallas seemed to sense she was holding back. She thought that would upset him; instead, his eyes lit with admiration.

"Loyal and a rider. You see my daughter, Dallas?" Senior bragged.

Dallas studied her, giving her an approving nod. "I see her."

Heat filled her face and chest. Senior's claim had something dangerously close to emotion clogging her throat. She went back to filling jars, unable to meet either of their gazes.

"We heading out, ladies," Senior announced. "Deena, I put my number, Sabrina's number, and even Michelle's in your phone. You got people now, so you call if you need something, hear?"

She nodded, blinking away the tears threatening to fall. She didn't know who either of the women were, but if Senior deemed them important, then they were possibly a part of Julian's family. Senior walked back over and kissed her forehead, leaving out with Dallas.

Fuck.

"I need a moment," she told Celine.

Deena walked into the hallway bathroom and sat on the toilet, letting the tears hit her cheeks finally. She had a family now? She'd been by herself for so long. But then Celine had come into her life, and now that Rocco was mated, Julissa made it a habit of checking in on her as well. Her phone had never rung as much as it had in the last year.

This, though? Senior's words, him calling her his daughter and meaning it... She buried her face in her hands as emotions she'd long buried erupted. Over the years she'd watched so many families with a sense of longing. Now, Senior was offering her that and so much more.

ten...

Deena was nervous as she pulled up to Julian's office. He'd called her this morning to let her know he needed to work for a little bit before their date. She worried that he would cancel altogether, but he'd reassured her he would be ready on time. She was excited about their date. She'd been wanting to go to Washington Park for a while now, especially once they cleaned it up. It had been dangerous before, but the city had really turned it around. With all the new features they'd added, a lot of families hung out there on the weekends. Every time she passed by, she would remind herself to visit. When she pulled up to the employee parking lot of the Knights' department store, Julian was standing outside, leaning against his truck. He waved and walked over to her, getting into the passenger side of her sedan.

He leaned over. "Good morning, shortcake."

She couldn't help her smile. "Good morning, Julian."

Julian stayed in place leaning over on her side. She rolled her eyes and pecked his lips, giving him what he wanted.

"You so spoiled."

He smiled and her heart thumped. Lord, this man. He buckled in and settled back into his seat.

"We doing bougie today, my baby?" he asked, turning to eye her fancy picnic basket in the back seat.

"It'll be a vibe," she assured him as she pulled out of the lot.

She expected him to protest being in her car, but he didn't. He adjusted the passenger seat so he could lean back and have room for his legs. Once he got into a comfortable position he relaxed, setting his hand on her thigh. Butterflies took flight in her stomach at the sight of his tattooed fingers against her leg. The one on the back of his hand was her favorite, a lion head with a crown atop its mane. Something about it exhibited his power. She shivered in pleasure. She was glad she'd worn a pair of cutoff shorts. Paired with a thick cardigan on top, it would be enough to keep her warm on the mild November day.

"You need to tint these windows, ma. You riding around in a fish tank."

She snorted and ignored him. "Are you sure you don't have to work?"

He turned to her. "I'll always make time for you, Deena."

She smiled, knowing he was serious enough to use her name. Traffic was thick downtown around the park. She'd expected the crowd to be small this early, but there was a fair number of people. She found them a spot in the parking garage, dividing up the stuff she'd brought with her. He grabbed the heavier items, and she didn't argue with him about it. Julian greeted and was greeted by a lot of people as they walked to the park.

She bunched her brows. "You know too many people."

He laughed. "It's the business that I'm in. I gotta know people to do my job."

She settled them in an area on the faux grass near the water, setting their stuff down. The weather was perfect, just cold enough for the sun to be a blessing rather than an annoyance. Deena pulled out her blanket and spread it on the ground.

Julian smiled. "Oh, we doing a for-real picnic."

She laughed. "You so silly."

It didn't take long for Deena to set everything up. She was nervous about what he would think, but his smile never wavered as he helped her. There were kids and families around, as well as other couples spread around the park on the grass. There were even some shifters in their animal forms prowling the area. She pulled out the different finger foods she'd made, and Julian hummed in pleasure.

"Oh, my baby finna spoil me."

Laughter spilled from her as she shook her head. "I didn't think to ask if you had any allergies."

"I'm easy, shortcake. As long as you got something sweet in there."

Deena covered her face and laughed. "Guess what I brought for dessert?"

He smiled and settled onto the blanket. "What?"

She reached into the small cooler and pulled out the mini shortcakes she'd made. Her cheeks burned as she showed him, and he busted out laughing.

"I'll take these for now, but I hope you know I'll want the real shortcake soon enough."

He tugged on her shirt until she was close enough to meet his lips. His kiss was soft and made her heart flutter. She pulled back and cleared her throat.

"Don't get comfortable just yet," she told him, pulling out her camera.

Taking some pictures of the picnic setup, she paused when she realized he was leaning into some of the shots.

"What are you doing?"

"If you posting these on your socials, I'm trying to be in the pictures. You ain't finna hide me."

She busted out laughing. He was so silly and so easy to like. Besides the fact that he was one of the most beautiful men she'd ever seen, his personality would sink her faster than anything else. She put the camera away and went to sit down, but her jaguar moved through her body in warning. Looking around with a frown, she didn't spot any reason for her cat to be on edge. Deena cocked her head when she spotted a familiar face...but she could've been mistaken. She put it out of her mind when she lost sight of them in the crowd.

Julian looked around the park, pleased with the date Deena had chosen. They'd been out here for a couple of hours, talking and eating. She was easy to talk to. Right now, she sat cross-legged, tucked into his front with his legs surrounding her. She fit snug against him, right where she belonged, sheltered by him. It felt natural and settled his lion. Lifting her hand, she fed him another bite of the mini shortcake. It was good, and though it was not a thought he'd ever say aloud, he loved that his mate knew how to cook. He especially loved that she'd taken the time and brought smaller versions of some of the dishes he'd added to the heirloom cookbook he'd bought her. It showed him that she, too, was a woman of her word. She'd told him she would take care of him and so far — even though she gave him a hard time about it — she was doing it.

Deena was still playing hard to get, but she was receptive, and that was all he could ask for right now. He leaned down and inhaled her scent in the crook of her neck. His lion rolled over inside of him, basking in her closeness. She was humming to the music coming from the small speaker she'd brought. She'd thought of everything for their date. It made him hopeful.

He rested his chin on her shoulder and looked around at all the other families. "I never thought to come out here," he commented.

"I've wanted to for a while," she admitted. "I just didn't want to come alone."

"So, you like to do this kind of stuff for dates," he said as a note to himself.

She shrugged. "I don't really date like that."

"You mean the dusties who've taken you out ain't did shit."

She laughed. "I don't date dusties."

"So you say, shortcake."

She scoffed and fed him the last piece of cake. He chewed and then leaned over her neck, kissing her softly.

"When I'ma get a taste of you?"

She snickered. "Does that game work on other women?"

"We ain't talking about other women, we talking about my mate."

Her breath hitched, and he could see her pulse drumming at her neck. He nuzzled against her skin, nipping her softly. She always smelled so damn good. It was a little different every time he saw her, but heavenly all the same.

"What are you wearing?"

"What?"

"You always smell good. And not just your scent, it's whatever lotion you're wearing, maybe?" He took another deep inhale at her neck.

"I make my own body butter. It's probably that," she told him.

He hummed, going back to his original question. "You ain't answer the question, my baby."

A familiar voice cut into their conversation. "Julian?"

He looked up with a frown. A woman he dated a while back stood over them, a warm smile on her face.

"I thought that was you."

Deena stiffened in his arms. He placed a hand on her stomach to stop her from moving.

"What's up, Carrie?"

"Nothing much. We never did get together again." Carrie acted oblivious to Deena's presence, which irritated him. He didn't like mess.

"I know you see me sitting here." Deena sat up straight. "Please run your thirsty ass along."

The woman sucked her teeth. "Girl, simmer down. He'll be back in the streets as soon as he's done with you."

Deena laughed, but there was no amusement in the sound. "Oh, you think?" She turned her head to him, her jaguar showing in her gaze. "You plan on leaving your mate to play with women not smart enough to understand their position?"

Now, Julian hated drama. He didn't start shit and for sure didn't mess with women who did, but there was something about Deena claiming him out loud that made his dick hard.

"Nah, my baby. I'm happy right where I am," he assured her.

"Mate?" Carrie asked, surprised. "My bad, sis. I thought Julian didn't do serious."

Deena nodded, dismissing the other woman. Carrie rolled her eyes and stomped off. His mate watched her go, then sighed.

"Let's go." She sat forward.

He pulled her back into his chest. "No. We're enjoying ourselves." He kissed her neck softly. "Don't let her mess up our day."

"I don't share," she said.

He chuckled, the sound humorless as he didn't find anything amusing about the thought of another man anywhere near his mate. "Neither do I, shortcake."

She turned to him and studied his face. He made sure she saw how serious he was.

"Remember how I told you my parents divorced?" He continued when she nodded. "When I was thirteen, Senior met his mate and left my mother, his wife of nearly fifteen years, for her. I saw the way that shit did my mom. I have never been serious about another woman because when I found my mate, I didn't want any of that kind of drama in my life. So, all this shit I'm doing with you is new for me. Making time for you, wooing you, all that shit new, you understand?"

She sighed but nodded her understanding. She turned her gaze from him, but he gripped her chin and brought her face back to his.

"Can't another woman tell you I did half this shit for her. I'm yours."

She swallowed, her eyes getting dewy before she nodded again and pecked his lips. "Okay."

He kissed her again, deepening it. She was breathing hard when he pulled back.

"You still gon' give me a hard time, aren't you?"

She smiled. "Maybe."

"Brat," he grumbled, pulling her back into him. A growl rumbled his chest and she laughed, relaxing into his arms.

eleven...

Julian sat in his office, finally able to focus on work. For most of the morning, he had Deena on his mind, which wasn't surprising. When they weren't together or talking on the phone, his attention was never far from her. Most of his thoughts circled around their date days ago. It was the most fun he'd had with a woman, ever.

He wasn't sure how he thought their mating would go. Some part of him had assumed his mate would fall in line when he was ready, and he was finding out Deena was not the woman to do that. She was a brat, and he was honestly turned on and frustrated by that in equal parts. When she followed orders, it was...

He shook his head because if he went there, no work would be done. Everything about the woman made his dick hard.

Noah hadn't reported any issues and so far, besides the fan mail, they hadn't had anything else spring up. It didn't stop him from worrying about her, though. The gifts from her stalker had stopped coming in the mail and it had been at least a week without them. That should've relieved him, but he was waiting on the other shoe to drop. They were trying to track down the letters and gifts, but so far, they weren't having any luck. For now, he would keep Deena's detail. Her safety was his top priority...well, that and convincing her to mate with him.

The wooing was working so far, so he would keep applying pressure where he could. They were going to a fundraiser together next week, and he looked forward to showing her off. She was a little apprehensive about the whole thing, but he'd been able to soothe her with the fact that both Celine and Julissa would be attending. It helped that she wouldn't be alone. Not that he imagined she would have any issues. Deena was not a person who would let others bully her or make her feel less than. He liked that shit a lot. She reminded him of his mother.

His phone rang and he smiled. That woman seemed to always know when he was thinking about her.

"What's up, ma dukes?" He turned his chair to watch the passing traffic outside of his office window.

"Excuse the hell out of you," Michelle predictably snapped.

"Hey, mama."

"That's better. Now, explain to me why I had to hear from Iris that you met your mate?"

He winced. "I'm sorry, Ma. You and I both been busy."

"That's not good enough, Junior. Has your father met her?"

Julian sighed. He did not want to get in the middle of that.

"No need to huff and puff over there, it's just a question."

"You can meet her at the fundraiser."

Since his parents had divorced before Senior became a part of the Motsi, Michelle was not included in the insular community. Though his mother was not in what she called "Bougieville," she was on the board at Winnie's House and attended every event thrown for the children's home. Adina and Michelle were best friends, and the two women were very serious about making sure the kids that lived at Winnie's House were taken care of.

"I'm out of town for the next couple of weeks with a client. I thought I could fly back for the event, but it's too much," she lamented.

Julian was proud of his mother. She'd understandably taken it hard when his father had left, but she was thriving now. She was a hairstylist with a few celebrity clients that she traveled to, so she was often on the road now he was grown and out of her house. He was a self-admitted mama's boy, so he missed Michelle when she was out of town.

"When you get back, I'll make sure to bring her to you."

Michelle sighed. "Ugh, that means Sabrina will meet her first. Make sure you tell my daughter that *I* am your mother."

"Ma," he groaned. "Deena knows our situation."

"Fine. I love you. Send me pictures of your tux."

He laughed. "Mama, you ain't tired of seeing me dressed up?"

Julian attended most Motsi events and yet Michelle always asked for a picture.

"Also, give me my daughter's number so I can call her and introduce myself."

"Goodbye, Michelle. I love you." Julian laughed and ended the call with his mother.

She was audacious, almost as bad as his father. He remembered the shit the two of them used to get into, each of them egging the other on. He didn't miss it. As much as his mother resented Sabrina, the woman had calmed his father down a lot. His parents were like tinder to a fire, feeding each other's bad habits.

He rubbed his temples, feeling a headache brewing. His lion rolled through his body, reminding him it had been a couple of days since he'd shifted. Looking at the clock, he decided he would leave work early today. He got in his truck and dialed Deena.

"Hello, Mr. Chase."

Jesus Christ, the velvet tone of her voice soothed his soul. He closed his eyes and let the comfort of her wash over him.

"Where you at?" he asked, opening his eyes so he could get on the road.

"At home, working. Noah can attest to that," she grumbled.

"You want to be safe and grumpy, or stressed about a stalker?"

She sighed. "Fine, sorry. You're right."

"This will all go so much better if you just keep admitting that."

Deena laughed. "You get on my nerves."

"I'm going running. Want to go with me?"

She paused, and he wondered if she would tell him no. "Okay," she said softly.

"I'll be by you shortly."

"I'll be ready," she told him, and though he understood what she meant, it didn't stop his heart from racing.

He drove up to her house and frowned as his lion stilled within him. It felt eerie, something off, but he couldn't put his finger on it. He parked and got out, looking around. He'd made Noah keep track of the cars that frequented her street so they would be able to tell if there was anyone new. He would make him go over it again just to be sure. Julian walked over to him, sitting on Deena's front porch, his watchful gaze on the street.

"You outside, you must feel it too," he said in lieu of a greeting.

Noah nodded. "Shit feels off. I got out the car and been in the house the past few hours. I came out here to see what got my panther on edge."

"I appreciate that." He took another cursory glance around the street.

"You taking her with you?" Noah asked.

"Yeah, I'll stay with her tonight, so you can take off."

Noah nodded but still made no moves. Julian smiled; he hired good people. That made him proud of what he was building. He knocked and Deena answered the door immediately in yoga pants and a sports bra. He took a deep shuddering breath, restraining his lion as he pinched her chin and brought her face up to him. He'd meant for his kiss to be short and gentle, but once she opened her mouth, he swept his tongue inside, devouring her.

"Ready?" he managed to get out.

She gave him a dazed nod.

He led her to his truck and helped her inside.

"Why in the world do you drive this big monster truck?" she asked, buckling her seat belt.

"It matches the monster riding inside," he said with a grin and a wink. "I let your detail go tonight, so you want to stay at my house, or do you want me to come back with you?"

She looked up from her seatbelt and narrowed her eyes. "I like how you just tried to finesse your way into my bed."

He laughed. "You'll know the exact moment I'm trying to get into your bed, shortcake, don't even stress about that. And trust me, that lil pussy will welcome me right in."

Her mouth dropped open and he laughed, pulling out of her drive-way. He lived a little bit outside of the city, so their ride would take a while. There was silence as he drove, Deena tapping away at her phone. He understood that her job dealt a lot with social media so he didn't stress it. When he pulled up to the gates of his house, Deena sat forward and gasped. He inputted his gate code and waited as the metal swung open. She turned in her seat to look out the window.

"Oh, this is bomb!" Her eyes widened as she faced him before quickly turning back.

He smiled, pleased she liked it. When he rolled up the driveway to park, she sighed in pleasure.

"Julian, it's so beautiful."

He took in the three-story place with new eyes. He'd chosen every part of the luxury cabin himself. It was built to his specifications and his dream of what he wanted his family house to be like, from the façade of cedar planks making up most of the construction to the touches of stone that comprised the front stairs going up to the second floor where his front door was. The porch went the length of the front, built on top of the garage, which took up the whole of the first floor. She reached for the door when he parked, and he gave her a look.

Deena chuckled. "I forgot I need a ladder to get down from this truck."

He snorted and went around to let her out, gripping her hand as he let them into his house through the laundry room. They went up the stairs into the kitchen, and she whimpered.

From the outside appearance, it would be expected that the inside would look as rustic, but he'd switched it up, blending the cabin feel he wanted with modern touches. The kitchen was filled with modern appliances and had a sleek Scandinavian vibe. The stairs that led to the third floor were made of chunky wood, but the railing was a mix of metal and glass. He was pleased with the result and happy to know Deena felt the same.

"How did you find yourself way out here?" she asked, running her hands along the butcher block countertops.

"I used to come here in the summer in the days of my misspent youth. It used to be a horse ranch. When the guy who owned it retired, I convinced him to sell it to me. I knocked down the old house and built this." He kissed the back of her hand. "I can give you a tour after our run."

She nodded eagerly.

"I'll show you to our room. I need to get out of this suit first."

"Our room." She tutted. "Very presumptuous, Mr. Chase."

He pulled her into his arms and nuzzled under her chin. "There you go, calling me Mister. You asking for it."

She laughed. "Is that all I have to do to ask for it?" She wrapped her arms around his shoulders.

"Just say the word, mama, and it's up."

"There's no slow with you, is there?" she whispered against his lips.

"Not when it comes to you."

She shuddered and stepped back. "Go change so we can burn off some of this energy."

It didn't take him long. He threw on some basketball shorts, forgoing a shirt. Deena was waiting for him at the bottom of the stairs. He walked her to his back patio, inhaling the cool air, and his shoulders automatically relaxed, scenting the pines that filled the forest of his backyard. Julian needed this run more than he realized. Stress had his muscles tense and his mind foggy. Turning to Deena, he sucked in a sharp breath.

What had he been thinking, inviting her to run with him?

Deena slipped her bra over her head and Julian wiped his mouth in case he was drooling. She revealed her lithe body, not even in a way meant to entice him. Sensing her and her cat's excitement, he knew the show wasn't for him, but he couldn't help but be riveted. He turned his back as she slid down her yoga pants.

He wasn't a saint.

And he knew he was already hanging on by a thread. Peeking over his shoulder, he saw her cat staring at him with its head tilted, eyes curious. He walked over to her, wanting to get to know her cat himself before he released his lion. Her jaguar was smaller than a normal shifter, but bigger than the natural animal. Her beautiful spotted coat was shiny and sleek. Julian stooped and the jaguar sniffed him. Its eyes lit moments later, and he smiled as she nuzzled against his legs.

"Shortcake been denying me, but not you, huh, minx?" He rubbed his hand down its sleek fur. The animal's head went back, exposing its neck to him, giving him the submission he knew the woman would never.

He butted heads with the cat, rubbing their cheeks together, and hummed in satisfaction. His lion bucked, eager to be released. Her cat licked his cheek, pawing him in impatience.

"Alright, you two," he chuckled when she knocked him down. "I'm coming."

He'd barely got his shorts down when his lion pushed forward, forcing his shift. It rushed to greet Deena's cat, the two animals rubbing their sides together. His lion was much bigger than her jaguar, mirroring their human forms. He inclined his head toward the forests, and they took off.

<h1 style="text-align: center">twelve...</h1>

Night had fallen by the time the two returned to Julian's massive house. Deena was still in awe of the place. She knew he had money, but this was a whole other tax bracket. A part of her wanted to be intimidated, but Julian was so down-to-earth that it was almost easy to forget they were not the same. She sighed, stretching her body as she pulled on the t-shirt he'd thrust in her hand when she went to take a shower. She'd brought her own clothes, but of course the man wasn't satisfied with that. She lifted the shirt and inhaled, smelling him all over the fabric. It was clean — she could smell the detergent used to launder it — but something told her he'd put it on before handing it over to her.

Possessive man.

She rolled her eyes and continued her perusal of the pictures lining the hallway, recognizing Julian and his friends, and his father. She assumed the woman who looked so similar to him was his mother. They looked happy. She liked that. She walked down the stairs, her eyes taking in everything. Something about this place was calling to her. Her jaguar was settled, content that they were here, which was... Well, she didn't know what to make of that. Her cat never really settled in any place that wasn't theirs.

She'd had to stop the reckless animal from leaving her scent markers on his property. Julian had already told her he had every intention of mating with her, but she was still wary of that. Not so much her jaguar. The ill-mannered animal was intent on leaving her mark on his place so that if any other female entered, they would know he was theirs.

She followed Julian's scent into the kitchen where he was pulling out a bottle of wine. He looked up and smiled as she entered.

"What's going on in your head?"

"Deena's thoughts," she answered flippantly.

He snorted. "Smartass."

She smiled. Not a lot riled him, and she found that very attractive. The way she talked to people could be off-putting, but he didn't seem to have an issue with it. He was patient and tolerant, but firm if she went too far. She shivered. Julian didn't take disrespect, and that shit turned her on, big time.

"You're missing a Christmas tree," she told him.

He looked around as though he hadn't noticed, and she rolled her eyes.

"You should get on that then, mama."

"This ain't my house."

He smirked. "Did you tell your jaguar that? Because she got marks all over my shit."

She growled. *He got on her nerves!* She stared at his profile as he grabbed them glasses, marveling at his beauty. The man was just fine. He was shirtless in a pair of jogging pants, and she wanted to rub against his chest and just inhale the scent of him. That wasn't even the wanton cat talking.

She shook those thoughts away. "I'm hungry."

"You want to go back to your place?" he asked, setting a glass of wine in front of her.

"Nah, I'm good here. Is there food in your fridge, country boy?"

He chuckled. "Yes."

She smiled and washed her hands, getting comfortable in his big kitchen. It was a dream, really. She'd made do with the small one at her house, but she couldn't wait to play in his kitchen. He sat at the island and watched her.

"You want me to help?"

"I got it." She opened his fridge and assessed what he had. It was surprisingly stocked. "There's nothing thawed, but you have ravioli. I can make some with spinach and tomato. That sound good?"

She looked up from the door when he didn't answer and caught him staring at her. "Jules?"

He shook his head. "Yeah, ma, that's fine."

"What's wrong?"

"Absolutely nothing. I'm trying to figure out how I'm supposed to let you leave here when it feels so perfect."

"Julian," she said softly.

She shook her head. This man would have her fully head over heels if she wasn't careful. She cleared her throat and changed the subject, pulling out the ingredients she would need for dinner.

"You said you spent summers here?"

He nodded. "Yeah. It started that first summer when Pops met his mate."

"That's rough," she murmured, heartbroken for his mother.

"He didn't cheat on my mom, but she was… It was rough there for a moment. They'd been together since they were teenagers. She was bitter and refused to get along with him. I was an angry kid there for a while."

"You acted out?" She sliced the tomatoes.

Julian chuckled. "That's a very nice way to put it. You know my father and Dallas were in the streets together."

She nodded, well remembering the way both of their names were bandied around in their neighborhood.

"So, as far as we were concerned, nobody could tell us shit. Between me and my friends, we were menaces. Senior and Dallas got tired of bailing us out of trouble, so he sent us here. It was some kind of reform camp at the time. Bullshit, really, but I loved the horses. Mase and them stopped going after that first year, but I kept coming back."

She frowned and looked up. "Y'all were still getting into shit." She knew that for a fact. Just like Dallas Knight's name rang bells, his sons and their friends were well-known throughout the community. For good now, but once upon a time, it wasn't that way.

He smiled. It was full of danger and dark menace, and why did that make her hot?

"Yes, but we stopped getting into trouble. We became a lot slicker with our shit."

She snorted, starting the water to boil the ravioli. "And as long as y'all weren't getting caught, your fathers didn't care?"

He shrugged. "They had their hands full at the time with their plans to take over the council seat."

"So that left four teenage boys free rein of the south side."

He nodded. "There were five of us."

She paused her stirring. "Five?" She frowned, trying to think back to who else they were hanging with.

"Devon." He shook his head. "He lived at Winnie's House with Rock. He was older than us, so when he got knocked, he got sent away."

Her eyebrows lowered. "Declan's brother Devon?"

"You know him?"

"Not Devon, but Declan." She pursed her lips in thought. "It's funny that you bring him up because your father was asking me about him the other day."

This time, Julian frowned. "What did he want?"

"Nothing, really." She shrugged. "He just wanted to know the last time I talked to Declan." She looked up at his silence. "What?"

"Just wondering what Senior is up to."

"He and Councilman Knight both," she warned him.

He groaned and dropped his head to the countertop. "Those two will be the death of me if it ain't you."

"Hey!" she protested with a laugh. "Speaking of... My new daddy invited me to the Motsi fundraiser for Winnie's House."

"I'm your new daddy. He can be your father, though."

She rolled her eyes, smirking.

"He beat me to it, I guess."

"Oh, you were going to invite me?"

He sucked his teeth. "Why wouldn't I take the opportunity to show off my mate? I already picked out your dress."

She warmed. "You're too audacious, Mr. Chase."

He growled and rounded the counter faster than she could take her next breath. Crowding her body, he trapped her between his arms and the sink. His canines lowered, and her heart rate sped, thundering in her ears.

"What I told you about that?" He scraped his teeth down her neck.

Her stomach clenched as lust filled the space between them. His teeth should've been ample warning to her that he and his animal were on edge, but she wouldn't be her if she didn't push him just a little...

"Remind me," she taunted.

Julian growled and lifted her, carrying her to his living room. She used her feet to try and push his pants down, ready to give in to her jaguar's needs. He dropped her onto the sofa and growled. "We finna handle this right now," he murmured, lifting her shirt and ripping off her panties.

Deena gasped, her heartbeat thundering. "What do you think you're doing?" she asked in a haughty tone.

Why she was challenging his animal, she didn't know, but her clit started thumping, wholeheartedly onboard with whatever she was on. Julian grabbed her ankles and opened her legs wide, his eyes flashing between gold and dark brown.

"You gon' have to back up all that shit you been talking, shortcake," he warned as he wrapped her legs around his waist.

Deena's chest rose and fell with rapid breaths. Julian looked danger-ous, damn near feral as his eyes roamed her body. Growing out a claw, he used it to cut her shirt in two. He spread the fabric open, and licked his lips, bending over her. His tongue trailed Deena's skin up to her breasts. She moaned as he pulled her nipple into the warmth of his mouth.

His fingers dipped into her sex and she exhaled roughly, fighting a moan. He twisted his hand and her eyes rolled back. She knew Julian would know his way around a woman's body, but *goddamn.* She should shut up and let him do wonderful things to her. Instead…

"Whenever you're ready to start…"

His dark chuckle sent shivers down her spine. "We love an unruly woman."

Deena opened her mouth to respond, but before she could say anything, he flipped her over and pulled at her waist until her ass was high, a deep arch in her back. Julian smacked her ass before running his claws down her thighs. A moan she couldn't contain left her lips when he shoved his tongue into her pussy. He ate at her until she screamed, an orgasm sweeping through her body.

Deena had no time to react, could barely catch her breath before Julian replaced his tongue with his dick.

"Fuck," she hissed as he filled her.

Her jaguar liked his roughness, the cat making her chest rattle with a purr. He pressed his hand in the middle of her back so that she couldn't move, his hips slamming into hers. He was deep, his dick running over her g-spot with his every stroke. She wanted to talk shit, to taunt him more, but the only thing leaving her mouth were whimpers as pleasure swamped her.

"I can't hear you, shortcake. I thought you had said something about me starting," he teased, drawing out slowly before driving deep.

His fingers brushed the top of her mound, caressing the lips of her sex before circling her clit. His touch was soft, contradictory with the ruthless strokes he delivered to her pussy. The opposing sensations pushed her right to the edge of climax. It built in her core, the ferocity of it making her legs tremble. She knew it would change her. Already, she understood that there would be no one after Julian, and she accepted it, but the intensity of the feelings building up with the orgasm tightening her body… For a moment, it scared her.

"Let it go, my baby. I'm here to catch you," Julian coached, undulating his hips, driving deeper into her.

Deena buried her face into the sofa cushion as shivers took over her whole body. She tried to run, but he held her ass tight against him.

"You can take it, mama. Let that nut go."

His words released the floodgates and she came, screaming. "Jules!"

"I'm here, baby." He didn't stop fucking into her, and it prolonged her orgasm. He rode her until he wrung out another and Deena was hoarse from screaming.

"Done," she whispered.

Julian leaned over and scraped his teeth against her skin. "If you done, why she squeezing on me, ma? That pussy pulsing on this dick, and you say you done?"

What did it say about her that his taunting words tightened her body with another climax? She didn't care, but she was determined to drag him over with her this time. She contracted her pussy and squeezed, and a rough, primal growl rattled his chest. Smiling tiredly, she did it again, rocking her hips. Julian cursed, his strokes speeding. Throwing her ass back, Deena moaned as another orgasm barreled over her. This time he froze, shoving deep before cursing and gripping her hips tight as he exploded inside of her.

Her body collapsed as she dragged air into her lungs. She would not be moving from his sofa for the rest of the night. She didn't care what he thought about it.

Of course, Julian had other plans and spent the rest of the night showing her.

thirteen...

One thing Deena could say about the Motsi...

They did not skimp on the alcohol. She snagged another glass off the tray of a passing waiter, humming as she sipped the god-tier champagne.

Celine snickered next to her. "You're about to be wobbling on those sky-high heels."

Deena smiled at her friend and did a quick two-step. "I'm true to this, not new to this."

The designer heels on her feet were a gift from Julian, along with the gorgeous scarlet red dress poured onto her frame. She'd gasped when she saw the label after the stylist he'd hired dropped it off to her house. Diamonds had also accompanied the other gifts, but she'd skipped them in favor of a simple thin Cuban link that he'd slid in with the other jewelry. He'd pulled out all the stops for her, and it was extremely flattering. The bodice was in a low-cut V, though the sides came up into two points. The gown was cinched at her waist, the skirt falling down to the floor in a beautiful pleated waterfall. A high split showed off her legs, the red satin making her skin gleam. The man had immaculate taste.

"I'm surprised Jules left you to stand alone with me," Celine teased.

Deena chuckled. From the moment Julian had seen her in the dress, his eyes had been glued to her. His gaze had immediately dipped to the small gold *J* that hung from a thin Cuban link around her neck. It was nestled in the valley of her breasts, and with a growl, he'd traced his finger across the warm metal. Seeing his pleasure, she knew she'd made the right choice.

They'd been at the fundraiser for the last two hours, and up until ten minutes ago, her mate had been welded to her side. He'd introduced her to so many people, she knew she would never remember their names. Senior had made sure everyone within a foot of him understood that Deena was his daughter. From some of the looks they'd gotten, she realized that Senior's claim carried a lot of weight.

It had taken Councilman Knight pulling them to the side before Julian planted her next to Celine with instructions to stay put. She was already getting antsy standing still, so she looked around the crowded ballroom.

"Where's my baby?"

Celine smiled. "He's in his grandfather's office with about a dozen guards. We're leaving soon." She sighed. "Just as soon as I can sneak out from mama."

Deena smirked. Celine hated being out and limited her attendance of Motsi events. Her shy friend didn't like interacting with the public much. It's partially why Deena had become the face of their company online. Celine was an amazing business woman, but her social anxiety kept her from enjoying these types of events. Deena could understand. The whole thing was intimidating. The lavish décor and food, the hundreds of people milling about; it was so different from anything she'd ever experienced.

Coming from her upbringing, she couldn't imagine she would ever be a part of something like this. She sighed internally. Thoughts of her time at Winnie's had been on the top of her head since they walked in. It wasn't that they were bad memories, but sometimes the thought of the precariousness of her situation would bring back some of that insecurity. She couldn't sit still and let the memories consume her. She needed to move around.

"I'm gonna check out the auction items," she told Celine.

"Okay. If you can't find me, check the balcony." Celine breathed out a relieved sigh.

Deena smirked, knowing her friend would rather be anywhere than in the crush of people in this room. Her steps were slow through the ballroom as she admired all the items. Luxury surrounded her, and a part of her was irritated at the excess, but she consoled herself with the fact that the funds would go to Winnie's House. She thought briefly of bidding on something. After all, she'd spent the last years of her childhood in the children's home.

She'd always wanted to contribute but didn't know what to do. It was hard for her to go back. She'd thought about volunteering, but it always made her sad and want to scoop all the kids up. It wasn't as though she had a terrible time there. They were treated nicely and the house always felt safe. But, as with anything, there were always people and situations that were outliers to the norm.

She shuddered as she thought about her friend.

Dana should've been as safe as the others in that house, but it had taken just one person with evil intentions. Deena couldn't even say that it was one of the kids in the house who had killed her friend, but after Dana's death, the house had never felt as safe as it once had.

Her breath caught at one of the items. The whole display was from a jeweler, so an array of diamonds sparkled under the light, but the rose gold and diamond link cuff reached out to her. Lord, the price was more than her mortgage cost in a year. She shook her head, though her eyes lingered for just a bit longer.

"I finally get the chance to talk to you alone."

The voice startled her enough that she nearly spilled the contents of her glass. She turned, and her eyes widened at Adina Knight. The woman was stunning, her trim figure in a fire red mermaid gown with a train. The square neckline was flattering, showcasing her collarbone. Her hair was pinned into an elegant chignon at the back of her head, and her makeup was flawless. Deena was speechless. For so long she'd admired this woman, and now with her in front of her, she was at a loss of what to say.

As Adina said, though they'd seen each other at various points in the past couple of years, they'd never had the chance to talk. The last time she'd seen Adina Knight had been at Antonio's first birthday party.

"I love your channel. I tell Celine all the time, but I wanted you to know as well. Me and my cousin Iris tune in every chance we get." Adina smiled.

Deena swallowed the lump in her throat, her heart hammering. "Wow, that's…thank you. I'm a huge fan of yours as well."

Adina cocked her head to the side. "Me?" she chuckled. "I haven't done anything."

"I grew up at Winnie's House. I used to see you walk in all the time. You always looked so elegant, but you were so sweet and accessible to us all. I would tell myself that I would grow up to be like you."

Adina made a soft sound, and she teared up. "You never know if it matters until someone who's gone through it can validate. Thank you, honey." She gripped Deena's forearm.

"Thank you!" Deena let out a shuddering breath. "You and Councilman Knight. He always came through if we had trouble. It was the safest place I'd landed. I don't know what I would've been without that place."

"Oh, sweetie." Adina reached over and pulled her into a hug, nuzzling her cheek.

Deena could feel the woman's powerful animal, and hers responded.

Adina stepped back and patted the tears from her cheeks. "Let me not break down in front of these people." She took a deep breath. "How is Julian treating you?" Her eyes now held sparkling mischief.

Deena's cheeks heated, and she looked around for him. "Umm, we're getting along."

Adina laughed. "Okay, well, if my nephew gives you any trouble, you come to me. Me and Michelle will get him together."

She joined her laugh. "I'll remember that." She cleared her throat. "I…do you think it would be okay if I dropped some items off to Winnie's?"

"Oh, God, yes. You know firsthand how much we count on the community for help."

"It's just soaps and body butters that I make. I wasn't sure if anyone would want something like that."

Adina squeezed her shoulder. "Is it something you would've wanted while you were there?"

Deena thought back, nodding quickly. She would've loved it.

"Well, there you go. You can call me and we can go together," Adina told her. "I'll leave you to your perusing, but Jules has my number."

Deena nodded and gulped the rest of her drink as Adina left her. She hid her smile in her glass, still a little giddy at having talked to Adina Knight. She composed her face when she felt someone stand next to her. She looked up with a polite smile, but then her eyes ballooned as she recognized the male standing next to her.

"Oh my God, hi!"

Callan turned to face her, his smile wide. "Deena?"

"Callan. How have you been?"

Along with memories of her time in the children's home, it seemed the fundraiser was bringing up people from her past as well. Callan had been at the home at the same time as her, though she wouldn't have called them friends. The house pushed all the kids in close proximity, and sometimes that forced a sort of false intimacy between them all. It was one of the reasons Deena was so stingy with her space and who she claimed as friends.

He nodded toward the diamonds. "Could you have imagined all this while we were in that house?"

She chuckled. "I couldn't imagine anything past surviving, to be honest. Winnie's was one of the best things to happen to me, though."

And that was very telling of how chaotic life after her mother's death had been.

Callan nodded. "Same."

"So, are you a part of the Motsi?" Deena asked, changing the subject. She'd spent enough time down memory lane.

"Well, I just got back into town a year ago, and now I work for Councilman Knight. So, not really a part of the Motsi, but I do attend some of the events," he answered.

"Good for you! That's so great." She was always happy when someone from their situation won at life. "You know something so weird? I thought I saw you the other day at Washington Park."

He frowned in thought. "Maybe. I go to lunch out there sometimes on the weekend." His face relaxed, and he gave her a sheepish smile. "I follow your blog and channel," he admitted.

"Thank you." She smiled.

"I'm so happy to have run into you. We should get together," he said, stepping closer.

Deena started to answer, but the presence heating her back made her snap her mouth closed. Her mate had arrived, and from the feel of his animal, he was agitated.

Julian dropped a kiss to her shoulder. "I thought I left you with Celine."

She heard the warning beneath his words. Was it bad that it turned her on? Julian was so sweet that it was easy to forget how he got down. The hard edge he displayed when he was displeased was something that she and her cat very much loved. Her current debate was whether or not to ignore the warning so that she was punished later or heed it, heading off any trouble.

Decisions, decisions.

"Julian, I don't know if you know Callan, but we were at Winnie's House together."

"You standing a lil close there," Julian said in lieu of a greeting.

Callan stepped back, his smile dropping. "I've seen him around Councilman Knight's office."

They didn't shake hands, and she didn't want to figure out what the weird tension between them was.

Julian's arm snaked around her waist, his lips touching the shell of her ear as he whispered, "Mama, my lion finna knock all this shit over if you don't take another step back from this male."

She shuddered, fighting to keep her eyes open as a wave of lust clenched her stomach.

"So…" Callan's jaw flexed before speaking. "I hope to see you again."

"Same," she told him.

He left, and Deena swallowed her smile before turning around to her aggravated mate. "You be doing too much, Mr. Chase."

Julian collared her throat lightly, aware of their surroundings. "I don't like the way he was looking at you."

She rolled her eyes. "Okay, love."

He smiled, kissing her lightly. "You gon' get enough of rolling your eyes at me. You going home with me tonight."

It wasn't a question. She would normally challenge him on it, but she was more than ready to go home with him. Still…

"Don't act like you run shit over here, sir."

"Whatever helps you sleep at night, my baby."

She snorted.

"And why you only got male friends from Winnie's?"

"My best friend was a girl," she reminded him.

He kissed her temple. "I'm sorry, love, I forgot."

She waved him off. "I'll give you a pass because I can feel your cat's possessiveness."

He nodded and guided her toward where she could see Celine standing.

"Junior," Sabrina called out.

Deena snickered as Julian winced. He hated being called that in public. She'd met his stepmother within minutes of stepping into the ballroom, and Deena liked the brash woman.

"Brina," Julian sighed. "Why must you call me that while I'm out?"

"Not you worried about these bougie ass people!" Sabrina cackled. "Your father is looking for you."

He groaned.

She laughed and Deena joined her, the boisterous sound too contagious not to. "Go, so I can get to know my new stepdaughter."

Julian looked at her, and she nodded. She had no issues with the woman. He pulled her into his arms.

"I'm finna go see what your sickening father wants and then we're leaving, hear?"

"Is that an order?" she teased.

He growled, and she hid her amusement. "I'ma take it out on your ass tonight, shortcake," he promised.

She shuddered, ready to leave right this second. He took off, and her gaze followed hungrily.

"You're good for him," Sabrina told her, sliding her arm through Deena's as they walked.

Deena turned her gaze back to Julian's stepmother. "You think so?"

"He needed someone who challenges him. He's a bit of a control freak."

Deena snorted at that bit of exaggeration. Julian liked order, sure, but he wasn't to that level.

"Ju tells me that you grew up in Greenridge. I'm glad he didn't end up with one of these prissy women around here," Sabrina said with a mischievous smile. "No offense, Celine," she said as they joined her friend.

"None taken," Celine smiled and shook her head, used to Sabrina's mouth. "Your filter gets thinner every year, Mrs. Chase."

Deena could only laugh at that. If she was worried about keeping her mind off of her time in Winnie's House, Sabrina was the way to do it. She would let the woman distract her until Julian came back.

fourteen...

Though her laptop was wide open, Deena was getting no work done. She was supposed to be setting up their social media for the week, but her mind was in the clouds. She'd been at Julian's house for the last four days, just now getting back to her own. He'd driven her home only after she threatened to block him for a month so she could catch up on work.

It wasn't that she hadn't been out to the farm; she had. But all the administration stuff that was her half of the work was unfortunately being neglected because he had Noah dropping her off at his house. Well...technically, she still could've been working, but she'd been admittedly dickmatized.

She needed to focus.

Instead of focusing, she got up and started lunch. She could take him lunch, and then that would get him out of her system so she could work.

Yeah, right.

She looked up half an hour later as her doorbell rang. Noah was up before she could move, his phone out, checking the camera at her front door. She rolled her eyes because she couldn't even answer her own door anymore. She'd finally told Noah to quit sitting in his car outside when he could do the same job inside her townhouse. It was a big concession, sharing her space with someone else. She thought it would aggravate her, but she and her jaguar were relaxed.

She was resigned to Noah's position in her life. She didn't imagine Julian would call him off, even after he handled the stalker mess.

She'd gotten a glimpse of what life would be like with Julian at the Motsi function, and she understood that the security was necessary. It was almost like being on a TV show. Palace intrigue and backstabbing seemed to be the norm. No wonder Mason never let Celine go anywhere without Lance. It seemed she would need to get used to the lifestyle.

Now that she'd had Julian every which way but up, she knew giving him up was out of the question. So, dealing with a security detail when they went out was a small price to pay to be with him. Noah came back into the house with two vases of flowers.

What in the world?

She smiled, giddy, and got up quickly, dancing as Noah put them both on the kitchen counter. The peach and white hydrangeas were her favorite, and she immediately stuck her nose in the flowers to inhale their scent. Julian knew they were her favorite flowers; she wondered why he also sent the red roses. She pulled the card from the hydrangeas, cheesing at them being addressed to Mrs. Chase. God, the man knew exactly the kind of pressure to apply. The note was simple, sweet.

It's always you

Deena clutched the card to her chest. She almost didn't want to put it down, but she set it in front of her, curious about the reason for the second bouquet of flowers. Her smile dropped, replaced by a frown of confusion.

Are you happy I found you? Must be fate.

— your biggest fan

Her hands shook as she dropped the card. Noah looked up from his seat with a question on his face. For a moment, she debated what to do. She could wait until tonight to tell Julian, but all of a sudden, the house she'd felt so secure in moments ago felt stifling...scary.

She cleared her throat. "Hey, can we go see Julian?"

Noah cocked his head to the side. "You need something?"

"These flowers aren't from Jules," she told him.

Noah rushed to her and lifted the card. He cursed. "I can get someone to come take care of this."

"I'm sure, but I want to see him," she told him. Hell, she needed to see him. She wanted out of the house most of all. "You want to ride with me, or drive?"

He scoffed. "I'll drive. You act like you drive an indestructible tank."

"Not too much on me." She forced levity into her voice as she packed up Julian's lunch.

"Let's go."

He peeped the box in her lap. "You made him lunch and didn't offer me none. Cold world, Dee."

She laughed, the tension from the bouquet shedding now that they were leaving the house. "You can eat when we get back. I made some for us too, greedy."

"That's what's up, then."

They drove the rest of the way in silence. Noah gave his keys to the valet and walked her through the department store. She slowed down when she saw a familiar face. Callan smiled as he approached them.

"Twice in a week. Must be fate," he drawled.

She flinched at his words, her smile forced as she greeted him. "Hi, Callan."

"I'm glad we ran into each other again. We need to exchange numbers." He stepped closer.

She inclined her head at her full hands.

"Those are beautiful," Callan told her, pulling out his phone. "Let me plug you in."

Noah stepped between them. "We gotta move, Dee," he said, gently grabbing her elbow.

"I'll have to catch up with you later, Callan," Deena called over her shoulder. She shuffled after Noah. "What was that?"

Noah nodded up toward the cameras around the store. "Take it up with your mate," he told her, swiping his card at the employee elevator.

She rolled her eyes. "He's so overprotective," she grumbled.

She sighed and rode up in silence. Julian met them at the elevator car, his eyes flashing between dark brown and gold, his cat clearly irritated.

"Shortcake," he greeted. That hard tone had a shiver of need sliding down her back. "I got her, No." He dismissed Noah, turning them toward his office. "What's that?" He frowned at the flowers.

His words took away her last shred of doubt that they hadn't come from him. "They showed up at my door."

Julian paused their walking. "What?"

"Yeah. I thought you'd want to know."

"You told Noah that?"

She nodded. "He said he would take care of it, but I wanted to see you."

He called Noah back. "Aye, run these down for me."

Noah gave her an 'I told you so' look. "I told her to let me take care of it."

Deena sucked her teeth and threw up her hands. "Oh my God. I can't win for losing with you two." She stomped off to Julian's office.

Julian entered his office a few minutes later, trying to control both his temper and his lion. He'd questioned Noah about the flowers, wanting every detail of the interaction with the delivery person. But when he got a moment, he would be going over the footage to check for himself. Running a hand over his face, his mind spun through the implications of the flowers being delivered to her door. The note had his blood boiling.

"You still mad at me?" she asked.

He fought to fix his face, suppressing his cat. Pulling her into his arms, he breathed in her scent. "You did the right thing bringing them to me."

"I also brought you lunch, but I don't know if I want to give it to you since you fussed at me."

Julian smiled at her attitude. "I'm sorry, love." He rubbed his hand down her back. "Thank you for taking care of me."

She sucked her teeth. He leaned down and kissed her, his lion demanding it. When he'd peeped her talking to Callan on the security monitors, his animal bucked, feeling very possessive. Perhaps if Deena had taken his bite, he wouldn't be so insecure. Some of his grumpiness could be attributed to that. Setting the box she'd packed his lunch in on the chair, Julian lifted her into his arms. Her legs wrapped around his waist as he swung her around, sitting her on the edge of his desk.

He kissed her, delving his tongue inside her mouth. She returned his kiss, her tongue tangling with his.

"I miss you," he murmured, coming up for air.

Deena rolled her eyes. "I don't see how. You talk to me every ten minutes."

He chuckled at the exaggeration, sliding a hand underneath her shirt. The feel of her skin beneath his palm soothed and inflamed him in equal measure. He lowered his head to suck on her neck. She was still a little peeved and her jaguar bucked at him, the bite of her power displaying her displeasure with him.

"Nah, I got something for that attitude." He unbuttoned her pants and slid his hand inside. "I told you I miss you and you still playing like you mad."

Deena hissed as he cupped her pussy. "Jules," she whispered. "What are you up to?"

Even as she asked, her hips lifted to help him ease her pants down.

"About to fuck away my mad and handle this lil attitude." He fit himself at her center and slid inside, hissing. "Two birds... one...fucking...stone," he said, shallow stroking into her on every word. He pulled out roughly before pushing back in, this time burrowing deeper into her warmth.

She shuddered, her arms wrapping around his neck as he leaned over to kiss her. "Is your door unlocked?"

"Ain't nobody bold enough to walk into my office without my permission," he whispered, kissing her.

He closed his eyes as her warm pussy wrapped tightly around his length. She felt like home, and the peace she brought to him was something he would never be able to replicate outside of Deena.

"Mine," he growled, fucking into her roughly. "It's been hours since I been inside this good pussy," he murmured against her skin.

His lion was urging him to mark her. She wasn't ready to mate, but he wanted anyone within eyesight of her to know she belonged to him. Julian sucked on her neck, scraping his teeth against her skin, hissing in pleasure at the marks. Deena whimpered and squeezed down on him. He knew he didn't have the time to savor her, but damn if that sped his strokes. Instead, he slipped in and out of his mate in a slow, methodical manner, making sure to hit the spot deep inside that had her whimpering beneath him.

Deena's nails raked down his neck, and he shivered as his lion filled his body. She never played fair. He lifted off of her, straightening his back so he could watch her fall apart beneath him. She canted her hips, rushing him, and he growled when his phone rang, reminding him he didn't have all day to play with his mate. It didn't stop him from teasing her as payback for her attitude.

"Please, love," she whispered, back arching, her chin lifting in submission.

That's what the fuck he wanted. He pulled her to the edge of the desk so he could stroke her harder, deeper. Deena moaned, her nails digging into his arms as she gripped him.

"Please what, baby girl?"

Her pussy pulsed and he nearly lost it.

"I wanna come, Mr. Chase," she whimpered.

Goosebumps lifted all over his skin at her words. The woman was his kryptonite. He reached between them, using his finger to strum her clit. Deena whimpered, her face going lax in ecstasy. Her pussy clenched, pulsing around his dick as she climaxed. He lifted her hips and drove in and out of her, chasing his own nut now that he'd satisfied his baby. Deena pulled down on his shoulders, demanding a kiss. He obliged her, their tongues dueling frantically as he thrust into her.

Her kiss was all it took to send him over the edge. His back bowed as pleasure pulled him under. Julian cursed as he emptied himself into her. He collapsed on top of her, nuzzling into her neck as he tried to catch his breath. Her hands traveled up and down his back in a soothing manner, and Julian considered ignoring everything happening outside of his office and keeping her trapped in here for the rest of the day.

His phone rang for the fifth time and he sighed, corralling his breath back under control. Deena pushed at his chest.

"Handle your business," she told him.

He grunted, reluctantly pulling from her body. He went into his bathroom and came back with a warm towel, cleaning her off.

"Come home with me," he ordered as he helped her back into her pants.

"You have a problem asking for things, Junior."

He bit her shoulder, and she laughed. "You be playing in my face, shortcake."

Deena smiled impishly, and his heart turned over. She was a brat, but damn if he wouldn't enjoy taming her. She fixed her shirt, tucking it into her jeans as she jumped from his desk.

"I'll see you later, love," she said, headed to the door.

"Pack more than a spennanight bag too," he called after her.

She laughed and shook her head. "Watch them orders, Mr. Chase."

His dick bricked like he hadn't just had her splayed across his desk. God, that woman.

fifteen...

Julian looked up as his best friend knocked on his office door. He'd barely been in his chair for an hour. He welcomed the distraction though because his mind was anywhere but work. He frowned as he took in Mason's face. His friend looked aggravated, if not a bit worried.

"What's good?"

"You talk to Unc about what he and Pop are up to?"

Julian shook his head. "It slipped my mind, honestly."

Mason looked surprised for a moment before a smile spread across his face. "Oh, Deena got you gone."

He chuckled, unable to deny it at all. "She won't take my bite yet, so it's got me distracted," he admitted.

Mason smirked. "You need some advice?"

"Man, whatever. What's happened?" He turned the subject back to their fathers.

"Celine told me this morning that the two were out at the farm questioning Deena about Declan." Mason sat in the chair in front of Julian's desk.

He nodded. "Deena told me."

"Lovebug said it wasn't much, but the fact that they're asking..." Mason left the rest unsaid.

But Julian knew what went unspoken. He sighed. "You think?"

"After this last spy, I definitely think. Pop's fed up, and we both know how Dallas gets down."

They stared at each other, both of them understanding that a war between the wolves and cats would turn the city upside down. It wasn't that either of them had the power to stop it, but they could hopefully stall it.

"I need to talk to Unc anyway." He shut down his computer. "What do you know about Callan Frasier?"

Mason frowned. "I don't know who that is."

"He works in your dad's office."

"In what capacity?"

"Paper pusher of some kind. He doesn't work directly for Dallas, so I didn't really do a deep dive into him," Julian told him.

"What you worried about?"

Julian shrugged. "He keeps popping up around Deena."

Mason snickered. "I thought you was finna say something."

Julian laughed ruefully. "Shit, that's enough for me, but something about him irking me."

"I bet," Mason joked. "Until your lion marks her, you'll be on edge about everyone."

He knew that was true, and there was nothing he could do about it. "Where they at?"

"At the gym, more than likely," Mason answered, knowing he was talking about their fathers.

He stood to leave. "A'ight. I'll see what's what and give you a call."

He walked his friend out, letting his assistant know he would be gone for the rest of the day. He made sure she understood that as soon as they heard word about the flowers, he wanted to know. Once he left the gym, he would track his mate down and work from home with her.

He headed into the afternoon traffic and was at his father's gym in no time, surprisingly. When he got there, it wasn't full, just the OGs sitting around with his father. He smiled, seeing Silas's daughter seated at the table. She was surrounded by hardened shifters, the flowery jumpsuit standing out. Dapping up his father's friends, he walked over to Riyah. He noticed they were playing Uno instead of their usual spades or poker.

He lifted the little girl, rubbing his cheek against hers. "Hey, lil bit. Your mama know you in here?"

"I'm hanging with Poppa," she told him, returning his greeting.

He set her back in the chair and directed his attention to the two men he came to see. Dallas and Senior shared a look before smiling at Julian.

"What's good, Junior?" his father asked. "How is it going with my daughter?"

Julian grimaced, and they all laughed.

"Lil baby giving you a hard time?" Dallas asked.

"She stubborn as hell," he answered.

"Dick her down and that'll straighten her out," Senior told him.

He laughed at his dad. "Pop."

"Just saying, I like a female that'll bust her guns. Can't ask for much more in a daughter. I called her and invited her to dinner at the house. I guess you can come if you want."

The men around the table laughed, and Julian could only shake his head. Senior stayed with the jokes. He didn't even want to ask how his father got Deena's number.

"I don't know if dinner with this one will help your case, nephew."

Senior busted out in laughter. "Fuck you, Dallas Knight."

"Pop, quit cursing like that in front of the baby," he fussed.

"I've heard cursing before," Riyah informed him, concentrating on holding all the cards in her hand.

"That's right, lil mama. Now, gon' and lay down a card," Senior told her.

"Uncle Senior, I'm still thinking."

"What's the problem?" Dallas directed the question to Julian.

Senior shook his head. "That boy want a soft and compliant woman."

Julian sucked his teeth. "Don't nobody want to be fighting for the rest of their life."

"Keeps the blood pumping," was Senior's response to that.

He scoffed. Dallas eyed him, waiting on his answer. He sighed, hating to admit it in front of so many people.

"She's not ready to take my bite."

"Could be she doesn't trust you enough to show you her soft side," Dallas told him.

He frowned. Did his mate not trust him?

Dallas continued. "She grew up at Winnie's. She done probably dealt with shit her whole life. Be a soft place for her to land and once she trusts it's not going away, you'll get there. She's looking for the same thing you are."

"Peace," he murmured.

Dallas nodded.

Julian digested that. He would think about it later when he had the leisure to. "Thanks, Unc. I need to holla at you two about something else."

Dallas and Senior shared another look. Dallas inclined his head and the other men cleared out. "Ya-Ya, put your headphones on for Poppa, please."

She put down her cards and did as asked. Julian waited until the others were farther away, staring at the two men for whom he had the utmost respect.

"Mase said he saw your detail over on the West side," he started, settling in one of the abandoned chairs.

Dallas smirked but said nothing.

"Add to that you two questioned Deena about Declan." Julian paused, waiting on them to step in.

"That's all you came for?" Senior spoke up. "You and Mason over there worrying like mother hens."

Julian sucked his teeth. "Y'all ain't finna be worrying my auntie to death with shenanigans," he tried to joke.

"I don't know when you and Mason designated yourselves our nursemaids," Dallas chastised.

"Unc, I'm never gon' stop any moves you're making, but I'm just… You know I like to be prepared."

"That's what's wrong with going legitimate. You got shit to lose," Senior said, shaking his head.

"Pops, what could possibly be wrong with that?" he asked, exasperated with his father, which wasn't new.

"Gotta keep your edge, Junior."

Julian sighed again. "Unc." He turned to Dallas. There was no use in even bothering to talk to his father sensibly.

"The game is the game, nephew. You know how it goes. Now that you done got Cyrus's spy out of my office, I can move comfortably."

Julian stared at Dallas before nodding. "Alright then. Just let me know when you need me."

"Once you finish this little dance with your mate, I'll have something for you."

He could only nod because he knew he would get nothing more from either of the men. "I also wanted to ask you about Callan Frasier."

Dallas frowned. "What about him?"

He debated what to say. He knew a part of him was a little perturbed about his closeness to Deena, but it felt like something else was going on.

"He has my lion on edge," he hedged.

Senior sat forward. "Does it have something to do with my daughter?"

"Yeah. Have you heard any rumors about him?"

Dallas shook his head. "He keeps his head down, does his work. I barely notice him."

The fact that Dallas knew who he was even though he was lower level was testament to how close an eye his uncle kept on his staff. The spy had been an anomaly, one they'd caught and got rid of quickly. He knew the rest of the staff would be under heavy scrutiny for a while behind it.

"I don't be in my staff's personal life to that extent. I'll ask around, though," Dallas added.

That's all he could ask for. "I'll get out of y'all's hair then."

"Michelle been by the house telling DiDi that she hasn't met her daughter yet," Dallas warned him in a teasing manner to change the subject.

He winced. He hadn't realized his mother was back in town. He expected her to pull up on him at any moment then. He needed to get on that because his mother would only be so patient, especially since both his father and stepmother had met her.

"On that note, I'm out." He got up and walked around the table, lifting up Sariyah. "I'm gone, Ya-Ya." He kissed the top of her head. "Keep your granddaddy out of trouble."

She smiled and nuzzled under his chin. He left them and called Mason as soon as he got in his car.

"Yeah?"

"You were right."

Mason cursed. "I'll talk to Silas."

"I mean, we should be straight for a while. Dallas won't really make any moves until he's sure he won't get caught."

Mason sighed. "Still. We'll prepare."

He hung up, totally in agreeance with his best friend. Until Dallas and Senior made their moves, they could only prepare and wait. Instead of worrying about it, he called the woman he couldn't keep off his mind.

<h1 style="text-align: center;">sixteen...</h1>

Deena sighed in pleasure the moment she slid into her car. Her feet were killing her, and her arms would be sore tomorrow from carrying all the supplies she'd snagged, but she would count this visit as a success. The open-air farmers market had been packed as usual, but Deena had arrived early so she could get in a little shopping before their booth opened. The vendor who sold her favorite essential oils and soap bases sold out early, and she did not want to miss her.

Usually, she and Celine attended the market together, but she'd let her friend sleep in today. Their herb booth was a relatively new idea and it was a lucrative one. They only did their supply overflow, so it was helping them cut down on waste as well. They'd hired a young woman to run it, and she and Celine took turns helping her in the mornings. The booth closed once they'd sold out, and Deena was happy with how quickly that had happened today. It was barely after noon. During the week, their customers were usually small restaurants around the area.

She couldn't wait to show Celine all the jars and props she'd been able to find when she'd walked around. They normally did their Christmas content in October, but with this stalker stuff, they were behind. They would be busy over the next couple of weeks, and Deena was actually excited. Despite not having a lot to celebrate growing up, she loved Christmas and all the crafts that came with it.

Making her way out of the packed parking lot, Deena smiled as her phone rang. Her heart fluttered when she saw it was Julian. She wondered for a sec if he was calling to fuss because she'd arrived at the market before Noah had gotten on duty. She knew she should've waited for him, but she needed to get there early. Champ, her night guard, was not as personable as Noah, so she'd drove separately. Noah had fussed when he got on duty, and now she was wondering if he'd told his boss.

"Hi, love," she greeted.

"Where you at, my baby?" His deep voice filled the interior of her car, and she sighed in pleasure.

"I'm on my way home from the farmers market."

"Noah with you?" he asked.

She paused. "No. Well, I mean yes, but like in his own car."

He hummed. "I'm working from home today. You want some company?"

Her pulse sped, giddy happiness bubbling inside of her. "Umm, yeah. I'd love that. But we both have to work, sir."

He growled low. "I won't make any promises. See you soon, shortcake."

She couldn't help the smile that covered her face when he hung up. She merged onto the highway on the way back to her house, her foot on the gas. Her phone rang barely a minute later, Julian calling her back.

"What's wrong?" Her stomach pitched with worry.

"Nothing for you to worry about. Noah got into a fender bender. Are you going straight home?"

"Yes." She breathed out a sigh of relief.

"Okay, I'll meet you there. Don't make any stops," he ordered.

Her brows lowered as her car started to slow down. She cursed when all the lights on the dash came on. "Umm, that's gonna be hard. The car is stopping by itself."

"What do you mean, stopping?" Julian asked.

She groaned and pulled over to the side of the road. "The car is dead."

"You're still sharing your location with me, right?"

She nodded, forgetting he couldn't see her. "Should I try and make it to the exit?"

"No. Stay on the crowded highway. I'm not too far from you. Stay on the phone with me."

She sucked her teeth at that order but made idle chitchat with him while she waited. Fifteen minutes later, she was bored and ready to go home. Hungry and getting irritated by the minute, Deena searched her car for a snack.

"Babe, I can just like walk to the exit and see—"

"Don't get your ass out of that car, shortcake. I'm like five minutes away."

She growled but sipped from her water bottle. A minute later, she did a little dance as she found a bag of chips in her back seat. She paused as something else caught her eye. There were flowers in the seat. How hadn't she noticed that when she'd put her boxes in? In her defense, there were other flowers in her box. Now that Julian had been buying them for her, she liked having the fresh buds on her coffee table. She reached for the sunflowers with shaking hands.

I thought these matched your dress today

She took a shuddering breath, looking down at the yellow sweater dress she wore. Her stalker was able to get in her car?

"What's wrong, mama?" Julian asked.

Before she could answer, she noticed a car slowing down and parking on the shoulder in front of her.

"Someone pulled up in front of me," she whispered.

Her heart started racing and her eyes flew to the flowers. Was this all a setup? What should she do? She dropped the note and reached into her glove compartment, pulling out her gun.

"Fuck, Julian, he's wearing a mask," she hissed.

Julian cursed. "You have your gun on you, right?"

"Always," she told him.

She always carried a gun on her. With her work with battered women, she was always careful. Plus, after everything that had gone down with Celine, she promised herself she would never be caught slipping like that again. She wouldn't hesitate to defend herself.

"GPS has me still a minute out. Hang on, baby," Julian soothed.

She let out a yelp when the man reached her passenger side and grabbed the door handle. He jerked on it, slapping his hand against the window when he couldn't get in. The menace in his eyes made her shiver. She raised her gun, prepared to fire it. She couldn't let him get to her. If she had to choose between the two of them, she would choose herself every time. Removing the safety, Deena damn near dared him to try her. Julian was calling her name, but she blocked it out, needing every ounce of her concentration.

They stared at each other, and as long as Deena lived, she would never forget the malice in the man's eyes. There was nothing human in them. They flashed green, the shape of them telling her he was a cat shifter. He shook her car before punching into her window. The glass broke, and Deena pulled the trigger. He ducked down and ran off back toward his car. She didn't know if her shot had hit him, but she kept a tight grip on the gun until his car spit out dirt as he peeled out.

She yelped as the window behind her head was tapped, whipping around, her Sig still clutched tightly. Noah lifted his hands and everything she'd blocked out filtered back in. Julian's frantic voice sounded around her.

"Deena, talk to me!"

"It's Noah," she croaked out past her dry throat. "I'm good. Noah's here."

She put the safety on her gun and dropped it in her lap, turning to her guard. She unlocked the door and Noah pulled it open.

"You good, Dee?" His eyes raked her frame.

She could only nod as her body started trembling. His eyes took in the broken glass on her seat, and he growled low and long.

"Come. Get in my truck."

Her legs were shaky as she followed him. Cars were slowing down around them and it was making her all the more paranoid. She got into Noah's Tahoe, and he locked the doors before heading back to her car. She could feel her body going numb, the surroundings fluttering in and out as the realization she could've been kidnapped settled over her. She could've lost her life. She flinched when the click of the locks disengaging sounded. Julian opened the door next to her and it was as though the floodgates opened. She sobbed as he grabbed her. She clutched him tightly as he lifted her from Noah's truck, carrying her to his own.

She didn't know what he murmured as he deposited her into the passenger seat of his truck. He pulled back and cupped her chin, his eyes flashing gold as he examined her. Her jaguar responded to his lion, rising up and filling her with magic. Julian kissed her softly.

"Are you okay to sit while I handle this?"

She looked around and noticed the blue and red lights. "I'm pretty sure I shot him," she told him in a panicked whisper. Were the police there for her?

"Good girl," he growled and kissed her forehead. "I got you, hear?"

She nodded. He draped a blanket over her, and she settled deeper into the seat, closing her eyes. All the toughness and adrenaline that had been propping her up for the last few minutes dissipated, and she passed out.

seventeen...

Julian paced his bedroom, his lion shredding him inside to come out. He would go running once he'd taken care of his mate. Right now, she was in the shower, the temperature set on hell. Steam filled the whole room, some even escaping under the door of his bathroom. He was anxious to be out on the streets looking for whoever was bold enough to try and take his mate. It wasn't like he had even so much as a starting point. That was the most frustrating part of it all.

He'd been on the phone all afternoon moving his schedule around. He wanted to guard Deena himself, but Noah had talked him down from that ledge. Too many other people and accounts were dependent on him keeping his head on straight. Still, it didn't stop him from arranging it so he could at least work from home. With how volatile his lion was at the moment, he didn't want her out of his sight. She came out of the shower in his t-shirt and nothing else. Rushing to her side, Julian pulled her into his arms.

"Better?"

"Some," she whispered. "Are you hungry?"

"Lay down and rest, shortcake. I can order us something." He followed her as she walked downstairs toward the kitchen as if he hadn't spoken. "Deena."

She sighed and gave him a small smile. "Cooking helps me relax, Mr. Chase."

He couldn't help his body's reaction to her calling him that, especially in that soft and docile tone. She paused as she saw the boxes he'd cleared out of her car.

"What's wrong? Did I leave something behind?"

She shook her head and cleared her throat. She pointed at the sunflowers on the counter. "This was in my car and I didn't put it there."

He growled, understanding the implications of that. "I'll take care of it. Anything else?" He scrutinized the rest of the stuff.

She shook her head and headed for his fridge. He sighed. There was clearly nothing he could do to get her to sit down. He texted Noah to come into his house and pick up the flowers. Next, he called his friend.

"My shop called and said Deena's car is there. What's wrong?" Rocco didn't bother with a greeting.

"Get them to go over that shit with a fine-tooth comb," he said instead of answering.

"Looking for?"

"A tracker," he reluctantly said.

Deena's shoulders stiffened, and Rock growled in his ear.

"Explain," Rock ordered.

He ran down what happened, angry from even recounting it.

"Who the fuck is this guy?" Rocco snapped.

"You already know what's going to happen the moment I find out," he promised.

"Count me in," Rocco told him before hanging up.

Julian sighed and put the phone down. He watched his mate putter around the kitchen, thankful she was safe, though it didn't stop his lion from prowling around his body.

She looked up at him from the stove. "I can feel your distress," she said quietly.

His brat was much more subdued than she normally was, and he didn't like that at all. He walked over to her and lifted her onto the countertop. She rubbed her head underneath his chin, her jaguar seeking comfort from his lion.

"You want to go running?"

"No. I want to lay down in your lap," she murmured.

His heart turned over. She was never soft like this. Dallas's words came back to him. Her softening was proof she was feeling more secure with him.

He cupped her cheeks, bringing her face up to his. "What else you need, mama?"

"Do you think I killed him?" she whispered.

He hadn't realized it was bothering her. His mate was hard, but the soft spots she hid from everyone else were finally being revealed to him.

"First, you did what you needed to do. Never regret that. Second, I've been checking every hospital, human and shifter, and he hasn't turned up, so my guess would be no."

Her shoulders dropped in relief. Her eyes were wet, though no tears fell. "You think he was tracking me?"

"That's for me to worry about," he told her, kissing her softly. "I love you." He wanted to change the subject.

"I'm ready," she told him.

His lion bucked in anticipation. Though she'd not said what she was ready for, his animal knew. "You're emotional right now," he tried to caution her.

"I love you, Julian. When I thought I would be taken, all I could think about was how much time I'd wasted instead of taking your bite."

"Deena." He kissed her and she opened her mouth, welcoming his tongue.

She pulled back and settled her cheek on his chest. He rubbed her back, using his lion to send her comfort. Lifting his shirt, she nuzzled against his skin before trailing kisses across his stomach.

"I want to wear your mark, Mr. Chase," she whispered.

He raised her chin and studied her eyes. "You're sure?"

"Positive."

He lifted her off the counter and put her down on her feet, grabbing her hand as they walked together upstairs. He gave her plenty of space to change her mind, staying silent until they reached the bedroom.

Deena stripped the moment she crossed the threshold, tossing her shirt over her shoulder.

"I'm sure, Julian. I promise," she told him as she lay in the middle of his bed.

Julian took his clothes off before approaching her. He slowly laid his weight on her, giving her time to reconsider. He kissed her, begging his lion to give their mate patience. His animal was ready to bite her. No foreplay, no preamble. From the way her power reacted to him, her jaguar was on the same type of time.

"No teasing," she told him, rolling her hips beneath him.

He chuckled and lifted one leg, kissing her knee gently. Deena reached between them and gripped his dick, guiding him where she wanted him to be.

"Impatient," he chided.

"Now you're the one playing in my face," she pouted.

Julian nipped her lip, sliding inside. Deena was wet and ready, her warmth accepting him inside with no resistance. They sighed together. He closed his eyes and prayed for control. Already his canines were lowering, his lion demanding he get to marking. Julian took his time though, basking in the connection between the two of them. Deena hugged him tight to her, her hips canting to take him.

The anticipation made every stroke intense. Julian slid his hands over her reverently, every touch soft as he worshiped her body. He kissed across her skin and down her neck until he got to her shoulder. She tensed beneath him, her jaguar's power flaring in anticipation. Before he bit her, he lowered his shoulder so she could reach. He wanted them to do it together. Deena latched onto his shoulder and he moaned, doing the same. Nothing prepared him for the ecstasy that flooded his body the moment her teeth broke skin. He followed suit, biting down, moaning as her blood entered his mouth.

Her jaguar's power flooded his body and his lion rushed forward. Their souls intertwined as their animals collided against each other. Julian's hips thrust into her as their magic consumed them. His skin heated, power sending electricity dancing across his body. The orgasm that slammed into him caught him by surprise, and Julian could only hold his mate tight as it swept him away.

He carefully licked across his new mating mark on Deena, contentment filling him. He looked down, his heart thumping erratically at her beauty. He rubbed their cheeks together before kissing the tears trailing her face.

"I can feel you," she whispered in awe. "Your love for me..." She buried her face in his chest. He rolled them over onto their sides.

"I told you I love you, woman," he murmured, slowly stroking in and out of her body. Now that impatience no longer rode him, he could take his time and enjoy her.

Deena whimpered and gripped his shoulders. "I love you."

"I can feel it," he whispered against her lips, pulling her hips into him. "It was worth the wait." She smiled, gasping as he thumbed her clit. "I'm gon' spend the rest of the night showing you."

eighteen...

Despite all the excitement from yesterday, Deena woke well-rested. It more than likely had to do with the fact that she felt safe at Julian's house — and sleeping in his arms. She reached for their mating bond, contentment filling her body as she felt Julian in the back of her mind. Even with the distance between them, her mate's mood was discernable. That would take some adjustment on her part, but she did like being able to feel him. The weight of their connection was comforting, and peace filled her at the presence of him.

As she descended the stairs, she debated what to do with her day. Celine had told her not to come in to work, and she was grateful. Though what had happened at the farm was years ago, after yesterday, she was afraid it would bring up a whole host of memories from that chaotic day. It could've been because she'd had to fire her gun. The only time she'd gotten into any kind of gunfight had been that day when Celine's family had tried to have her killed.

She shuddered just thinking about it.

She froze on the bottom step as she heard noise coming from Julian's kitchen. Had Noah come in? She didn't think to ask if she would need Noah since Julian lived so far outside of the city. She inhaled deeply, hoping the scent would give her some information.

Deena frowned.

She didn't recognize the scent, though it carried notes of Julian's. Hurriedly rounding the corner, her eyes widened when she saw a petite woman rifling through his cabinets and writing down on a pad of paper. Was she making a list? Did he have a maid?

She cleared her throat and the woman turned. Deena released her breath as she recognized her. Julian had pictures of the two of them together everywhere. She was gorgeous, her power raw and untamed. Long stiletto nails graced her fingers, and her wig was laid to perfection, parted down the middle. Julian was the perfect mix of both his parents, but he got those thick pouty lips from his mother, and his light caramel skin tone as well.

His mother was wearing a pair of baggy distressed camo pants with a bodysuit that showed her curves. It also showed a tattoo across her chest of Julian's name. She wondered if it was Junior or Senior but would mind her Black ass business. Either way, Deena was stunned at her appearance.

"Good morning," Deena greeted.

The woman smiled at her. "Good morning. Aren't you beautiful? DiDi did not exaggerate that."

"Thank you. I can see where Julian got all his fineness."

The woman barked out a laugh. "He still got enough of his bighead ass daddy to get on my nerves."

Yep, minding her business on that too. She held out her hand. "I'm Deena."

"Michelle." Julian's mom reached across the counter that separated them.

Michelle gave Deena her full attention, her gaze tracking across her body. Her eyes drifted down to Julian's mark, very visible due to the tank top she wore. Michelle narrowed her eyes a moment before she straightened her face. Was she displeased?

"How do you feel about kids?"

Deena was thrown off by the question. "Umm…"

Michelle waved her hand around the house. "My son built all this to fill it with kids. How do you feel about that?"

"I want kids." Deena didn't even have to think about it.

The woman smiled. "Would you like some breakfast?" Michelle asked, but then chuckled. "Look at me. Offering you food in your own house."

"Oh, that's..." Deena's cheeks heated.

She hadn't even thought that far ahead about their mating last night. Julian had made it perfectly clear that what was his was hers. And her cat had certainly put her mark all over the place.

"Breakfast sounds nice. I'll make it, though." She rounded the counter.

Deena didn't even know what to make of this woman. She had all that contained energy in a small body.

Michelle leaned against the counter and stared, her eyes sparkling with mischief. "Are you going to have a problem with me popping up on my son?"

Deena snorted. "So long as you don't have a problem with anything you see when you bust in here."

"Put me in my place then." Michelle laughed. "I'll add that in the pros column."

Deena smiled, really liking his mother. She pulled out the ingredients for pancakes.

"I heard a lot about you from DiDi, but I would love to hear it from you," Michelle prodded.

"Umm, I grew up on the South side, Greenridge to be specific." It was one of the rougher parts of the city, but she would never be ashamed of where she was from. "My mother passed away when I was eight, and after bouncing around between foster homes, I finally ended up at Winnie's House."

Michelle's smile was wistful. "Ms. Winnie was good people. How was your time there?"

"Better than the years before I got there," she admitted as she cracked eggs.

His mother squeezed her shoulder in empathy. "We used to live in Greenridge. Did Junior tell you?"

She nodded and handed his mother the fruit she'd washed.

Michelle continued as she found a knife, cutting up the fruit. "Yeah, we all grew up there. Before Dallas went after the council seat, we all used to roll together. You can't imagine the shit me and Adina had to get them two out of. Julian and them boys ran the streets 'bout as bad as their fathers did."

"I remember them, even though I kept my head down in them days," Deena murmured as she started cooking.

"Well, at least he found somebody who can rock a good buss down," Michelle said dryly.

Deena cackled and swept her hair over her shoulders. Noah had complained the whole time she had to be at the stylist. "My hairdresser is still in Greenridge."

Michelle smiled. "I watched your channel after Junior told me who you were. I like your content."

"Thank you," she told her. Deena liked the way the two of them worked together. It felt natural, as though she'd known Michelle for a lot longer than the few minutes they'd just had.

"I talked to Senior too. He said Julian was helping with some kind of stalker?"

Deena plated their food and stalled for a moment. Yesterday came back to her, and with it, for a moment, fear. She shook it off and set their food down.

Michelle's hand was warm on her back. "My baby will figure it out, don't worry. Do you want to go shopping with me after breakfast?"

Deena nodded quickly, happy for the subject change. She would love to spend the day with his mother. Julian's family was so warm and inviting to her, she couldn't help but be happy about that. She couldn't imagine not getting along with her mate's family, especially since she didn't have one of her own. It felt amazing to be a part of one. She'd been without that feeling since her mother had died. Not that she was trying to replace her, but it would be comforting to have that closeness with a woman again.

After breakfast, Deena took a shower and dressed, matching her new mother-in-law's fly. She smiled at the matte black G-Wagon when she came outside.

"You and Julian have the same taste in cars."

Michelle snorted. "He got his good taste from me, baby girl." She handed her keys to Noah and hopped into the back seat.

"Dang, Ms. Michelle, now what if I wanted to be a passenger princess?" Noah joked.

"Boy, please. Don't be driving my baby wild neither," she ordered.

Deena laughed, jumping into the back seat. She loved Julian's mother.

Hours later, Deena was catching up on the work she'd missed while out. She was on the couch, her legs kicked up, the laptop on her knees. She and Celine split the tasks for the business side of things equally, but marketing was where Deena flourished, so she handled that mostly. Right now, she was processing orders, making a list of all the herbs they'd need to harvest and dry to fulfill them. She was speeding through work because she was happy. Spending time with Michelle had been fun and had gone a long way to improving her mood.

They'd hit a grocery store as well as some other places. Michelle was well-known and as charismatic as her son. People waved and spoke everywhere they went. His mother had included her in everything, introducing Deena as her daughter. Even now, thinking about it gave her the warm fuzzies. She'd always wished that she'd been able to do things with her mother as an adult, so doing them with Michelle soothed that part of her. The woman was funny as hell, and they got along well. All the worries she had about meeting his mother had been gone within the first few minutes of them talking.

She heard the beep of Julian's kitchen door and looked up. He came in, not in the suit he'd left in that morning.

"Where you been?"

"The gym with Mase."

He sauntered over to her, the power of his lion reaching her well before he did. The feral energy sped her heartbeat and had her squirming in her seat. Julian lifted her laptop and placed it on the floor. He stretched out on top of her, laying his head on her stomach.

"My mama cussed me out today."

She snickered. "Why?"

"Because I marked you before she got a chance to meet you."

She kissed the top of his head. "She felt left out of the process. She said she's taking over the wedding because of that."

His head lifted. "She told you that?"

She nodded, laughing when he groaned. He nuzzled his head against her stomach. She closed her eyes and basked in his closeness.

"I like your mama." She rubbed the top of his head, and he purred in response. The sound coiled her stomach with heat. "We went grocery shopping, which… You too grown for your mama to be buying your groceries."

He laughed. "Try stopping Michelle."

She snorted, agreeing wholeheartedly that his mother would do what she wanted with no input from anyone else.

"Yeah, I like her a lot."

"I love that old lady." He tightened his arms around her waist.

"She does not give old lady."

He laughed. "What was her fast ass wearing?"

"I want to be like her when I grow up," she said instead of answering.

"You bought a tree, but it's empty," he noted as he spotted the Christmas tree she'd put up. "It's not even Thanksgiving yet."

"So?" She smiled and shrugged. "We're going to decorate the tree together."

"I like the sound of that," he murmured against her stomach. "It smells good up in here. You cook for your man?" He slid up her body, sucking on her exposed collarbone.

"Oh my God, Junior," she fussed.

He nipped her shoulder before licking across his mark. Her body went up in flames, her nipples tightening.

"Quit calling me that."

"Quit trying to sneak and leave more marks on me," she countered, mushing his head.

He bit down on her neck, and she laughed before moaning when he pulled the skin into his mouth. She squirmed, trying to push him off.

"Nah, let me go 'head and leave some more marks so all the dusties know."

Her stomach hurt from laughing as she fought to roll from beneath him. "Trust me, between your parents, everyone in this town knows who I belong to."

She squealed as they landed on the floor. He growled low and pushed her leg up so he could fit himself between them. His eyes darkened when he realized she wore no panties beneath his shirt.

"I like the sound of that shit," he said absently, trailing down her body, nipping her skin, leaving more marks.

She moaned when he licked across the folds of her sex. Her back arched as he devoured her. He was gon' always get what he wanted from her. She didn't know why she kept trying to deny her mate. She called his name as he set her body on fire. By the time he wrung the first orgasm out of her, she was ready to agree to whatever.

nineteen...

Julian had seen some shit in his line of work. Hell, he'd even done some shit, but when it involved his mate, it was knocking him off his square. Not that he'd never felt empathy for his clients, but from this experience, he better understood their anxiety. He knew they were doing everything they could to find out who was stalking Deena and yet, it never felt like it was enough. Not fast enough, and not enough information. It was frustrating to say the least.

It was stressful in a whole other way than the stress he had dealing with his clients. He didn't look forward to telling his mate about the tracker on her car. The packages to their PO box had stopped, but only because they were showing up at her house. He'd kept them from her, but he knew it was another thing he'd have to tell Deena. He sat in his car in the garage for a second to catch his breath. Mason had offered to meet him in the gym again to relieve some of the stress, but Julian was anxious to get home.

He remembered the reason the moment he stepped into their bedroom a few minutes later. His mate was on the bench in front of their bed, a towel wrapped around her, applying the body butter she made to her skin. He sat at her feet, rubbing his face against her legs.

"Your skin is always so soft and smells so good," he murmured, kissing her thigh softly.

"What's wrong, Mr. Chase?" Her voice was soft, the sensual note soothing his agitated lion.

He gave her a tired smile before kissing her knee.

She lifted his chin, her eyes raking his face. "What's wrong, baby?"

He had a lot of shit to go over with her, but he wanted just a little time to bask in her. "Long day."

"Up. Take a shower and I'll have a surprise for you when you come out." She stood and helped him up.

He pulled her into his chest, kissing her softly. He would normally tease her, but instead, he closed his eyes and let her jaguar's power settle his cat's.

"Go, baby," she whispered against his lips.

He nodded and stripped on the way to the bathroom. The hot water felt amazing against his skin, taking some of the knots in his shoulders out. He didn't take too long, eager to see what kind of surprise his mate had for him. He came out of the bathroom with a towel slung around his hips. His eyes widened when he saw the candles lit in the darkened room. It smelled of lavender and some kind of woodsy scent.

He growled as he got a look at Deena. She was in a black lace bra with high-cut matching panties. His mouth watered, his day fading into the background.

"Lay down, Mr. Chase."

Fuck.

He followed her instructions, forcing his lion down. The animal wanted to ravish her, but he would let the scene play out. He laid out on the bed and closed his eyes, taking his first relaxed breath of the day. Her weight on his back helped, as did the warm, strong touch of her hands. Deena expertly worked the muscles on his back, the soft music in the background the only sound in the room. She didn't try and engage him in conversation, instead allowing the magic of her hands to push away his stress. He could feel her pleasure in caring for him down the mating bond and it touched him. By the time she was done, his dick was hard, but he was damn near asleep. His lion was completely settled. She leaned over him, and he could feel her face inches from his.

"I'm not asleep, shortcake. Just content." He didn't bother opening his eyes.

She kissed his cheek. "You can sleep for a little bit. I'll rewarm your food."

He turned his body carefully so he wouldn't dislodge her, settling her across his torso when he faced her. "Thank you, my baby."

He pulled her down so he could kiss her, gripping her hair as he slid his tongue between her lips. She sighed, cupping his cheeks. There was never a time when she touched him that he didn't melt.

"You told me you would take care of me, and you have been. I appreciate that shit, mama."

"You're spoiled, you mean," she teased.

"That's finna be your fault," he murmured, closing his eyes as his hands slid up and down her thighs.

"My fault, Michelle's fault..."

He snickered. "I smelled her and Mama Di when I came in the house. Them two been through here?"

"Planning the mating ceremony. Michelle said she finna spend all Senior's money."

He opened his eyes and sucked his teeth. That woman. "I'm sure you ain't even try to control her."

"Control who? Mama getting her lick back and that ain't my business."

He laughed hard, pulling her into his chest. "Fuck, I love having you in my life," he said after a moment.

The light in her eyes soothed all the troubles from his day. "You taking a nap?"

He shook his head. "Nah. I'm hungry as hell."

She lifted from him and pulled on a robe. "Come then. Let me feed you."

He could only shake his head as he slid a pair of briefs up his legs. "I'ma be big as hell fucking with you, my baby."

She snorted and left the room. Deena could cook her ass off but for the most part, she cooked healthy. In the couple of weeks they'd been living together, he was getting spoiled. No wonder his best friend never wanted to leave his house no more.

Julian followed her to the kitchen, licking his lips at the sensual sway of her hips as she walked. The woman was effortlessly sexy. He managed to pull his eyes up from her ass when she ordered him to sit at the dining room table. His stomach growled as the scent of their dinner filtered through his lust.

"Garlic butter chicken with lemon asparagus," she announced as she set it down on the dining room table.

He grabbed her waist and brought her between his legs. "Thank you."

She kissed him, running her hands across his hair. "You're worried about keeping me safe, but I trust you, Julian. Don't take on too much stress. I take care of you because you take care of me," she told him, bending to kiss him again.

"I'ma always do that, my baby," he assured her.

He eyed her as she walked around to sit. Love for her overwhelmed him for a moment, leaving him speechless. She smiled at him, holding out her hand. He cleared his throat and gripped it as she said grace over their food.

They ate quietly for a few moments until she broke the silence.

"Have you found out anything new about the stalker?"

He pondered what to tell her. "We still don't know who it is."

"What about the flowers?"

He shook his head. Frustration burned through him. Everything they did led to a dead end and it was infuriating. It had been a full week since the flowers were left in her car and still, nothing.

"Only thing I've managed to find out is that someone put a tracker on your car." And it had taken days for Rocco's shop to pull the car apart to find it.

Her eyes ballooned. "I was hoping you were wrong about that."

"It's gone for now, but I did want to run something by you." He studied her, debating his next words. She was stubborn and independent. "Your stalker recognizes your car. I want to get you a new one."

She paused eating. "You're going to buy me a new car?"

"I'm actually asking this time, shortcake."

She smiled. "Can I pick it?"

He was shocked. "Yeah. Whatever you want, love."

Her eyes turned mischievous. "And if I want one like your mother's?"

"Blacked out and everything?"

Surprise had her eyes wide. "I don't…that's too much. I was kidding."

He sat back in his chair and licked his lips. "I told you it's whatever you want with me, shortcake."

Her gaze heated, and she squirmed in her chair. She cleared her throat before speaking. "I've always wanted one of those Jeeps with the top that comes off."

He nodded, grabbing his phone off the table. "What color?"

"I want to suck your dick so bad right now," she said instead, and he damn near pushed the table from between them.

He shook his head and chuckled. "I swear you unruly. Color, mama."

"Black so we can match," she said, getting out of her chair.

"Deena…" he warned.

She pulled his chair from beneath the table and dropped to her knees in front of him. Julian could only stare as she pulled him from his boxer briefs. She looked him dead in his eyes before taking him into her mouth. His head lowered to his chest, a sigh releasing as all the tension left his body. Not that he had a lot after her earlier massage. He hummed the moment his dick touched the back of her throat. Deena didn't move, simply holding him in her mouth. She was waiting on him and *goddamn,* that turned him all the way on.

"I'm ready," he ordered.

She slid up his shaft, smiling before licking around the head of his dick. Her next stroke had him clenching his teeth. Caressing him with her tongue, she sucked him into the warm cavern of her mouth. She cupped his balls and slid her tongue along the bottom side of his dick.

"Deena," he growled out, a warning at her teasing.

She slid him out of her mouth. "Yes, Mr. Chase?" she asked softly, looking up at him with those dark eyes.

He was fucking done for. Gripping her under her arms, he lifted her body.

"Sit on that shit, mamas," he ordered, sliding her panties to the side and bringing her down on his dick.

She hissed, throwing her head back as he fought through the tightness of her pussy. They moaned together when she was fully seated on his dick. Deena twerked on him slowly, working her hips as she rode him. He played with her clit, hissing as she ran her claws down his neck. Julian wrapped her hair in his hands and tugged until her back arched, her breast a veritable offering to him. He sucked on her nipples, alternating until he could feel her fluttering on his dick.

"Coming," she whispered, grinding her hips onto him.

He released her nipple, going to his mating mark and biting down. Deena moaned loud, wetting his lap as she came. She stood and pushed his plate to the side as she bent over the dining room table. Julian growled and dived right back in, slamming into her until the table scooted forward. He rubbed her back, luxuriating in the feel of her soft skin as he drove into the pussy that had him beyond whipped.

Julian got lost in her, the passage of time meaningless as he fucked his mate from the dining room, into the living room, all the way up to their bedroom. By the time he was done with Deena, she'd passed out on top of him on the floor. Julian pulled the blankets off the bed and over them. Fuck, he loved this woman.

twenty...

Deena chewed her bottom lip as she double checked the contents of the two boxes on the kitchen countertop. She'd gotten a headcount from Adina about the kids that were currently housed at Winnie's House, but she wanted to be sure she wasn't leaving anyone out. Julian had assured her that even the boys would appreciate the gifts she was dropping off, but she was nervous all the same.

She was anxious about the lotions and soaps, yes, but she was more scared because it was her first time going back to that place. She'd had good memories there, but there were so many laden with trauma. Could she easily walk the halls her and her best friend had before she'd been killed? That was the question. She took a deep breath and stepped back from the boxes. They were done and all that was left was to drop them off. Stressing over it wouldn't help anything.

She squinted at the time on the microwave and sighed. Julian would be leaving soon, and she needed to talk to him about driving. She could easily get Noah to chauffeur her around, but she liked to drive and missed controlling that aspect of her life. Especially when so much else was out of her hands. She texted Noah to let him know she was driving.

"Junior," she called, walking into their bedroom.

He growled and grabbed her ass, lifting her in his arms. "What I told you about calling me that?"

"I'm sorry, Mr. Chase." She softened her voice and in return felt his dick prodding at her center.

She couldn't even lie, she loved that reaction.

"You play all day in my face, shortcake," he growled, nipping her neck.

She laughed. "Fine. I need something to drive until my Jeep is ready."

"Why can't Noah drive you?"

"I want to drive," she insisted.

He studied her, and she kept her face clear, not backing down. Finally, he sucked his teeth. "You can drive my truck, I guess."

"I'm not driving that big ass Transformer."

He sighed. "So damn unruly."

She laughed at his fake pout. "I can't even see over the steering wheel of that thing."

His smile made her want to drop to her knees. "But you not short though."

She mushed his head. "You get on my damn nerves, Julian Chase."

He kissed her deeply, stealing her senses before setting her down on now wobbly legs. He crooked his finger, and like an eager puppy, she trailed behind him, following him to his garage. He flipped on the light and grabbed the keys for his Mercedes coupe he drove when they went out on dates. She was unsuccessful at hiding her smile.

"I don't know why you insist on driving that redneck truck when you have this hiding in your garage."

"Alright, not too much on my baby."

Deena snorted.

"Be careful in my car, Deena. Don't scratch my rims," he said as he mashed the garage door opener.

Noah slid under, whistling when Deena shook the keys at him. "Oh, we riding in the coupe today."

"Aye, watch your hands. I don't want no fingerprints on my shit," he barked at Noah.

She laughed outright, letting out a whoosh of air as Julian pulled her to him. He kissed her hard, his tongue spearing her mouth. She couldn't contain her moan.

"Text me when you get to Winnie's. And be careful," he ordered.

"I will," she whispered, dazed by him as always.

He headed to his truck, and she went back into the house to get dressed. She and Noah left a little under an hour later, headed toward Greenridge. By now, she was used to his company, so the silence between them was fine. Her body tensed the closer she got to Winnie's House, so that by the time they'd arrived, her shoulders were tight. She parked along the curb in front of the house and took a deep breath.

On the outside, not much had changed. It had originally been a triplex that had been converted. There were eight bedrooms inside, with three kids to a bedroom. There were times when it wasn't full and didn't feel so crowded, but even to this day, Deena treasured her own space. The lawn was immaculately maintained, though littered with bicycles and various toys. The home took kids from ten years old up to eighteen. It was supposed to mimic a giant family, and sometimes it did. Other times...not every kid that came through was meant to be around others.

She took a deep breath and exited the car, popping the trunk. She looked up as she heard her name being called and frowned, spotting Callan coming from the house.

"Hi! What are you doing on this side of town?" he asked as he got closer.

She waved to the boxes in the trunk. "Bringing some stuff by for the kids. What about you?"

"Same." He smiled and stepped closer, his hands out for a hug.

Noah stepped between them. "No offense, bruh, but back up off shawty."

"Oh, it's okay, Noah."

"Julian said no one close, Dee, and you know how your mate gets," Noah said with a shake of his head.

"Mate?" Callan frowned, his eyes dropping to her neck before scanning her shoulder. "I didn't realize."

Deena chuckled to cover the awkwardness. Julian had gone out of his way to mark her, so she could only imagine what he was seeing.

Callan gave her a strained smile. "Well, I don't want to hold you up."

She nodded. "It was nice seeing you again."

He waved and stepped back. Deena gave him a small nod as she lifted one of the boxes from the trunk. She closed and locked it as Noah grabbed the other. They lugged them to the front door, moving aside as someone walked out. He was a street guy for sure, gold fangs glinting as he smiled in recognition.

He nodded his head toward the Mercedes. "Julian letting you push his baby, huh?"

"Doesn't happen often, I take it?" Deena asked with a smile.

She wouldn't pretend not to like the thought of that. She would've felt some type of way if he was letting women drive his shit around.

"Try never," he laughed. "You got that, lil mama?" He pointed to the box.

"Yes, thank you, Noah's helping."

"What up, No?" The man bumped elbows with Noah.

"Ain't shit, Shine," Noah answered back.

The guy raked his eyes over Deena, lingering at the marks on her neck. "You might want to watch out for that one," he said, pointing to where Callan was just now getting into his car.

She glanced back and shrugged. "We grew up here together. He's not that bad."

"Just saying, shawty. I imagine Julian don't play 'bout you. Just watch yourself." Shine held the door so they could enter the house.

She nodded at his warning, taking it for what it was.

"I'll get up, No," he told Noah, swaggering off.

"Who was that?" she asked as they headed toward the front office to check in.

"Shine's good people," was all he said in answer.

She dropped it because she already knew how they operated on this side of town. It was the reason this facility was so safe. It was heavily protected by the street hustlers in the neighborhood, at least from outside trouble. Dallas Knight had long ago deemed it a safe space for their kids to grow up, and everyone on the South side had honored that. She smiled when she saw all the familiar hangout areas, some of the better memories popping up. Bittersweet nostalgia hit her, and she was glad she'd come back. She'd had her reasons for staying away so long, but she promised herself she wouldn't do it again. She would be back to help support the kids that would pass through these halls.

twenty-one...

Julian growled as he got another message on his phone from some-one in the old neighborhood. He'd been getting them all morning from people who'd seen his car riding around Greenridge. They wanted to know why he was in the spot and not stopping by. He'd let them know there was precious cargo inside. It was the reason he'd relented and let her drive, knowing she would be protected once people saw her in his car. He cursed as another message came in, this one congratulating him on his "thick shawty." He was about to act a fool.

He called Deena's phone, drumming his fingers on his desktop. She answered quickly.

"Hello, my love."

And shit...that almost derailed him. He loved when she talked to him all soft. Still...

"The fuck you got on, ma?"

"Excuse you?" she snapped.

"I been getting messages about you in my car all morning. You and Noah must've made more than one stop today."

"I made a couple. Hair store, lunch, nothing big."

"So, answer the question. Why I'm getting compliments on my mate?"

She sucked her teeth. "I got on some jeans and a t-shirt."

"Them shits painted on, though," Noah spoke up.

"Mind your damn business, Noah," she laughed.

Julian sighed. "Deena Chase."

"Not you calling me by your last name already," she teased.

He had to smile. "Where you at now?"

"Headed to pick up my new car from Rocco's shop," she said excitedly. "They're finished with whatever you had done to it. Then, I'm going out to CeCe's before coming back to my house for some supplies."

"Get your fast ass out of Greenridge. I bet not get nan 'nother message about my thick mate being out in the streets."

She cackled. "I'ma go put on a sack right now, love."

He laughed at her smartass mouth. "Bye, girl."

"I love you, Jules."

His heart stuttered and his breath caught, love for her overwhelming him. "I love you more, shortcake."

She hung up, and he stared at his phone. He was glad she was picking up her Jeep. He'd had Rocco's shop add some modifications to it that made him feel like she would be safe enough separated from him. It had taken everything in him to leave this morning, knowing she would be out and about in town. He would've preferred to limit her movements between his house and Celine's farm, but he could admit that something could happen to her at either of those places. Nowhere was one hundred percent safe.

"You look a million miles away," Mason commented, startling him from his thoughts.

"This shit with Deena bothering me," he admitted to his best friend.

Mason walked into the office, sitting in the chair in front of Julian's desk. "You'd rather be there with her."

"Shit, I'd rather her be here in the office with me," he muttered.

Mason snorted. "Do you hear how you sound? That girl got shit to do instead of sit up under you."

Julian sat back and sighed. Mason was right, but it didn't change his stance on the matter. They both looked toward the door when his assistant cleared her throat. Champ, Deena's night guard, was standing behind her with one of his HR employees between them. He frowned when they entered his office.

"What's going on?" he asked.

His assistant sighed. "I brought Champ in because once I show you what InfoSec found, you're going to want this one" — she used her thumb to point at the woman behind her — "escorted off the premises."

He reached for the folder his assistant was holding out and opened it, his frown deepening. It was the information he'd requested on Callan.

"What did they find?" he asked, but he was already going through the file. Impatience was riding him as he skimmed across the words. He growled as he read through the report. There were police reports from different women who all said that Callan was abusing them. None of the reports had made it to the Motsi. The why could be explained away by the fact that the human police didn't like to interact with the Motsi, but he still sensed someone was hiding these reports from Dallas Knight. He slid the folder over to Mason, the pictures in it pissing him off. All of the women resembled Deena. How had Callan gotten away with what he was doing for so long? Why had no charges been brought up against him?

"Where did you get these?" Mason asked, looking over his shoulder.

"Contacts," Julian answered succinctly.

Everyone that worked under him cultivated their own. It was how they did their job so well.

"How the fuck did he pass the background check to be working in my father's office?" Mason growled.

It was the same question he had. He stared at the HR rep.

She shuffled her feet and looked down. "His pass barely has access around the Motsi. I ordered the same kind of background check a vendor would've gotten. Nothing too deep."

"And why is that? He's working in the same suite of offices as my uncle, why the fuck was it so lax?" Julian sat forward and braced his elbows on his desk, working to calm his temper.

She cleared her throat and avoided his gaze.

"You let him finesse you out of doing your job correctly?"

"I'm sorry," she whispered. "I wasn't—"

Julian held up his hands. "You already know what needs to happen."

She nodded, tears cresting her eyes. "I'll clear my desk out."

It was an egregious oversight and allowing her to keep her job was out of the question. He didn't employ people he couldn't trust. She left the office with Champ behind her.

"Find him. Now," Julian ordered his assistant.

He trusted her to put someone on it immediately. Before he could say anything else, his phone rang. His heart sped when he saw Deena's number. His lion moved through his body, Deena's spike of adrenaline pushing through their mating bond. Something had happened. He answered quickly.

"What's wrong, mama?" She paused a little too long for his liking so he sat forward. "Deena, what's the matter, baby?"

"Someone got in the house," she finally managed to get out.

"Are they there now?" He was already out of his chair.

"No." She cleared her throat. "Me and Noah just got here and the door to my house was open. Noah's making me wait in the car while he checks it out." He heard the sound of rustling before she came back. "Wait. Here he comes."

"Put him on the phone," he ordered.

"Yeah, boss?"

"What happened?"

Noah sighed. "They broke in, trashed her shit, and left a message. Deena…you can't go in." He growled. "Boss, I gotta call you back."

Julian cursed as the call ended. He grabbed his suit jacket. "Mase—"

"Let's ride," Mason said, headed for the door. "I'm on what you on."

Julian appreciated that his friend would ride for him. They headed toward the employee garage, him trying Deena's phone over and over. It kept going to voicemail. Between the calls to Deena, he was texting his people to get them to her house. He needed to collect every piece of evidence he could and find out who was behind this.

He finally got through as he slid into his truck. Her face popped up on the screen and she was angry, her eyes flashing between gold and dark black as her animal tried to take over. There were spots along her neck where her fur was pushing through her skin, her jaguar damn near close to coming out.

"Talk to me, shortcake," he said in a soothing tone, hoping to reach her cat.

"My stuff is everywhere," she whispered. "They fucking destroyed my kitchen."

"I'm on my way, baby," he assured her.

She wouldn't meet his eyes, her gaze on the ground.

"Deena," he called softly.

Her head lifted, her eyes gold. There was no hint of the woman in her gaze. He didn't know what Deena's animal would do if she freed her jaguar, so he punched the gas.

It took him thirty minutes in the traffic to get to her townhouse, and he was pissed at himself for being so far away from her. He arrived there the same time as the rest of his team. They would check the place for prints and whatever they could find to identify the intruder, and they would make sure her stuff was cleaned. His lion bucked the moment he saw the damage.

"Deena," he called.

He found her in her jaguar form pacing in the small backyard she had outside of her townhouse. Noah was watching over her, and from the healing scratches along his arms, he'd tried intervening. If he touched her... Julian pushed down on his anger. Noah sighed in relief when he saw him. Jules nodded toward his arm.

"She shifted before I could stop her. She was trying to leave without me."

"Did you hurt her?"

"Boss, you see these fucking scratches?"

Jules said nothing because the question still stood as far as he was concerned.

Noah sucked his teeth. "Nah, I barely touched her."

Deena's cat growled at him, and Jules inclined his head toward the house. Noah got the message and vacated the backyard. Julian squatted down and stared at the pacing animal. He let his cat fill his eyes and watched his mate. Her tail swished in aggravation.

"Come, my love," he ordered her. She stopped pacing and studied him intently. He held out his hand. "Now," he said softly, putting power behind his words.

The jaguar moved slow, her sinewy movements haughty, still show-casing her pique, but she followed his order. The cat sauntered up to him, and he rubbed a hand down her back. Deena's back arched, and the animal nipped his chin.

"Behave," he admonished, nuzzling against her head.

Her body shuddered, but her muscles relaxed the more he pet her. Julian hugged her to his body and murmured assurances until Deena finally settled, pushing him down so she could sit in his lap. He wanted to be inside, checking through any evidence his crew had found; in-stead, he let his mate have the time she needed. His lion pushed to come out, but her yard wasn't nearly big enough for what his cat wanted to do. There would be no running and chasing out here. He'd remedy that once he got them home.

Her jaguar sighed and Deena shifted in his arms, her naked body splayed in his lap. He cupped her cheek and brought her gaze to him.

"Better?"

She nodded and nuzzled her head into his neck, breathing in deeply as she took in his scent. He liked this soft Deena. If only she'd let him spoil her like this all the time. He took off his suit jacket and handed it to her. She slid her arms into it and it enveloped her. It still didn't cover enough for his liking, knowing she would have to go back inside with all his men wandering around.

She chuckled. "I can feel your cat's jealousy. I didn't think I would ever like something like that."

"Come on. I want to get you home while you're in this kittenish mood. It's probably the only time you'll let me baby you."

She sighed and stood. "What is your obsession with babying me, Mr. Chase?"

"You give off prickly, shortcake, and that makes me want to smother you in love."

She chuckled, but her face hardened the moment she spotted the condition of her house through the glass of the sliding doors. He buttoned the two buttons of his coat and growled at the way it draped over her body. God, this woman was fine as hell. She tugged it closer together, probably feeling his lion's displeasure through their mating bond.

He snarled and pulled her into his arms. "Stay behind me because I'm liable to lose my shit if I see any eyes on you."

It wasn't the time for jealousy really, but his lion was on edge. He needed to focus on getting his mate back to his house before his animal started raging.

twenty-two...

Deena's heart was racing, her jaguar damn near inconsolable as she took in the state of her house. All of her hard work had been reduced to garbage. She couldn't help the tears that clogged her throat and blurred her vision. She'd understood that with being mated to Julian, she would have to move, but this townhouse was hers and hers alone. It was a huge accomplishment and she'd had no plans to give it up. But now...

She didn't think her animal could settle here again knowing someone had violated it.

Julian gripped her hand tight, walking her back to her bedroom. Her knees buckled as she saw the state of it. She'd barely made it into the living room before her jaguar had taken over, so she hadn't been in her room yet. The mattress was turned over, the sheets and blankets everywhere. Her clothes were strewn across the room, scent marks that didn't belong to her covering the walls. She wanted to throw up.

"I'll replace everything," Julian promised her, pulling her into his chest. "Leave it all here, my love. I'll buy it ten times over."

Her shoulders shook with rage and grief. The amount of damage done meant they'd been in her house for a while. She and Noah had gone to Celine's house to film some content after she picked up her Jeep. Three hours at the most, but whoever it was had made the most of the time she'd been out. She clutched Julian's waist, hating the tears that fell from her eyes. He pulled back and lifted her chin.

"For every tear you drop, I'll get that back in blood," he promised.

His animal was angry, though none of it showed on his face. The lion was thrashing, the energy in their bond chaotic, feral.

She shuddered at the resolve in his voice.

"Get dressed and let me get you out of here."

She went in her closet and picked up the first shirt she found, throwing on a pair of leggings. Reaching in the back, she grabbed the box that she kept all her papers in, thankful it was untouched. It held pictures of her mother and her from when she was a child. She went into the bathroom to get the stash of cash she kept under the sink and gasped when she stepped inside. Her makeup was scattered everywhere and written on the shower stall in red lipstick were the words *He can't have you.*

Julian cursed as he entered her bathroom. He grabbed her shoulders. "Go, baby."

She stooped to reach under the sink for her emergency funds, clutching it tight. Leaving the bathroom on wobbly legs, she stood at the door of her bedroom, observing Julian's men as they went through her house. So many strange scents and shifters unknown to her and her animal all up and through her space. Her jaguar would never again settle in the place. And she understood her own trauma enough to know why she held such attachment to her house, but the hurt was still sharp. They were things, just inanimate objects, but every piece lovingly chosen had been a declaration of her independence, and it was gone.

Julian guided her out the front door. Mason was there pacing. He walked up to Deena and studied her.

"Anything you need from us, okay?" He rubbed his cheek against her, his panther's power aggressive but soothing.

She nodded, swiping at the tears on her face. Once Mason told his mate, Celine would be calling her to check on her. She was so thankful for the friends that she'd made. She was headed to Julian's truck when she heard something that made her pause. Julian and Noah were talking in the front driveway next to Noah's SUV. Noah's words had drifted to her, and she put her stuff down on the hood of Julian's truck, making her way over to them.

"What did you say?"

Noah shared a look with Julian. "Dee."

"No. Repeat what you said," she demanded.

"Deena, baby." Julian grabbed her arm.

She shook him off. "You said you smelled Callan's scent?" Fury had her hands shaking. Incandescent rage burned through her chest. Had she not been out of her mind with grief, she probably would've realized how familiar the scent marks were along with Noah. "Why the fuck would he do this?"

Noah shrugged. "I don't know, but I know that it's his scent on all of your shit. We saw him earlier today. When I told him Julian was your mate...maybe he snapped."

Mason cursed. "I'm calling Pop." He walked off to do just that.

"You think he's the one who's been sending me fan mail?" she asked Julian, her eyes wide, shock sending shivers down her spine.

Julian nodded. "What are the chances there are two separate people fucking with you?"

"Oh God," she whispered, pacing her driveway.

Julian talked with Noah and Mason for a few more minutes, but she tuned them out, her thoughts spinning. What reason would Callan have to do this to her? That thought circled her mind the whole way out to his house. Julian cursed when they pulled up. Both his parents' cars were in his driveway. He helped her into the house with a sigh. When they entered his kitchen from the garage, they found Senior pacing and Michelle sitting at the counter, her fingers flying over her phone's keyboard. They both looked up when Deena and Julian walked in.

Senior's face was enraged, his lion's presence very pronounced. The power of it filled the kitchen. He pulled Deena into his arms.

"How are you, love?" his voice rumbled.

She nodded. "I'll be fine."

"We're putting an end to this shit, hear?"

She completely believed him. Julian's lion seethed down their mating bond, and she had no doubt that the two men would burn the city down looking for Callan. For the moment, shock had her at a standstill, unable to make any decision, rational or otherwise. Calming the two men was the furthest thing from her mind. She and Callan hadn't seen each other in years. What would make him single her out for his obsession after all this time?

Michelle wrapped an arm around Deena's shoulder. "I got her from here, Junior. Come, mama, let me take care of you." Julian's mother guided her upstairs to their bedroom. "What do you need right now?"

Deena didn't know. She was so staggered by it all. "I just don't understand," she whispered as she sat down on the edge of the bed. "Why would he do this?"

Michelle made a humming sound. "We may never know the why for something like this." She squeezed Deena's shoulder. "I'm going to run you a bath and then make you something hot and sweet. It will help with the crash that's surely coming."

Deena could only sit docilely by while Michelle puttered around their bedroom, gathering supplies.

Thirty minutes later, Deena had to admit that the bath had made her feel better. She found Michelle in the kitchen as she descended the stairs. The woman set a hot cup of tea in front of her. With a wink, she tipped in a generous amount of brandy.

Deena could only smile. "Thank you. Where are the Julians?"

Michelle chuckled. "In Junior's office. Did the bath help?"

"It did, thank you."

"I'm sorry your sanctuary was violated. I can't imagine what that's like," Michelle said softly.

Deena took a shuddering breath. "I worked so hard to get there."

His mother gripped her hand in sympathy before passing Deena her phone. "It's been ringing off the hook."

Deena looked down and saw all the missed calls. For a second, she sighed because she wasn't in the mood to talk to anyone, but then she remembered who her friends were. Their text messages asked her to call them, but only when she was up to it. They understood what didn't have to be said, advising her to take her time. A wistful smile tilted her lips. They knew her well. The phone vibrated in her hand with an incoming call. She winced, knowing this person would not wait to talk to her.

"Hey, Dec."

"You good?" His voice was deep, gruff.

She didn't bother asking how he found out what happened so fast. Instead, Deena forced her voice to sound normal. "I'm fine. Julian is taking care of it."

Declan grunted in answer. "Does he know who did it?"

Her heart thundered as fear and confusion battled within her. "Do you remember Callan from back at Winnie's?"

"Frasier?" His voice raised in surprise.

"Yeah, I guess. I didn't really know him like that." She didn't know if that was his last name, that's how much she hadn't interacted with him.

"He was messing around with your friend Dana."

Deena frowned. "I didn't know that. When?"

Declan growled. "I could never prove that shit, but I think he was the one who beat her."

Deena's stomach dropped and her hands went numb. "Are you sure?"

"Don't even worry about it. Tell your mate I'll be in touch." Declan hung up before she could say anything.

Which was fine because her ears were ringing.

Michelle cupped her cheeks and brought her face around to hers. "Breathe for me, baby. Julian!"

Deena could do nothing as her vision went black.

twenty-three...

Julian sat on the edge of his bed, his lion thrashing around in his body. Deena was finally asleep. His mother's panicked scream still echoed through his mind and would for some time. To find his mate slumped in Michelle's arms was an image he would have burned into his memories. Deena had woken right after and told him what Declan had told her. Her body had been trembling, confusion and aguish flooding their mating bond. His heart ached for her, and it had taken nearly an hour for him and his mother to convince her to take a sedative.

It had been even harder to convince his parents to leave his house. Senior was set to stand over his mate while she slept to protect her. Julian shook his head. He loved those two and loved that they'd taken Deena into the fold of their family.

His phone buzzed in his pocket. He had people out looking for Callan so he couldn't ignore the call. He did frown at the number, not recognizing it. There was a bounty on the motherfucker's head, so he wasn't the least bit surprised. He suspected he would get many calls from people wanting that money.

"Yeah?"

"I got a present for you," a familiar voice told him.

"Dev?"

"I heard you was looking for someone," his friend said in answer.

Julian sighed. "How the fuck you hear that from inside?"

"I got my sources."

Julian knew that. His friend had gotten knocked when they were teenagers, but it hadn't kept Devon from running his little empire from the inside of the state prison. He cocked his head as he realized why Devon would be calling him.

"Declan got him?"

Devon chuckled. "You ain't the only one watching out for lil mama. Congrats, by the way, on your mating."

"Tell your brother I owe him."

"Nah. It's but one of many we owe you. I ain't never needed for shit in this cage," Devon said.

"I'ma always hold you down," Julian told his friend.

"Oh, no doubt," Devon said. "You want my peoples to drop your present at your door?"

"At the gym," Julian answered.

"Bet," Devon said. "See you when I get home."

"I'll be ready," he promised the wolf.

Devon hung up, and Julian leaned down and kissed his mate softly. His eyes traced her face and he sighed. He needed to make moves, but he was reluctant to leave her. He had one more call before he could do what he really wanted. Dialing his uncle, he headed down to his garage.

Dallas answered on the first ring. "Mason told me what happened. How is your mate?"

"She's good now. He gotta go, Unc."

"Do what you need to do, Jules. I taught you boys how to handle business, but if push comes to shove and you need me, call, hear?"

Julian nodded, though Dallas would not be able to see it. "You know I don't leave a mess."

Dallas chuckled. "Indeed, nephew. Be safe."

"Always," he answered and hung up.

It only took him thirty minutes to change and make sure that the security he'd set up at his house around Deena was in place. Another ten minutes and he was on the back of his matte black motorcycle, speeding off toward Greenridge. When Julian reached the gym, he found Mason, Silas, and Rock posted against Rock's Lincoln.

"You sure you want to be a part of this, Silas?" he asked as he removed his helmet. "You got a lot more to lose than the rest of us."

"Man, if you don't shut your lightskin ass up."

Rock and Mason laughed.

"I ain't finna be too many lightskins tonight," he grumbled, parking his bike.

"We fixing to get caught standing out here in the open because of your light bright head ass," Rock joked.

Mason cackled as Julian shoved Rock.

"Fuck all y'all," he said, thankful for the teasing.

It took him off the brink. His lion was ready to rampage and his friends were keeping him from making impulsive, dangerous moves. He could've told them what Declan had told Deena about Callan killing her friend, but he kept it to himself, already knowing how they would react. It would then be four people on edge versus just the one.

Instead of going inside, they waited. Soon, he spotted an old-school box Chevy, candy apple red on chrome wheels. Flashy as hell for someone that needed to be hiding.

"Aye, man, them wolves wild as shit. Ain't even trying to be discreet," Mason said, shaking his head.

"That goddamned Devon," Silas sighed.

Julian snickered but sobered when the car stopped in front of them. A bulky wolf got out, not bothering to turn it off as he prowled to the back. The music got louder as the wolf opened his trunk. Out of habit, all four friends touched their guns, waiting to see what would happen. Only Julian relaxed his hold as the male pulled out a bound Callan. The wolf tossed him to the ground, gave them a head nod, and got back in his car, pulling out of the parking lot. Not a word was exchanged.

Callan looked up at them with panicked eyes. Julian let his animal take over his gaze.

"You stayed in the city and thought you wasn't gon' see me about my baby?"

Callan growled but said nothing.

Julian stooped over the panther. "A little birdy told me you like to put your hands on women. Women who look an awful lot like my mate."

"I ain't telling you shit," Callan spit out, his false bravado easy to see through.

"You sure you don't wanna cleanse your soul before Julian sends you to hell?" Mason taunted.

Callan narrowed his eyes. "You talking all that shit because I'm tied up."

"Say no more, friend," Rock growled. He grabbed Callan's arms and dragged him to the gym.

Mason held the door opened and they entered. Rock threw Callan to the floor and Silas cut the ropes over his hands and feet.

"We ain't pussies, so we'll let Julian give you a fair shot," Silas told the panther as he crossed his arms over his chest.

Callan flinched but said nothing, rubbing his wrists as he stood.

"Should've picked someone else to fuck with. You don't know this, but Julian's lion likes to play with his food." Mason snickered. "His ass is unhinged."

Julian shook off their words, loosening his muscles. "Shift," he ordered Callan.

His lion was excited about the fear he could see in the other man's eyes. Mama Di had drummed into all their heads the rules around fights in the Motsi after what went down with Celine and Mason. He knew there would be no consequences to them if he killed Callan in his animal form, especially defending his mate. Not that it would matter. He didn't plan on leaving evidence that Callan ever existed, never mind died.

Callan spit on the floor in front of Julian. "You don't deserve Deena."

"You killed her friend; I know you don't think you do." Julian shook his head as Callan stepped back. "Oh, you didn't think we knew that too, huh? So many women you used trying to replace my mate."

Callan growled and balled his fists. "We can fight like men."

Julian scoffed. "Why? I'm a beast, bitch. Don't worry, I'll leave enough of you for the police to get DNA. And when I'm done, I'm going home to Deena — something you've never been able to do."

That snapped something in the other male, his eyes changing into that of his panther's. Julian growled as Callan finally gave in and shifted. He rolled his shoulders and smiled. He was finna get in his ass for the old and the new.

Julian hung his head in the shower, his mind still. There was no trace of guilt for what he'd done. If he could dig Callan up and kill him again, he would. Not only for terrorizing Deena, but for the crimes he'd been getting away with for so long. His lion roamed his body a moment before he felt Deena's conscious touch to their mating bond.

She was awake and checking up on him.

He smiled and turned the water off, stepping from the shower as she entered the bathroom.

"Looking for me, shortcake?" He wrapped a towel around his waist. She rushed to him, her arms going around his body. "I'm still wet, my baby."

"Don't care," she murmured, laying her cheek against his chest. "I was worried you were gone."

"Gone where, love?" He lifted her chin and stared into her eyes.

He probed their bond to discern her mood. Her worry was easily read, though it was rapidly dissipating. He used his lion to cover her with reassurance. Julian nuzzled his cheek against her.

"I thought after I told you what Declan said… I worried you would go after Callan." She paused and shook her head.

He hummed, not answering her unspoken thought. Her eyes widened, and he remembered how well his mate knew him in the little bit of time they'd been together. She searched his face, her jaguar probing their bond. The silence lengthened as she came to terms with whatever she saw in his gaze, and she took a shuddering breath.

"Okay then." She tiptoed and kissed him softly. "Want me to make you something light before you go to sleep?"

There was not an ounce of fear tainting the bond between them. Instead, her love and care was there, along with relief. Her animal was perfectly relaxed, and that told him everything. His mate understood the world they came from and would have no problems with the darker side of his job.

They were well-matched.

He thanked fate for putting her in his path and choosing her for him. Lifting her shirt from her body, he kissed her softly.

"Food can wait. I know a better way for you to put me to sleep," he murmured against her lips.

"I love you," she whispered.

"And I love you."

Julian counted himself lucky he'd been able to find a woman who fit into his life. He'd gone into their relationship wanting to be her peace, only for her to turn around and become that for him.

She was home.

His peace.

<h1 style="text-align:center">epilogue...</h1>

Julian crossed his arms over his chest, watching his mate with a smile on his face. Right now, she and Celine were in the kitchen at Winnie's, doing a Christmas special on cooking for big groups. It smelled like heaven, and he was grabbing a plate for sure before they left. He was so impressed with the work both of them did. The kitchen had been transformed into a warm and homey Christmas set. He could see Celine's nerves and feel his friend's tension as he stood next to him.

"She's fine, Mase, and they're almost done," he said to reassure him.

Mason only grunted.

They were both worried for the same reason. The two friends were pregnant, and after a lot of squealing and crying from them both, Mason and Julian realized getting either woman to sit down during their pregnancies was going to be a big task.

Julian smirked and kept a close eye on Deena as she handled the hot turkey. Everything in him wanted to rush forward and grab the heavy dish from her, but he was minding his place. Besides, she would get in his ass if he interrupted their live. Another thirty minutes later, the women wrapped it up and ended the filming. He and Mason both took a deep breath.

He'd worried that the news they'd received before arriving would throw her off, but Deena was handling their live like a pro. No one on the other side of their devices would know that she'd finally gotten closure on her childhood friend's murder. Though they had no body, Julian had called some contacts he had in the police department, dropping hints about the cold case. They'd used Callan's DNA and compared it to what they'd found on Dana's body, finally closing the case. It couldn't bring her friend back, but he and Deena had visited Dana's grave this morning before coming to Winnie's. Though she'd been emotional, she'd pulled it together and was now breezing through her cooking. There was no hint in her voice or manner of the tumultuous morning she'd had.

He could see the exhaustion when she finished, though. It didn't show on her face, but he could feel it through their mating bond.

"You did it, my baby," he told a radiant Deena when she sauntered over to him.

"How was it?" she asked, kissing him.

"I thought it was dope," he answered honestly.

Her smile widened, and she hugged him tight. He stepped back and placed a hand on her barely-there stomach. They'd only just found out she was pregnant yesterday. Neither of them had been expecting it, and after his mother screamed in excitement, she'd slapped the back of his head for ruining the plans she had for their mating ceremony. As if he'd purposely gotten Deena pregnant within weeks of their mating...

"How are you two feeling?" He nuzzled her neck.

"I'm feeling fine. Once we clean up, I'm ready to lay down. Your bigheaded child is wearing me out."

He snickered. "You should be home resting, then."

She hummed, which could've meant anything. He had a feeling it didn't mean she agreed with him.

"An hour."

She rolled her eyes but nodded and headed off to start. He was behind her, helping because despite what she thought, he would put his foot down if she started doing too much. They finished in less than an hour, and he got a plate out of the deal, so he was happy. By the time he pulled into their driveway forty-five minutes later, Deena was asleep in the passenger seat. He smiled and shook his head. The woman was hardheaded and he didn't foresee that changing. She only woke once he lifted her into his arms.

He carried her inside, depositing her onto the couch. He didn't bother turning on any lights in the house. Deena had Christmas lights all over their living room and kitchen, festive colors dotting the walls and keeping the rooms lit all on their own. She'd gone from getting a tree before Thanksgiving to completely filling their home from top to bottom with decorations by the time December had arrived. With his mother's help, of course, because those two were as thick as thieves now. With a grandbaby on the way, Deena had a plan to slowly establish a relationship between Michelle and Sabrina so his stepmother could be included as well. It would be tricky, but he was proud of her for trying and certainly happy not to be the only person in the middle.

Deena laid down and pulled a throw blanket over her shoulders, humming in pleasure.

"Before you drift off again, I have a present for you," he told her, stooping so he was at her eye level.

Her eyes lit up. "Christmas is a whole week away."

He cupped her chin. "I'm so happy to be your mate."

"It's the best decision you've ever made, really," she teased.

He laughed and walked over to the tree to grab a box. He held it out to her as she sat up.

"This was never intended for Christmas. I bought it to celebrate you and everything you've accomplished despite the chaos you've been dealing with for the past month."

Her hands made fast work of the wrapping, tossing it to the sofa next to her. She gasped and looked up at him, tears cresting her cheeks.

"Jules," she whispered, handling the bracelet with gentle fingers. "How did you know?"

It was the same cuff she'd been admiring at the fundraiser for Winnie's House. Mama Di had given him a heads-up on how much Deena had loved the piece.

"I have my ways," he answered instead of telling her that.

He helped her put it on, admiring the way the diamonds glittered against her skin. His mate didn't have a lot of "stuff." He'd found that out when she'd finally moved in. He'd replaced all her clothes like he'd promised her, but she hadn't asked for anything else from her townhouse. She'd told him she was used to leaving everything behind when she moved. It broke his heart. He wanted this cuff to be the first of many treasures she would keep.

"Thank you, Mr. Chase," she whispered, kissing him softly.

He deepened the kiss, pushing all the feelings he had for her down their bond. She was right — mating with Deena was the best decision he'd ever made.

Also available from Dria Andersen

Chasing Savannah
Hers to Call

Destiny Series

A Destiny Awakened
Destiny Revealed
Escaping Destiny

Haven Series

Haven
Soulbonded
Hellbound

The Hamilton Brothers

The Friend Contract
The Alpha Accord

Georgia Arcana Series

Surrender to the Moonlight
Magic in the Moonlight

The Knight Series

To Her Rescue
For Her Safety

Short Stories

Porsha's Wolf
One Night One Bite

About the Author

I am a full time photographer, and a mom of two. I've been writing my whole life, and after the birth of my first kid, I decided I couldn't very well bring up a fearless human without first trying the things that scared me. So, I wrote my first book, and then subsequently more.

I try to write stories I love to read: love stories that feature brown girls like me. Some of my stories feature gods and goddesses, and creatures I derived from old, African folk tales remixed and thrust into a modern world. Visit my website, www.driaandersen.com for more information on my other novels.

Join my newsletter for free short stories and more...